Coloring Outside the Lines

Alex Rasmussen

Gail,
Thanks for stopping
and supporting the art :
From one local to another!
enjoy!
-Alex

ISBN:1519624735
ISBN-13:9781519624734

THIS BOOK IS FOR THE DREAMERS.

PUSH ON.

1

I know there's something there, bouncing around in her head.
I can see it.
She says there isn't, but I know better.
At least I think I do.

Am I crazy?

That's beside the point.
But something's up.

There we were, sitting at a table full of friends at a bar in downtown Seattle. It was 80's dance night and we were dressed the part, neon colors and all, and she was giving me the silence again, and that little smile along with it—the one that said she knew what she was doing.

If I hadn't been so bent on trying to figure out her head games, I'd have told her she looked cute with that little ponytail on the side of her head. But there she was, laughing and carrying on with everyone else and then, the second *our* eyes met, her face turned to stone.

But she says there's nothing wrong, so fuck it.
Gimme another beer and I'll turn my chair, plenty of other folks to talk to.

I'm not gonna let her ruin "Thriller."

5

After another hour or so, the two of us said our goodbyes to the group and started to head home. She walked ahead in hot pink knee-highs. The bus ride to Fremont would've been quiet if we hadn't run into my friend Ben, on his way home from work. He took the seat next to mine, and the two of us started up a conversation while she screamed silently beside us.

Our stop came too quickly.

I said goodbye to Ben, and she and I stepped off the bus before heading up the stone stairs to the apartment. Once inside, she ducked into the bedroom to change into her robe—the fuzzy pink one with the cartoon monkeys all over. I walked down the hall, into the living room, and sat down on the couch. Leaning forward, I rested my elbows on my knees, placed my head in my hands, and took a deep breath.
The darkness was nice.
I stayed there for a while.

When I finally opened my eyes, I noticed my reflection in the sliding glass door ahead of me, still looking ridiculous in my 80's getup—neon blue shorts, high socks, a tiny blue tank top, and an oversized trucker hat that covered my shoulder-length hair and featured the figure of a cartoon Tasmanian devil. I looked beyond my sad 80's self to the lights on a distant hillside and wondered if somebody were out there, looking back.
Staring through that door made me think about the day she and I had spent together a few months before: lying there on the carpet, both naked in a patch of early summer sun, the door cracked just enough to let the cool breeze blow inside. The two of us took pulls off the whiskey when we felt like it, had sex when the mood struck, and passed the laptop back and forth, taking turns playing our favorite songs for each other.
I wished we could go back to that day.
I also wished that she'd stay in the bedroom for a while longer so we could have a little more time to ourselves, but, once robed up, she came into the living room and sat down on the couch beside me, facing me with that same smile on her face.

I could hear it, like the ringing in my ears after a loud concert, high-pitched and unforgiving—like one of those special whistles that could drive a dog wild.

I turned to face her and, as the two of us stared at each other, the shrill sound grew steadily louder.

Then she shattered the silence.

"I think you're just in this relationship because it's convenient for you."

The ringing stopped abruptly, and I could feel myself staring at her in disbelief.

After a few seconds of this, I realized I should probably speak.

"Are you kidding me?" I asked. "All night long I've been asking you what's up...and you've told me *nothing.*"

She offered no explanation, just that same smile.

I glanced toward the sliding door, inhaled deeply, and thought I heard the neighbor's dog bark.

"I can't keep playing these thought-guessing games with you, Brenna. We just wasted a whole evening...*again...* "I looked back at her, furrowing my brows. "And what do you mean, *convenient?*"

Brenna shifted atop the cushions and straightened her posture. "Well," she began, in a sweet southern drawl, "you have a place to stay, rent is cheap..." She glanced down at her hands, folded atop the monkey robe. "But I don't think you're here in this relationship with me anymore." She paused for a moment, taking a long breath. "I think you're somewhere else..."

Brenna looked up at me with some stoic confidence.

"You *want* to be somewhere else"

It crept along the corners of her mouth.

She knew

...and knew that she knew.

Shit...

Now what?

End it.

No.

Don't give up now. Try harder.

But she's right...
You're just delaying the inevitable...

I shook my headful of racing thoughts, hesitating for a moment.
"I'm sorry..."
No turning back now.
"...but I don't think we should continue this."

Brenna looked at me silently, clenching her jaw. Then, right when I thought she might punch me, she said calmly, almost sweetly, "You've wanted to say that for a while now haven't you?"
Brenna was from North Carolina and her accent, even in that moment, did things to me.
I focused and answered her question. "Honestly, yes. I have thought about it a few times, but I wanted to try and make this work." The words kept coming, whether I wanted them to or not. "But the further we go, the more I'm realizing that we're in two different spaces right now." Then the cliché rolled off the tip of my tongue. "I think this would be better if we were just friends."
Brenna glared at me, nodding slowly. Then, after what felt like an eternity, she stood up. "Me too, "she said. "You treat your friends better anyway."

Most of what I owned was already in my car, so packing my things didn't take long. All I kept in Brenna's apartment were some clothes, my guitar, a toothbrush, and two hand weights I rarely lifted.
She was more than happy to help me move them.
The two of us walked across the street to my old Nissan and threw everything into the back.
Brenna looked at me with sad eyes, arms folded to keep her robe closed.
"So this is it, then?"
The night air was cool and quiet.

"I think this is best for us."

Brenna took a deep breath, nodding slowly and biting her lip before mouthing, "Okay."
Then she said our last words as a couple under a Seattle streetlight:
"See you soon."

She knew she would.
We worked together.

2

I drove a few blocks down the sleepy street and came to a stop beneath the low-hanging branches of a large tree. Music blaring from the Nissan speakers was beginning to make my head hurt, so I shut the stereo off and rested my forehead against the steering wheel. This felt good, except for the vibrations of the idling engine rattling my brain, begging me to turn the car off completely and welcome the silence. I obliged, but, devoid of distractions, it didn't take long before I felt something brewing in my gut: a pressure, dark and heavy.

Head resting on the wheel, I began to release a low, rolling groan.

"Rrrrrrrrrrrrrrrr..."

Bubbling up and getting louder; flexing my stomach to push it harder:

"RrrrrrRRRRRAAAAAAAaAaAaAAhhHHHHHH!!!!"

My forehead pressed against the wheel, which I grabbed tightly with both hands before using my last bit of breath to scream,

"FUCK!!!!!!!"

I threw my head up and looked around, hoping I hadn't awakened anybody in the nearby houses.

No signs of disturbance.

Closing my eyes, I leaned back into the headrest and felt the floodgates in my mind open wide, allowing every conflicting thought imaginable to rush into my aching brain.

Did I do the right thing?
            Am I an asshole?
Yes.
      ...No!
Was Brenna right?
      Was I in that relationship for the right reasons?
            Should I go back there?
No.
      It's over.
            You did what had to be done
      Yeah...
            But what about...

"Okay, that's enough," I said aloud to myself and myself.

Sitting there with inner voices babbling back and forth wasn't going to cut it.

I started the car.

I needed to get my mind off of this, or at least talk to someone about it, and I needed to get out of those damn 80's clothes. I reached into the backseat, grabbed a T-shirt and some jeans, and changed into them, bumping my knee on the steering wheel a time or two in the process.

Once I was back in 2013, I threw the retro rags onto the passenger seat and gave Ben a call. The conversation he and I had had on the bus was still fresh in my mind, and it'd been a long time since we'd spent any time together. I felt this would be a good night to catch up.

Ben was the bass player in an alternative country band. He had moved to Seattle from Virginia a few years back and we'd met when he started working with me at a music store downtown. In those days I wore a goatee that accompanied my long brown hair, which is why Ben had strutted up to me on his first day of work, tipped the brim of his cowboy hat, and said, "Howdy, Jesus."

With that facial hair and those locks, I did look a lot like Christ. Throw a robe and some sandals on me and I was a dead ringer, something I'd definitely capitalized on a time or two as a last-minute Halloween costume.

Anyway, once every week or so a few of us from the music shop would go out after work for pizza and beers at a place called The Green Room on Blanchard. This was a great ritual, but sometimes a dangerous one, as the beers would mysteriously transform into shots of whiskey over the course of the night. I remember once, a few hours into one of these sessions, a friend of the bartender pulled a knife on Ben in a drunken rage and was thrown out onto the street by the beast-of-a-bouncer from New Zealand. Apparently the bartender's friend, part of some motorcycle gang, thought Ben was giving him the stink eye.

Those Green Room evenings led to some very painful mornings at the shop, fortunately none having anything to do with a knife wound, just our stomachs twisting themselves into knots and our eyes trying to hide in the back of our heads to escape the fluorescent light. But this pain was never anything that an unshaven, half-sick nod that said, "I feel you," couldn't push us through.

Neither Ben nor I worked at that shop anymore, so I felt it would be nice to see him again.
The man also loved his whiskey, which was exactly what I needed that night.

The two of us met at a spot in Ballard called Ramblin' Jacks.

We walked up to the bar and grabbed a couple of shots, two empty pint glasses, and a pitcher of beer. Then we made our way out onto the crowded patio. It was late August and, contrary to the widespread belief that Seattle is soaked in rain three hundred and sixty five days a year, we were blessed with a warm night after a day of eighty degrees and beautiful blue skies. (We Seattleites tell folks it's wet here year-round to keep this summer paradise to ourselves. You're in the loop now, and I trust you can keep a secret.)

Ben and I grabbed a tiny table amidst the chatter and wasted no time getting down to business.

"Cheers."

The whiskey burned good.

When Ben took shots, his features sucked toward some point in the center of his face like he'd just swigged lemon juice. Funny face or not, though, the man had style. Staying true to his roots (despite the warm weather) Ben wore a black button-up shirt, cowboy boots, wrangler jeans, and a cowboy hat. Always the cowboy hat.

"So, how you been?" I asked, setting down an empty shot glass.

Ben took a deep breath and nodded slowly, looking as though he were bracing me for something.
"Been a crazy couple a' weeks, bud."

"Yeah?" I replied "Why's that?"

"So you know that girl I've been seein'? The one I met down at the shop?"

I scanned my brain for her name. "Carmen?"

Ben pointed a finger at me. "Camille," he corrected, "but close." He took a sip of his beer and continued. "So everything was goin' great. We moved in together a few months back, a place in Fremont. Got ourselves a little puppy named Sue—"

I cut him off. "Sue?"

"Yeah," Ben replied, "Sue. He's a little Jack Russell terrier." Ben grinned like he was proud of something and waited for me to respond.

I didn't get it.

After a moment of silence, Ben held both hands up in front of his face, speaking to me like I was an idiot. "A boy named Sue?"

Leave it to Ben to name his dog after a Johnny Cash tune.

"C'mon, Jason..." he said, shaking his head in disappointment.

Jason Mayes. Pleased to meet you.

Back in high school, people used to call me "Purple Haze Mayes."

Feel free to use that nickname if you'd like.

"Anyways," Ben continued, waving his hand dismissively,

"Camille and I have always had our time apart. She has her friends, I got mine. But about a week after we move in together, she starts spendin' a lot of time with this friend of hers from work named Steve."

Ben took a swig, setting his glass down on the wooden table with a thud.

"Now I'd met Steve, and he seemed to be on the level, but on top of that, I trusted her, so I didn't make a big deal out of all the time they were spendin' together. Hell, I've got girlfriends." Ben paused. "Well, not girlfriends," he corrected, "but you know what I mean." Ben pointed a finger toward me. "Shit, you remember I was livin' with Amy when I *met* Camille."

I did remember. Amy was the fiddle player of Ben's last band. When the two of them had first started playing together, Ben had gotten drunk a time or two and tried to make some moves on Amy, but she wasn't having it. So technically, yes, now they were just friends.

"Camille was out at work one day and I ended up havin' the day off, so I decide to be a sweetheart and clean the whole apartment for her, top to bottom—make it sparkle. We'd both been really busy and things 'round there were startin' to look a tad rough. It wasn't a disaster or nothin', but definitely needed some love. So I cleaned the kitchen, cleaned the bathroom...even mopped the damn hardwood.
I was feelin' pretty good about things and just had the bedroom left."

Ben took another drink.

"So I head in there to start cleanin' off our dresser, and I'm movin' her little stack of books onto the bed and this note falls outta one of 'em, all folded up with her name on it, something you'd pass to that sweet thing in science class, askin' her to the eighth grade dance."

I tried to remember the name of a girl I'd danced with in middle school.

"Well, I kicked around the idea of just puttin' that note back;

matter of fact, I *did* put it back. I figured it was her note and I shouldn't mess with that. But as I kept cleanin', I couldn't stop thinkin' about it, wonderin'. So halfway through movin' stuff around in the closet I said, '*Fuck it.*' I grabbed that thing and opened it up."

Ben rubbed a hand across the five o'clock shadow that had sprouted along his jaw.

"I'm glad I did," he said, raising his eyebrows and nodding. "Note was from Steve. All kindsa talk 'bout their weekend in Chelan, wine tastin' and swimmin'...sayin' things about how he wants Camille all to himself. Made me sick." Ben clenched his jaw and slammed a fist on the table, raising his voice. "She told me she went to Chelan with her *sister!*" Realizing he'd startled a few people sitting nearby, Ben took a sip of his beer to calm down. Then he shook his head. "I waited for Camille to get home and threw that note right in her face." Ben lifted his hat and ruffled his hair with the free hand. "Bitch."

He set the hat back on his head and glanced down at his beer, placing both hands on the glass like it was a crystal ball or some little teleprompter showing him the words to say.

"I told her to pack a bag and get out," he continued. "She came by a few days later with her brother and his truck to get all her stuff outta there...lucky I didn't burn it all. They hauled it all off and she moved in with her friend up in Greenlake. I kept Sue."

Ben looked up at me. "You know what the kicker is, though?"

I was mid-sip so I raised my eyebrows in response.

"This Steve guy's got woman's handwriting," he said. "I thought that letter was from one of Camille's girlfriends 'til I really started reading it." Ben shook his head and spoke slowly. "She cheated on me with some *fuckin'* pussy."

Ben said this in all seriousness, but I couldn't help laughing. I also couldn't help asking, "You sure she doesn't have any girlfriends named Steve?"

Ben cracked a smile. "Eat shit."

It was good to see he hadn't lost his sense of humor.

"All joking aside," I added, taking on a serious tone of my

own, "I'm sorry to hear that, man. That sucks."

Ben slapped palms on the tabletop. "Yeah, Jayce." He shook his head. "Wasn't meant to be. Been a few weeks, though, gettin' a little further each day."

He took another drink.

"But let me tell you, this Steve's lucky. Lucky there was no envelope lyin' around *with* that note. Hell, if I'd a' had his address, I'd a' come right over, knocked on the door, and given him a big ol' Louisville kiss."

"Louisville kiss?" I asked.

Ben nodded and said, "Yuuuuuup," as he used both hands to mimic the swing of a baseball bat, making a popping noise at the end of the arc.

"Damn."

(If you're ever getting hot and heavy with a girl in Seattle and she takes a moment to tell you that she's dating a guy named Ben from Virginia, run!

For your teeth's sake.)

Our beers were running low, so I poured what was left of the pitcher between us. As I did, Ben peeked over my shoulder and gave me a nod.

"Hey, check her out, Jayce." He shook his head. "Good lord, I love that look."

I turned my head to see the look he loved.

She strutted across the patio carrying five drinks. Two in each hand and one pressed between her left side and forearm, vodka somethings with different colored straws. The girl cruised past Ben and me with a sexy confidence, looking like an old pinup model—Bettie Paige beauty—bright red lipstick, black hair, a white dress that whispered something but didn't tell the whole story, and a few well-placed tattoos.

She sat down at a nearby table with four giggling girls.

I wondered why none of those girls had helped Ms. Paige carry the drinks. *Maybe they were a surprise?*

Something else struck me too.

16

For the past year there had been a little voice living in my head, one that reminded me I was off the market every time I looked in a female's direction a little too long. But now, that little guy had checked out. I was single again, and if I wanted to, I could march right over to that table and start up a conversation with one of those girls.

That thought made me smile, made me feel free. But it also made me think of Brenna.

I was really going to miss being with her. But deep down, I felt that we had done the right thing.

My mind drifted and I thought about how I'd never get to sleep next to her again.

Sometimes the two of us would pass out with our foreheads pressed together...

Ben must've seen me spacing out and known what for.

"What's the deal, Jayce?" he asked. "Brenna seemed pretty out of it on the bus."

"Yeah." I nodded and stared at my beer, rubbing my finger up and down the side of the glass. It was still cold.

"Brenna's great," I began, "great on a lot of levels." I looked up and shook my head. "I just can't play her games anymore."

Ben took a sip.

"What kinda games are we talkin'?" he asked.

"Well," I said, "tonight we went out to Oasis for 80's dance night. For about a week now, we've had plans with a bunch of our friends to do this. Everyone was gonna get all dressed up and meet down there. So Brenna and I went out yesterday and bought some retro clothes, got all decked out..."

A flashback of dancing to Depeche Mode...

"Yeah, I seen those little shorts you had on," Ben chuckled to himself. "You gotta tan those legs up, bud. Lookin' pretty pasty..."

I grinned and continued.

"So, I met Brenna up there after work. Hadn't seen her since I left the apartment this morning and, right from the start, the whole night, she's giving me this silent treatment. At first I saw it as a challenge. I tried to make her laugh—nothing. Tried to give her a little kiss, rub her back, hand on her leg—nothing. Just this cold little smile she wears when something's on her mind."

That smile... I thought, shaking my head to a familiar high-pitched ringing.

"So I ask her what's up. She says there's nothing, but she still acts like this, all night long, all the way up until we get home and sit down on the couch. That's when she says—" I replayed the scene for Ben in my best North Carolina accent. "—'I think you're just in this relationship because it's convenient for you.'"

He smiled at my botched southern drawl. "She does that all the time, man. It's so annoying. I always have to try to guess what she's thinking, won't just come out and tell me what's on her mind." I thought for a second. "But then when she *does*...I wish she had just kept her mouth shut."

Ben nodded, while a corner of his mouth turned upward. "So what'd she mean," he asked, "'bout convenient?"

I took a sip of my beer.

"She thought I was checked out. And honestly, I'd been fighting it, but she was onto something. That relationship has been wearing thin for a while now. Brenna and I are both stubborn as hell, and we've been fighting a *LOT* over the past few months."

A montage of arguments...

"Over little stuff," I continued. "Stupid stuff, like..." I thought for a moment. "Like, I got mad at her the other night when we were out at a Mexican restaurant. She made some joke to the waiter about me being cheap, and I took it wrong. It was a funny joke, too, I was just being an asshole, some pent-up something trying to come out of me. I apologized to her after the fact, but I don't like being like that."

Ben shrugged. "Then don't."

I nodded in reflection.

"Yeah...I just don't think it's right for us to stay together, man. Things just keep getting worse."

"And why do you reckon that is?" Ben asked.

"Honestly?" I said. "I think both of us are in a place right now where we want something new, not even with the relationship, just new in general. A change of scenery. I know that she doesn't like it up here anymore, sick of the Seattle freeze. Wants to go check out New Orleans. And I'm diving deeper into the music, wanna start traveling around, playing more gigs out of town." I glanced toward the table of giggling girls before looking back at Ben. "You know, if I had a magic lamp right now, all I'd wish for is a Volkswagen van in decent shape with a full tank of gas and a mattress in the back. Travel around and play little shows all over."

A thick mental fog was beginning to dissipate.

"I think we're both feeling this longing to be somewhere else, but we're here together. And that's nice too, being together." I rubbed my palms together. "But it's causing a friction, like there's some pull inside each of us toward something unknown, and some secret resentment along with it, blaming our feelings of being trapped on the other person—a fight inside each of us between the comfort of now and the desire for something new."

"Those are big forces you're fightin' there," Ben said.

"Yeah, they are," I said. "And I've been trying to keep these desires of mine at bay, trying to balance them and the relationship. But honestly, a lot of the time, playing music is all I can think about, man." I scanned my brain for an example. "The past few months I've been sneaking out to the car for a few hours every day to be alone and strum my guitar, mount the metronome to the dashboard and practice. It drives her crazy, but it's all I can do to feel like I'm making some progress toward this dream of mine." I shook my head. "I think it's probably best I just go it on my own for a while...scratch this itch while I've got the fingernails for it..."

Ben held up a hand and curled his fingers into a claw.

"I do love her fire though, man," I continued. "Brenna's got this crazy enthusiasm for life, crazy fire. Living for new places and new experiences like she's trying to suck in the whole world, all at once. We've done so much in our short time together."

Brenna and I lounged on a beach in my brain.

We'd bring our pillows...

"But that fire is in her everything," I went on. "It's in her when she's feeling good and it's in her when she hits that other side. Brenna gets these ideas in that head of hers and runs with them. And if she *told* me about those notions before they had a chance to grow in there, then maybe the thoughts could be contained. But she gets something bouncing around in that brain and, before you know it, she's deconstructed our entire relationship based on something I said to her at her sister's dinner party three months ago."

Ben tilted his head to the side, adding, "Or something you didn't say."

I pointed at him. "Exactly!"

Ben paused for a moment before shaking his head. "Fire." He raised his pint and looked at the last sip. "That fire can keep you warm..." Ben tipped the glass, drinking what was left. "...or it can burn you alive."

Whether this was the wisdom of Ben or Jim Beam, I liked it.

"Amen," I said, following suit and setting down an empty glass of my own.

I took a deep breath and scanned the patio, feeling lighter, clearer, fogless.

Everything was alive—glasses clinking, people laughing, rock n' roll blaring over little speakers. Each one of us was a cell in some massive entity trying to drink itself into ecstasy.

"'Scuse me, Jayce," Ben said, standing from his chair. "Gotta go take a leak."

"Leak away," I replied, standing as well and grabbing the empty pitcher.

I walked to the bar and ordered a refill.

When Ben and I sat back down, we started to talk about music. He told me about a show that his band was going to be playing the next weekend in a little town east of the mountains.

"We're playin' at this place, The Anvil," Ben said. "It's one of two bars in this little nothin' town called Roslyn." He shook his head. "Crazy people out that way, Jayce. And boy, do they *love* us."

Ben filled his glass with fresh hop-juice as he continued. "Last time the band played there, the place was so packed we had people standin' outside watchin' us jam through the windows, beers and all. They don't give a fuck out there—beers inside, beers outside. Hell, the cops were even drinkin' *with* us! Everyone in the bar was dancin' and singin' and hootin' and hollerin'. And that bartender fed us so many shots I was seein' double by the end of the second set."

"Good thing you're just the bass player," I said with a smirk. "If you get too drunk you can just hang on that root note all night, and no one will ever know the difference."

"Damn right!" Ben said, pointing a finger at me. "And the asses still shake just the same."

Then he burst.

"Oh shit! Speakin' of shakin' asses..." Ben grinned big. "We had a couple girls dancin' up on the tables when we played 'Folsom Prison Blues.'"

"Yeah? Did Myles and Aaron do that solo battle again?" I asked. Aaron was a lap-steel guitar player, and Myles was the master of the electric. Each of them was great on their own, but it was really something to see them go back and forth, burning notes at breakneck speed and trying to out-play one another.

"Hell yeah they did," Ben said as he grabbed his glass and sipped quickly, lubing his mouth to shoot the next words with slippery efficiency. "So get this. There was this big girl and this little girl. They had been drinkin' together at the bar all night long, and as soon as we go into 'Folsom' they both get up and start dancin' on the floor together, you know, swingin' each other around and laughin' and all that. The other folks on the floor see this, and they're lovin' it, so they push out to make a circle around the girls. Then they all start clappin' and yellin' and cheerin' these girls on.

"Well, the little one gets excited and has the bright idea to climb up onto one of these little round tables, empty glasses on it and everything. And she starts dancin' up *there*. So the big girl sees this and decides *she* wants to do the same. Takes her a bit longer to get up onto the table, but she does it.

"So they're both up there, each girl is dancin' on her own

table...and everything is goin' great. These folks down below are still clappin' and yellin' and cheerin', gathered 'round these two. Myles is goin' off and Aaron is goin' off and the drums are poundin' and my bass is rumblin'. And we're already 'bout five minutes into the song; but we ain't stoppin' now, noooooo way—there'd be a damn riot. So we keep it rollin'. Hell, we'll go 'til our fingers fall off if need be.

"So we're rippin' and roarin' and blazin' and soarin' and searin' so hot the fuckin' walls are startin' to melt when, next thing I know, I look up, and who do I see but ol' miss biggie? And she's tumblin' right off that poor little table, and straight down onto the floor." Ben laughed hysterically as he slapped his leg, drawing some curious looks from a few folks seated nearby.

Ben didn't notice. He was in Roslyn.

"She was dancin' up there and the heat must've gotten to her," he managed through broken laughter. "Some kinda heat," he shook his head, "'cause she tried to take her top off, lost her balance, and ended up flat on the floor with one titty out and that shirt halfway over her head!"

I smiled, half at the story and half at Ben, who continued to chuckle uncontrollably with eyes squinted into slits.

Ben was just about to say something else when the pinup girl and her group walked past our table. Pinup must've shot a look over her shoulder at Ben because, getting serious all of a sudden, he looked at me, nodded, and stood up, taking a big sip of his beer as he dusted off his shirt.

"I'll be right back."

Ben was a man of his word.

A few minutes later, he *was* back...with a new friend.

Pinup's right shoulder was decorated by a large and colorful tattoo, a casino collage: full house (three sixes and two queens, to be exact), a whiskey bottle, some dice, a few slot machines, and a roulette wheel, everything laced with smoke that spelled "All in."

I'm pretty sure Ben fell in love with her the second he saw this. Ben's first passion was whiskey, but gambling was a close second. Once, at Snoqualmie Casino, I'd watched him blow a whole two weeks' pay in a few short hours. The guy is horrible at craps and stubborn as hell—a bad combination for anyone hoping to walk away from the tables in the positive. This being said, based on Pinup's tattoo alone, *I'd* bet that if Ben had had a wedding ring with him on that patio right then, he'd have given it to the girl. Unfortunately, this scenario isn't possible because if Ben *did* happen to come into possession of such a ring, he'd likely lose it because of some stupid move in a game of Texas Hold 'Em.

Ben and Pinup hit it off, and the three of us chatted for a bit before one of her friends walked out onto the patio and sat down to join us—a nurse in training, local girl. After about a half hour the ladies invited Ben and me to join them at their friend's party up the street. This was a very tempting offer, and it took me a lot to refuse, but all I wanted to do was stretch out in the passenger seat of my Maxima and pass out.

It had been a long night.

The four of us walked into the bar and paid our tabs. After that, we stepped outside and I said goodbye to Ben, who didn't seem upset about leaving with two beautiful girls. I knew that the next time I saw him he'd have a story to tell about the rest of the evening.

With one arm wrapped around Pinup's waist, Ben tipped his brim of his cowboy hat.

"Great seein' you, Jason. Always is."

I smiled and tipped the brim of an invisible cowboy hat.

"You too, Ben. Good catching up."

I waved to the ladies.

"Bye, girls. Nice to meet you."

The beauties waved and said goodbye as the trio turned and made their way up the sidewalk.

I walked back to the car feeling good.

Reunited with my vessel, I slipped inside and drove around, looking for a spot to park the Maxima Motel for the night. After a few minutes, I happened upon a quiet residential street not far from the bar where, about halfway up the block on the right, a developing lot sat silent after a long day of construction. Two-by-fours and tall stacks of plywood surrounded the freshly framed first floor of a new house.

Bingo.

I always try to park near construction sites when spending nights in the car; it's a lot less conspicuous pissing in a Honey Bucket than in someone's front bushes. Over the course of the night's conversation, I'd forgotten about my bladder. Once relieved, it was happy and ready for bed—well, sleep at least. No bed tonight.

I thought about Brenna, hopefully snoozing soundly in her monkey robe.

After changing into my sweatpants, I brushed my teeth, rinsing with a bottle of water I'd found lounging in the Maxima's back seat. Once my dental duties were done, I grabbed my pillow and blanket from the trunk and climbed into the passenger suite through the curbside door. Then, still warm from the whiskey, I reached down with my right hand, cranked the seat all the way back, and fell asleep to the image of some large girl falling off a table to the sound of "Folsom Prison Blues."

3

There was a moment of silence after we hit the last note of the song. Then, like the sound of thunder hits a few seconds after a lighting strike...

Applause!

They loved it...and we loved that they loved it.

The woman smiled and took a bow before turning to me.

"What else you got?" she asked, rubbing her palms together.

I could see she had a few more dance moves up her sleeve, and I decided to put them to the test.

"You know 'Billie Jean?'" I asked.

She dipped her head slightly and peered at me over glasses.

"Are you kidding me?"

I took that as a 'yes' and started playing the bass line from Michael Jackson's masterpiece on my acoustic guitar. The woman, who had been standing beside me, used this opportunity to move forward and showcase her moon-walking skills in front of the small crowd that had gathered to watch the two of us perform. For somewhere between the ages of fifty and sixty, she really could move. Folks in the crowd began to clap along, cheering to the beat.

I couldn't stop smiling and took a moment to let it all soak in.

The woman's name was Sparrow.

She was fit for her age, sporting a gray, flattop haircut with a braided rat tail dangling off the back. The two of us were performing together on a sidewalk in front of the "first" Starbucks coffee shop on an autumn afternoon at Pike Place Market in downtown Seattle.

The sun was shining, the people were smiling, and the air was crisp in the home stretch of a gorgeous Seattle summer. It was late September, a time of year when the entire city savors every moment of good weather we get, knowing that each sunny day could be our last for the next eight months.

I wrote "first" Starbucks like "this" because the first store was actually opened a few hundred feet away from this one in 1971 and moved to its current location at Pike Place in 1977, so the store at the market is one of the *oldest* Starbucks shops in existence, but it is also widely misunderstood to be the first. Either way, the tourists who come through Pike Place treat this spot like it's their holy land.

The line to get a cup of coffee at that shop usually stretches halfway down the block. The coffee tastes the same as it would at any other Starbucks, but at the Market you have to wait thirty minutes to get it. This lengthy lull can be made enjoyable by a few things, though, one of which is us—the street performers. (Disclaimer: One's level of audio enjoyment will depend largely on who is playing. Some of the Starbucks performers are great, but others are capable of turning the wait for that holy mocha into a half hour of torture.)

Along with the live entertainment, one can also experience all the sights, sounds, and smells of one of the country's oldest and most eclectic farmers markets—including the unique opportunity to bask in all the perverted glory of the original Starbucks logo: stamped onto a large sign hanging above the door of the shop are three bare-breasted cartoon mermaids, each facing forward and endowed with two tails. These mer-girls glisten, wearing a slight grin as they grab both of their tails by the fin and spread them eagerly over their shoulders like spry little sea whores.

Seriously, look it up.

Many a young tourist has seen their first pair of 2D boobs right there on that historic sidewalk—truly a magical place—and at that time (my twenty-sixth year), I made most of my living entertaining those very patient, mermaid-gazing coffee fiends.

Coffee fiends who, right then, were in for a surprise.

Those who had seen Sparrow and me perform our last song knew what to expect, but the new faces in the gathering crowd hadn't seen what this dancing granny had up her short sleeves besides her Mike-ish moves.

I started singing the first verse of "Billie Jean."

And, as she continued to dance back and forth to the beat, spinning every now and then when the moment called for it, Sparrow began moving her hands in front of her face with a flowing grace, interpreting the words coming out of my mouth and instantly translating them into sign language.

I hoped that there were deaf ears somewhere in the crowd. I'm sure they would have been thrilled.

Every now and then, Sparrow would accent a certain lyric with a spirited lunge or sudden raise of the hands, synched perfectly to the beat of the song. Folks watching began to take pictures and videos with their phones, wearing the same look of enchantment that I'm sure I'd had plastered across my face when I'd first seen her seven minutes ago. I had been in the middle of playing "Losing my Religion" and had glanced up from my guitar to see Sparrow doing exactly as she was doing now: dancing and moving her hands to shape every lyric while wearing a tiny smile of perfect contentment.

I beamed thoughts of gratitude to whatever may have been listening at that moment—god, the universe, Sasquatch, maybe just me. Regardless, I thanked something for bringing that experience into being.

Sparrow and I had never seen each other before, and knew that we may never see each other again. This spontaneity is one of the many beauties of street performing, or "busking," as I'll refer to it from here on out. Anything can happen, and anyone can become a part of the show.

Even the spell check on this computer doesn't recognize the word "busking." So I think it was best I explained it there—saved you a Google search.

At that point, I'd been busking at Pike Place Market for about ten months. I loved that little universe—the soul of Seattle. That market has been open almost 365 days a year since 1907 and sits on a hillside overlooking the Elliot Bay waterfront on the west side of downtown. It is home to hundreds of local artists, street performers, farmers, and merchants.

And yes, it's the market where they throw the fish.

In case you're out of the loop, I'll fill you in.

There is a seafood stand at Pike Place that has become famous for the workers hurling fresh fish at each other, about ten to fifteen feet through the air. One fish-pitcher, usually wearing an orange rubber apron, stands at the elevated counter and chucks the scaly football over bins of ice and various sea-foods down to another employee on ground level. This catcher then snatches the flying fish mid-air and hands it over, still hot from its high speed travel, to delighted and often screaming customers.

If you're ever sitting at a bar, find yourself in a conversation with someone new, and feel like having a little fun, try this. If the person asks you what you do for a living, tell the curious that you work at Pike Place Market in Seattle.

After this, seeing as most folks are hip to the Pike Place fish-chucking phenomenon (one of the market's main attractions) your new friend will usually ask you if you work at the seafood stand where they throw the fish. Say yes.

If your new friend *doesn't* ask you this, just tell them you work at the seafood stand where they throw the fish anyway. Then you can make up all kinds of stories about throwing trout around for a living, like how at your job interview you were butt naked and cold, forced to catch thirteen wet salmon in thirty seconds, hurled at you by drunken sea captains from all corners of a stinky room.

Or how you go home each night and have to wash your clothes in bleach.

Then ask your new friend to smell your sleeve.

Games like this keep the mind sharp.

Anyway, three to seven days a week, depending on how the money was coming in, I would hop on a bus full of smartphone zombies in West Seattle at seven in the morning for a thirty-minute ride downtown. This journey usually found me standing up, stuffed between sleepy commuters while carrying a guitar case in one hand and a folding metal stand in the other. The stand was used to elevate my open case to optimum money-catching height so that passersby wouldn't have to bend down to deposit their dollars.

Pike Place buskers are permitted to play an hour at a time at any of sixteen designated performance locations throughout the market on a first-come, first-serve basis. I would arrive at about eight in the morning to sign up for a ten or eleven o'clock slot at Starbucks. Other spots were profitable, but I liked the intimacy of the coffee spot, and the fact that folks standing in line there were able to hear an entire song or two while waiting, rather than just catching a few notes of a tune as they strolled past. I'd usually play two to four sets a day, providing my fingers and voice were up for the challenge.

On days that I wasn't busking at Pike Place, I sold product for a few local artists on the craft line, which is a series of metal tables and concrete slabs several blocks long that are divided into about 200 four- to five-foot spaces. These tables are housed in an open-air arcade, protected from northwest weather by large plastic windshields that can be raised or lowered with cranks. Local creatives show up each day to project their minds onto these tables with hopes that folks wandering through the market will take a piece home with them in exchange for their hard-earned cash.

On the north end of the market, there are also a few dozen concrete slabs that sit outside and are fully exposed to the elements. These slabs offer a beautiful view of Puget Sound, the Olympic Mountain range, and the colorful cast of characters who hang out at the nearby park.

Feline Fred is one of these characters. A tall, middle-aged man with shoulder-length, graying hair that always looks wet, like he's just stepped out of the shower. This Pike Place staple wears short skirts, fishnet stockings, and cat contacts as he struts through the market every now and then with a rolling suitcase. Out of this rolling suitcase, Feline Fred sells his unique artwork: colored pencil drawings of cats in human poses, usually in some ballerina stance, wearing various outfits and posing in front of different backdrops. Each outfit is tailored specifically to accommodate a set of six luscious human breasts which have been drawn bulging from the cartoon cat's body.

This, my friends, the common denominator between each and every Feline Fred drawing: a dancing cat with six human tits. And you'd better believe I bought one. Mine is a six-titted ballerina cat in space.

Best dollar I've ever spent.

There is never a dull moment at Pike Place—always something to see.

And in that moment, for the few folks standing on that Starbucks sidewalk, Sparrow and I were it.

She and I reached the end of "Billie Jean" and took a bow to the handful of applauding people before us. Releasing a satisfied breath, I looked toward the guitar case, sitting proudly atop its metal stand, and noticed that the dollar bills inside had multiplied while we were playing—a strange phenomenon.

Sparrow and I smiled at each other and came together with a hug.

"Thank you for having me." She beamed.

"Thank *you*," I replied. "That was awesome. Come back any time."

I offered Sparrow a few of the dollars that we'd earned during our performance, but she refused to take them. Sparrow instead placed one hand on each of my shoulders and looked happily into my eyes.

"That *was* my payment," she assured me.

Sparrow then winked before turning and making her way up the brick street, strutting to some groovy rhythm in her head.

After she'd gone, it was just me again.

Me and my Starbucks friends

...and the mermaids

I had time for one more song before the a cappella gospel quartet would take the spot, so I decided to end my set with "Heart of Gold" by Neil Young. Last time I'd played this tune, a woman had watched me perform the entire thing and then tipped me twenty dollars for "taking her back."

Take me back...
I've always believed that music could take you places.
I think music might even be the secret to time travel—memories trapped within the notes and the rhythm.

All it takes is hearing "Hotel California," and I'm back at a cabin in Cle Elum sipping summertime drinks with my first love out of high school. Or "Master of Puppets" and my friends and I are skateboarding on a homemade half-pipe in our buddy's garage.

It's nice to have such easy access to these places. All I need to do is press play.

A time travel specialist stationed on a Starbucks sidewalk with a few folks along for the ride.
"Heart of Gold." Neil Young. Set the device for 1972, Northern California...

About halfway through the song, a woman handed a dollar to her daughter, probably about three years old, with instructions to "put it in there," as she pointed toward my guitar case. Mom's pointer finger must've been angled slightly to the right because, instead of depositing the dollar in my guitar case, the little one walked up to me in the middle of the tune and stuffed Mr. Washington right into the sound hole of my acoustic guitar.

"No, baby!"
The girl's mom jumped forward in an attempt to grab the dollar before it ended up in the guitar, but it was too late. The wee one was quick.

I laughed and the little pigtailed ninja looked up at me, smiling proud.

That dollar still lives inside my guitar. Along with another good luck charm that I'll tell you about later, acquired almost a thousand miles away from that Starbucks sidewalk.

After the last note of the tune, I said, "Thank you," and "Have a good day," to the mother-daughter duo and pulled my stand and case aside while the gospel boys set up their show. During that hour, I'd sold two CDs at ten bucks a pop and made about twenty-three dollars in tips, not including the good luck dollar—a pretty solid set.

It was one o'clock. I'd play one more set at three and then, if that went well, pack up for the day.

I stuffed the cash into my pocket, laid the guitar in its case, and folded my metal stand. After throwing the stand over my shoulder, I began to walk south across the brick of Pike Place while the gospel boys broke into their first song. Instantly, a group of people swarmed the Starbucks sidewalk like moths to a porch light, clapping along and snapping cell phone pictures.

That Jesus guy must've been pretty cool.

It was only about a block's walk along Pike Place—between restaurants and shops on the left and the craft line on the right—to the coffee shop where all the buskers would hang between sets.

Outside the shop, on the corner of Stewart and Pike Place, was Terry, a longtime market staple. Terry was originally from Kansas and had been playing at the market for about eleven years. I leaned against a parked car to watch him dazzle a crowd of onlookers. People loved Terry's musical routine. For his grand finale, he would balance a guitar on his chin and simultaneously solve two Rubik's cubes, all while hula hooping—a true marvel in coordination.

Sometimes I would walk into that coffee shop on a slow afternoon, the music would be low, and I would hear what sounded like several computer keyboards being typed on furiously. Looking toward the counter, I would notice that the barista was nowhere near the register, and, as my gaze drifted to identify the source of the sound, I would see Terry and two street magicians huddled around a table in the corner, heads down and arms locked, hands moving at light speed. Another step closer would reveal a blur of color in each of their hands and a stopwatch placed between the three of them, then...

SLAM!!!!

Multicolored plastic would meet the tabletop at high speed, and the winner of the Rubik's cube race would snatch the stopwatch with an eager hand.

"Goddamn!" the champion would gloat. "Only twenty-four seconds!" (...or some other inhuman completion time.)

After that, the guys would talk for a bit, tell a few stories, have a few laughs, but it was never long before one of them would reset the stopwatch and the race would start all over again.

That shop was a great place to spend time in between sets, reading, writing, and chatting with various market folks as they drifted in on short breaks from their daily grind.

Before I went into the coffee shop, though, I wanted to say hello to a friend.

I watched Terry end his set to a raucous applause from an excited crowd. Basking in the immediate effect of his cultural contribution, Terry smiled before letting two hula hoops fall to his feet, catching the guitar as it dropped from his chin, and taking a bow.

The sound of applause faded to static as my guitar and I walked out of the afternoon sun and into the sea of people shuffling through the Sunday market craft line. There, an old blind busker was seated atop a white bucket, his gravelly voice belting "Itsy Bitsy Spider" to a small group of dancing children, attached by spaghetti arms to smiling parents.

I stepped to the right of the mini concert and continued through the arcade, bobbing and weaving between every type of person imaginable—man, woman, child...young, old...large, small, white, black, yellow, magenta—all of them walking or wheelchairing the craft line, scanning each passing table for that local nugget they couldn't live without.

I walked past the obsidian knives, the local photographer who still used film, the flower farmers, the honey stand, the handmade jewelry, wallets made from recycled truck inner tubes, sweaters made out of alpaca wool, spray-paint art...

Aha!

There it was, nestled between handmade hair wraps and matchbox dioramas. The table I'd been looking for, a rainbow of color shining bright beneath four clamp-on bulbs...

The blown glass art.

Pumpkins, hearts, starfish, ornamental orbs, each displayed in various colors—red, pink, blue, orange, yellow, green—and all shimmering simultaneously on that four-foot space. But these creations paled in radiance compared to the smile of the girl standing behind the table *selling* the stuff.

"Hey, Brenna," I said as I stopped in front of the table, carefully leaning my guitar case against its edge.

I break the glass, I buy the glass.

Brenna looked stunning, wearing the red dress I'd bought her at a thrift shop in San Diego. She'd also decorated her short, brown hair with a little red bandana and worn some stylish red earrings to match, not to mention that ruby lipstick.

Fire.

Brenna smiled through green eyes.

"Hello, Jason."

It'd been about a month since she and I had split up. Those first few weeks apart were strange—adjusting to being single again, getting used to seeing her around the market, and fighting the urge to call her anytime something happened that I knew she'd get a kick out of. After a while, though, she and I had started speaking again, and were now able to comfortably converse beyond formalities.

"How's the day so far?" I asked.

Brenna glanced over my shoulder. Behind me, a woman stood itching to get a peek at the cluster of glass orbs that dangled above the table like a balled-up rainbow.

"Excuse me," the woman said politely as she stepped forward to touch one of the ornaments. She then bent over and peered upward into the cluster, observing the way the lights hanging above the table beamed through the bulbs.

"Beautiful," the woman muttered to herself as she straightened her posture. She pointed at an ornament and asked Brenna, "How much are these?"

Brenna leaned forward to be heard over the chatter of a crowded arcade.

"One for twenty, or two for thirty-five."

The woman reached into her designer purse and pulled out a fifty dollar bill.

"If I give you cash," she said. "Can you sell me two for twenty-five?"

Brenna laughed.

"No, but I can sell you two for *thirty-five.*"

The woman processed this response and, as she stuffed the cash back into her purse, asked, "Do you have a website?"

"Nope," Brenna replied, accenting the solitary syllable with a single shake of her head.

The woman then reached out with her right hand and held one of the glass balls in her palm.

"Well," she said, "I absolutely love them. These are *exactly* what I've been looking for."

The woman paused for a moment and nodded quickly. "I'll think about it."

She abruptly scurried away.

Brenna laughed and looked at me, answering my question from a moment ago.

"It's been busy," she said. "Very busy. But I've only got..." she peeked down at her phone, resting between two glass candleholders, "three hours left, and then I'm FREE!" She raised her hands like the winner of the hundred meter dash.

"Nice," I said. "Any plans for the evening?"

Brenna flashed a tight smile. "That's none of your business now is it?"

I smiled back. "Shut up."

Brenna laughed. "As of now, the big plan is to go home, lie in a patch of sun on the floor, and fall asleep. After that..." She shrugged. "Who knows? You?"

Brenna mentioning the patch of sun on the floor had triggered a memory—whiskey, carpet, music...

Focus...

I snapped back—the market, the table, *the fire...*

"I'm gonna do one more Starbucks set at three and then head over to The Rusty Bucket for an open mic."

Brenna shot a quick glance over my shoulder. A few customers were lining up to get a peek at the glass.

"Cool," she said, looking back at me. "Sounds like a fine evening."

I nodded slowly, unable to remember why I'd come to the table.

I know there was a reason...

Brenna glanced down at my guitar case.

"You got some money for me today?"

Money! Right!

I reached into my pocket and pulled out the small bills I'd accumulated during my last set.

"Yes, ma'am," I said as I counted the money—four fives, ten ones, and a ten. "Forty."

Brenna pulled a small wad of cash out of a wooden box on the table. She peeled two twenties from the bundle and handed them to me. "I'll trade ya."

I took the twenties and handed Brenna the small bills, a hot commodity for any cash register.

The busker bank had delighted another customer.

"Thank you," Brenna said sweetly. That southern drawl always had a way of shining through her 'yews.' "Good luck at the open mic."

I grabbed my guitar case, saying, "Thanks," and "Enjoy your nap," as I stepped out of the path of ravenous consumers with glass appetites.

Squeezing back through the chaos of the craft line, my bulky case bumped into people the entire way.

"'Scuse me... 'Scuse me... Sorry..."

I exited the crowded arcade and crossed the sunny street to the coffee shop. A good-sized crowd had gathered inside. No Rubik's cube race today, but the place was packed with tourists—every seat caffeinated and a long line of folks waiting patiently for their afternoon fix. My guitar and I squeezed past the busy counter and chattering tables, making our way toward the back of the shop. This area was a small pocket of peace amidst a bustling market, and was also home to a very cozy leather couch—my favorite place to marinate between sets.

I planned on doing just that.

I removed the metal stand from my shoulder and tucked it, along with my guitar, into a corner behind the couch. Then I pulled the two fresh twenties of out my pocket, stuffed them into a wallet made of recycled rubber, plopped my ass onto the couch made of leather, and opened up a book made of words to pass the hour and a half until my next set.

4

"Is that one of your songs?"

I looked toward the girl who was leaning against the light post.

She looked to be about twenty. Wearing a pair of round sunglasses, like John Lennon's, and a multicolored band in her brown hair that reminded me of some sixties style. A sunflower patch had been stitched onto the black guitar bag that rested against her bare legs.

It was 3:45, near the end of my last Starbucks set. The sidewalk was quiet, and the steady stream of market customers had been reduced to a tiny trickle. Reacting to the low tourist traffic, some of the vendors had already begun to pack up for the day. I hadn't made much money myself, but figured I'd finish my hour anyways—never know when that wayward twenty dollar bill may find its way into the case.

"Yeah," I replied. "That's a newer tune."

The girl smiled.

"I like it," she said. "It's really catchy."

"Thank you."

I unhooked my leather guitar strap and reached into the elevated case, grabbing one of my CDs.

"I've got that song on this disc here," I told the girl. "My buddy Dalton plays second guitar on the recording and sings some harmonies."

I handed her the disc, packaged in a cardboard sleeve. She examined it with an enchanting curiosity.

The cover was a photo that my buddy Joey had taken on his

recent trip to New Zealand. A few cotton clouds hung in the blue sky above a vast, golden ground. Running along the left side of the picture was a small trail, burned into the sand and fading narrow into the horizon. A lone man stalked the trail with a black coat slung over his shoulder.

When Joey had shown me this picture, I knew it had to be an album cover. He was happy to let me use it.

The girl flipped the sleeve and read the text on the back before looking at me through those sunglasses. "This is super cool," she declared excitedly as she dug into the pocket of her jean shorts. "I'll take one for sure."

The girl pulled out a bill.

"Can you break a hundred?"

Seriously?

"I can if you wanna buy five of them," I replied.

The girl giggled. "I'm just kidding," she said, handing me a twenty. "Keep the change"

"Are you sure?" I asked.

The girl smiled and nodded.

I slipped Andrew Jackson into my pocket, said, "Thanks a lot," and reached into my case. "Here," I held another disc toward the girl. "Take a second CD and give it to a friend of yours."

The girl hesitated. "Are *you* sure?" she asked.

I nodded. "Mmmhmmm."

She and I stepped apart to let a family with a stroller pass between us. When we came back together, I handed her the CD.

"Awesome." The girl beamed. "Thank you!"

"Thank *you*," I replied as I held out my hand. "I'm Jason."

"Jaclyn."

Handshake.

"Good to meet you, Jaclyn."

I slung the guitar over my shoulder and began to tune while Jaclyn slid the CDs into her guitar bag. She then leaned back against the pole.

"Hope you don't mind me watching you play one more."

I strummed the first chords of a Tom Petty song.

"Not at all."

She tapped her foot to the beat, quietly singing along to "Free Fallin'." After the last note of the song, she clapped, slung her guitar over her shoulder, and waved goodbye with her fingers as she walked toward the south end of the market.

This is how I met Jaclyn Weber.

5

The way things work out sometimes blows my mind. I often wonder what makes everything line up the way it does.
What forces are at work, bringing all of this together?
All of us
Sometimes I find it interesting to trace relationships and circumstances back to their origins and explore those beginnings that gave way to the events of now.

I once spoke to a poet who called himself Firefly at a grimy midnight pub in Pioneer Square. He told me that someone had recently asked him how long it takes to write a poem.
Firefly had replied, "It takes me my whole life up until the moment I give birth to it."

I like that thought, everything feeding into everything, forever—gaining momentum and growing each second. The idea that what I'm experiencing now is a residual ripple from a rock I dropped in the big pond twenty years ago—a collection of ripples from every rock I've *ever* dropped—crisscrossing with ripples from other rocks dropped on adjacent shores... Everybody's rocks, everybody's ripples. Thousands of them, millions, billions, trillions—mixing, mingling, and co-creating shapes and patterns...
I think about this moment now being the product of every action I've ever taken, every word I've ever said, every word my *parents* said before conceiving me and every choice *they* made. Every slippered step my grandma took before she gave birth to my mother and every house my grandpa built before he shot my father out of his... Everything.
Then I think about that same equation applied to everyone else living on the planet, or who has ever lived—who ever

will live...
        Sorry...
                I'm going on a tangent here.
Back to a point of some sort; back to the story.

I'd had a lot of time on my hands to reflect and focus since Brenna and I had split—a lot of time to think about where I wanted to go and what I wanted to do. And the more I thought about it, the more I entertained the image of the Volkswagen van, of traveling around the country and playing little shows...street performing, exploring, meeting people, working odd jobs... Living.

That idea poked and poked at me—a relentless, stubborn little fucker—forcing me to listen, to think.

I didn't have a van, but I *did* have the Maxima, and it was running like a champ. Cozy enough to sleep in, too, and good gas mileage. I also didn't have anything chaining me to Seattle—no home, no romantic relationship, no kids (that I knew of).

With these things in mind, I began to formulate a plan. A plan that, to the untrained eye, probably looked a lot like a list of cities. Okay, it *was* a list of cities: Austin, Boulder, San Francisco, Portland, New Orleans, and L.A., to be exact, but once I scribbled the names of those cities into my little notebook...

That list became my mission.

6

Everybody screamed again.

I didn't realize there were so many damn Broncos fans in Seattle.

Looking up from my notebook, I saw that Denver had just completed a two-point conversion against the New England Patriots, putting the Broncos up fifteen to fourteen in the fourth quarter and leaving New England only a minute and fifteen seconds to answer. If anyone could make that situation work, it was Tom Brady.

The game went to commercial, and I shifted my attention again.

I'd been there at The Rusty Bucket for about a half hour, dividing my time between beer, Sunday night football, and my notebook, scribbling random thoughts as they drifted in and out of my head.

They can be tricky, those thoughts—hard to catch.

I like to think of them as little birds, flying into my head through the ears.

Usually, even if my feathered friends decide to hang around in there for a bit, they'll just get restless and fly right back out again. But they can only escape as long as there's an opening, so I've developed a method for capturing these little guys. All I have to do is become conscious of the fact that they're fluttering around in there—banging into my skull, squeaking and squawking and rattling all over—and, with will alone, I can close the shutters inside my ears tight.

Boom!!!

Sometimes those thoughts will try to fly out of my nose, but I can close those shutters, too.

Boom!! Boom!!

Then, once the shutters are closed and the thoughts are trapped inside my head, I can control them.

They're *my* thoughts after all.

I tell them not to be scared and send them down my arm, into my fingers, where I push hard until they bleed out the tip of my pen and live on some paper forever (in this case the word "forever" is relative to the lifespan of said paper). Those thoughts are happy on that paper, though: alive, transformed into the physical from some intangible energy.

I like to think about Fitzgerald or Kerouac, spilling swarms onto *their* paper. Paper where those thoughts could be read, shared, enjoyed, and pondered, allowing those speedy little birds to zip into the readers through the eyes and ricochet around inside their heads.

Once there, the thoughts had grown, duplicated themselves in new hosts where they could mate with other thoughts nesting in those fresh minds and create whole new species of ideas, birthed and bursting forth through conversation and other communications, colonizing minds worldwide, spreading like wildfire.

These thoughts love to travel, love growing bigger and stronger with each new mind they meet, so they thank me for bringing them to life, the little thought birds.

You're welcome, you noisy bastards.

Anyway, there I was. Me, my thought birds, and my beer; hanging out with a bar-full of other musicians, their thought birds, and their beers; along with the Broncos fans, their beers, and Tom Brady's right arm, at The Rusty Bucket in Ballard for what would soon be open mic night.

Walking in the door to a long wooden floor and brick walls, the bar ran most of the length of the room's left side, adjacent to a series of tables spread along the wall to the right. After walking past the bar, the room opened into an area with a few dart boards and a slew of small tables scattered in front of a four foot tall wooden stage. On that stage, nestled against the wall, a shy piano cowered beneath a massive chandelier. The Rusty Bucket's house lights were usually dimmed, and a single candle graced each table, illuminating the room just enough so that you could see who you were buying that beer for.

The sign-up process for The Rusty Bucket open mic was not for the weak.

Lives have been lost.

Folks would sometimes show up hours ahead of time, hoping to get fifteen minutes to share themselves on that coveted stage. Sign up was normally at 7:30, but you would begin to feel the hunger and tension building in the room at around 7:15. The host was rarely the same person two weeks in a row, leaving jittery musicians to scan the scene for fresh meat. Usually, one could spot the prey huddled in some nervous corner, clutching a pen and the almighty sign-up sheet. Other telltale symptoms of hostdom included gratuitous sweating and an attempt to remain inconspicuous while unable to conceal a look of impending doom.

At 7:30 sharp, the marked would rise paranoid from their shadowy safety and walk across the room to find a place to hold the sign-up (usually near the stage at the back of the room). Once spotted, they were trailed by a pack of bloodthirsty musicians, the swarm growing in number as it stalked across a beer-soaked wooden floor (ever seen a magnet dragged across flakes of metal?). Vampires would abruptly end conversations and leap from their seats, moving swiftly across the space to score a better spot, rushing toward the stage in a cloud of dust, tripping each other and jabbing sneaky elbows.

Once at the back of the room, the survivors were divided into three groups: newcomers (virgins always got first pick), folks who had been waiting at the bar to sign up for longer than an hour, and everybody else.

This particular night, I was everybody else.

By the time I was called to the sign-up sheet, the only spots left were some very early slots (around 8) and the very late slots (around 1 in the morning). I chose to play at 8:15, preferring early sets because I didn't have to wait long to play and played fairly well because I hadn't had time to sit around and drink six beers before my set. Then, when I was done, I could kick back and enjoy the rest of the night—and those beers.

Speaking of beer, mine was running low.

Before I went for a refill, though, I decided to go outside and smoke some pot.

It was a nice night, and I wanted to break in a new pipe I'd just bought from one of the glassblowers down at the market.

I walked through the door and turned toward an empty bike rack. Leaning against it, I loaded a bowl. The familiar scent triggered a brilliant idea: marijuana scented air fresheners.

Yes... Of course...

I wondered what it would take to get something like that off the ground.

Surely, I'd need an investor...

And what a hit the fresheners would be... Wait. Was that a pun?

I could sell them at all the smoke shops in the state... Make a killing...

But, I bet someone else has probably alrea—

"You gonna share some of that?"

The guy had stringy black hair hanging from beneath a red trucker hat and looked like he was about thirty. He wore torn jeans and a Black Sabbath T-shirt and was huddled beside a backpack in the doorway of a closed antique shop, twirling a drumstick in his right hand.

He seemed harmless enough.

"Sure, man," I responded. "Why not?"

I walked over and sat in the doorway with the guy, holding the pipe toward him. He accepted, saying, "Don't mind if I do," before lighting, holding for a bit, and exhaling.

A chalk dust cloud of smoke colored the chilly night air.

"Oh yeah..." The guy reflected as he returned the pipe and closed his eyes, spacing out like a heavy metal monk. As I sparked the lighter, he opened his eyes. They were very bright

45

green, focused on me.

"Thanks, dude," The metal monk spoke slowly. "That's *just* what I needed."

He unzipped his backpack—"Here,"—and offered me a bottle of rum.

I twisted the top and tipped the bottle in his direction. "Thanks."

The rum tasted good.

"What are you doing sitting in the doorway here?" I wondered aloud, handing the bottle back to him.

"Just waitin' on my girlfriend," the monk replied. "She's bartendin' over at The Cauldron there, and she's gettin' off any minute."

"Why don't you go wait for her in the bar?"

"Not allowed in there anymore," he answered, taking one more sip of the rum before returning the bottle to its backpack abode. "Me and my homie John were in there a few months back, hangin' out, and somebody did right puttin' Pantera on the jukebox. Fuckin' love Pantera." Metal monk pulled up his right sleeve. "As you can see."

On his upper arm, he had a tattoo of the letters *CFH*, forged from steel and surrounded in flames.

I responded with a slow nod. "*Cowboys From Hell.* Good album."

The fact that I recognized the acronym made the metal monk happy. He fist-bumped me before carrying on.

"Me and John were playin' a little pool and 'Walk' came on, so we both got stoked and started gettin' into it. We used to ride dirt bikes to that album out in Moses Lake back when it first came out. *Vulgar Display of Power,* you know, the one with that dude gettin' punched in the face for the album cover."

How could I forget?

"John was in the middle of shootin', and I wanted to fuck with him, so I started air jammin', you know, rockin' my pool stick like a guitar, right up in his space." The metal monk strummed an imaginary axe as he continued to speak. "I fucked him up so bad he scratched." He chuckled. "So John got pissed and turned around and gave me a shove, he's a little guy though—felt like my kid sister shoved me. So I said, '*No way, dude,*' and gave him a bigger shove with both hands, sent him flyin' off his feet. I thought that was that, but then he came back across the room and full-on tackled me into a table. Well, me and him started rollin' around on the floor—bad news for John 'cause I was on the wrestling team back in high school, and I've still got some serious moves. 'Bout six seconds and I had that little shit in an arm bar. 'Course, right as he was tappin' the big Samoan bouncer comes up and grabs me by my shirt collar..."

I laughed. "What'd your girl think of that?"

The metal monk grinned. "I looked over at her while they were escortin' me out. She was behind the bar with her arms folded, shakin' her head and smilin'..." He paused for a moment. "She's an angel, dude. I don't know what she sees in my dumb ass, but she puts up with me. I must be doin' somethin' right."

The metal monk started pounding out a beat, palms on his knees, as he continued to speak. "Me and her moved up here from Arizona two years ago. Met when she was workin' at a Duncan Donuts down in Tucson... Fuck." He shook his head. "We started livin' together and she'd bring boxes of those things home. I'd eat 'em breakfast, lunch, and dinner. Ate too many and ended up gettin' a bunch of cavities."

I laughed and took a long puff, looking up at the sky as I blew the smoke out.

In the city you can only see a star or two, even on the clearest nights...

"Hey, you know who you look like?" the metal monk asked.

I glanced back at him. "Jesus?"

He pointed at me. "Oh yeah! Him too!" Then he took on a serious tone. "But no, dude," he continued. "It's kinda creepy. You look just like Jim Morrison right before he died."

"Hmmmmmmm..." I thought for a second. "That's a new one."

I knocked on the nearby wooden door and slid the pipe back into my pocket before checking my phone: 8:10.

Show-time.

"Hey, I gotta run inside, man." I stood up. "Playing a set in five minutes and gotta tune the guitar." I extended my hand

toward my new friend. "Good to meet you."
He shook my hand and smiled. "You too, dude. Have a good set."

I'm convinced that because of the metal monk's well wishes, I did just that.

I walked inside, grabbed my guitar, and stepped up onto the stage, playing two songs that had been in my regular rotation for a little while—one tune about summertime in North Bend (where I grew up) and one venting frustrations about a school shooting that had permeated recent news. The folks at the Rusty Bucket seemed to enjoy both songs: I hadn't been booed yet, and no tomatoes had been thrown. But there was still time for all that; I'd saved my newest song for last.

I'd written the words to this song when Brenna and I had first started seeing each other. After our first few dates, I was really beginning to get into her but wasn't sure if I was ready to dive into a relationship. Those lyrics captured the inner tug of war I was experiencing, but for some reason I hadn't been able to write any music to go along with them until right before Brenna and I had split up.
I'd named the song "Symptoms of the Night"
It had a creeping tempo, picked with the fingers, and a haunting yet beautiful vocal melody.

Seated on the piano stool, which I'd pulled to the front of the stage, I leaned into the microphone and told the crowd I'd be playing a new song, hoping that if I butchered it, they'd understand.
Maybe they wouldn't even notice.
I'm always my own worst critic.

Here we go...
I took a deep breath, looked down at the neck of my guitar, and began playing the song's opening chords.
It took me a moment to control my breathing and slow the battery acid pumping through my veins, but once I got a hold

of myself, the song's opening tones flowed fluidly from my fingertips. Repeating the series of notes, I flubbed one part of the E flat arpeggio, but recovered quickly and rolled on.

Okay... So far, so good.

Time to sing. Deep breath. First verse...

"It lights the way... It flickers, don't let it fade away,
Dancing in the wind... today."

Breathe. From the stomach... Good.

"Stories that we told... Identities breathing bold,
Smiling through the flame... We hold."

Between each verse, a melody is hummed over a series of finger picked chords:

"Hmmmmmmmm... Mmmmmmmmm... Mmmmmmmmm... Mmmmm... Mmmmmmmm..."

Everything was flowing nicely.

Good. Looks like the practice paid off.

Hey.

Focus.

Next verse.

Wait... What are the words again?!

Shit...

I racked my brain as the verse approached.

Only a few notes left. No, no, no...

Oh yeah!

"It's all locked inside... Open up and open wide,
It's no fun to run...and hide.

"Symptoms of the night... Take my hand and let's go find
Some place we can be...alive."

During the second humming section, I noticed the place was silent. Everyone was listening.

They like the song.
   They're paying attention to it, connecting with it.

   Stop it.

      Focus.
         Last verse.
            Breathe...

"It's spinning this time... It's easier to leave your mind,
   When you put it all...on the line.

"And that's a risk I like to take... It's a reckless game with so much at stake,
   But I've got a heart that loves...to break."

I felt myself drifting as I hummed the final section of the song, eyes closed, voice shaking, excited but rolling through the motions, feeling everything: the good, the bad, the confidence, the fear—all of it.
   The final chords approached slowly.
   F sharp...
   F...
   E flat minor...

      Hold it... Last note... Let that ring out...
         Good.

I slowly opened my eyes and realized everyone in the place was staring at me, not making a sound.
   I felt good about the way I'd played the song, but didn't know what anyone *else* in the room thought of the performance.
   Shit. Did they hate it?
      Did my voice sound bad? Am I delusional?
         Is this a terrible song?
   The crowd exploded with applause—cheering, clapping, a few whistles thrown in for good measure.
   I let out a deep breath, one that had been lodged deep in my gut for fifteen minutes.

Awesome.

I leaned into the microphone one more time and said, "Thank you!" as I unplugged my guitar and walked offstage.
        What an amazing feeling.
        There's always a moment when I'm sharing a new tune where I'm completely in love with it, but I'm not sure if the sentiment will be shared. Playing that newborn piece feels similar to what I imagine it would be like sending my kid off to school for the first time, out into the big world on its own. I have control over that tune when it's in my head, my home, but the second it leaves there, it's at the mercy of the schoolyard. Hopefully, the song is strong enough to fend for itself.

I stepped down from the stage, laid my guitar in its case, and headed toward my table, where I was greeted by my beer and notebook—dear friends. I took a seat and frantically wrote down feelings of excitement and gratitude about everything that came to mind: the song I'd just played, my experiences leading up to it, Brenna, Pike Place, my friends, my family, my health, the flavored milk that's left after you've eaten all the chocolate cereal. At this point I was writing furiously, trying to keep up with the swarm of thoughts in my head. Those damn birds again, flying frantically, breeding and bursting out of eggs laid by feelings of accomplishment and release still stuck to me from the stage.

I think if I saw myself hunched over my notebook, scribbling like I was, I might think I was crazy.
Conscious of this, I came up for air...and beer. I enjoyed a big swig and took a moment to stare at the bubbles dancing in my glass. As I did, I tried to slow my mind and take in as much of the information and detail around me as possible. *Think of it all... So many sensations to experience at any given moment.*
        The sights.
                The sounds.
                        The smells...

Feelings.

Tastes.

    Thoughts...

        Wait...

Is thought our sixth sense?

"How's that beer?"

    I'd been spotted.

The lowering of my glass—and its bubbles—revealed a tall black dude. He wore baggy old clothes that hung from broad shoulders. Over his right arm, a faded brown leather satchel was slung over a dirty, potato-sack shirt. That shirt was tattered, but the guy himself was clean-cut, standing there with both hands in his pockets and a resonator guitar hanging by the strap over his left shoulder. Laser-beam brown eyes peered at me through slit eyelids, shaded by the ragged brim of his fedora.

    He was waiting.

    I looked at my beer, back up at him, and took a drink.

    "Delicious," I replied.

    The guy nodded, eyes still narrowed. I got the feeling he was smiling, but his mouth didn't move.

    "Name's Dante," he said, extending a large hand. "Just drove up from Portland last night."

    Handshake.

    "I'm Jason."

    Dante and the fedora nodded toward the table. "Mind if I join you?"

    I held up my beer. "We don't mind at all."

    Dante smiled, with his mouth this time, and carefully set his caseless guitar against the brick wall. "Cool," he said as he hung his satchel on a chair and pointed at my beer. "But first..." Dante pointed that same finger toward the bar. "The fuel."

    With that, he made his way to the pump.

The opening chords of a fresh song begged my attention, and I turned to face the stage where a new singer had just begun his set, a shorter guy, tilting his head back slightly to tickle the microphone with the hairs of his goatee. Under a San Francisco Giants baseball cap, a mop of brown hair hung past his ears. The player strummed a baby blue acoustic guitar and wore a blue jean jacket with matching jeans.

(Instead of referring to this songwriter as "The Guy" or something generic, I'm going to call him "the Jeanie." In fact, I may give nicknames to many people, places, and things over the course of this story when proper labels aren't available.)

The Jeanie had an interesting voice: very genuine (Jean-uine?), speaking on pitch with a subdued and somber drag about cruising down the California coast. I lost myself in the Jeanie's journey as he raked strings and wove words that made me feel like I was shooting through Santa Cruz in my Maxima. A few minutes into the sunshine ride, just as all of us rolled past Pescadero, the Pacific on our right...

POP!!!

A deceased string dangled sadly from the headstock of the Jeanie's guitar.

He'd blown the low E—the big one. The Jeanie continued to play his song, but the guitar was wounded, and the two of them wouldn't make it much further into battle without that string; too dangerous.

I reached for my case and popped it open.

Despite his guitar's mortal misfortune, the Jeanie finished his tune. After this, he addressed the room with a speaking voice nearly identical to the one that had sent us seventy miles an hour down Highway One.

"Hey everybody," he began, with a hint of embarrassment, "as you probably noticed, I just broke a string."

The Jeanie slid his guitar carefully over his head, making sure not to catch the brim of his baseball cap in the process. He then set the instrument against the wall before wheeling back around to speak into the microphone. "Does anybody happen to have—"

"Here you go man," I interrupted, standing in front of the stage with guitar outstretched. "Treat her right."

The Jeanie glanced down at me and smiled as he grabbed the instrument. Up close, he kind of looked like a young George Harrison. "Thanks, buddy."

"No problem," I replied. "Enjoy."

I walked back to the table just as Dante arrived with a bottle of beer, which he tipped toward the stage. "You save him?"

I nodded. "Yeah. Guy broke his E string."

Dante shook his head and made a clicking noise with his mouth as he raised the bottle to his lips.

We took our seats.

Watching someone play your guitar is like watching someone dance with your girlfriend.

There were a few thoughts running through my head during the Jeanie's next songs. The first was an appreciation of my guitar's beauty—a different view from the sidelines, different sound.

I sat back and admired the instrument's depth and richness of tone, proud to call her mine.

Damn, she looks great in that blue dress.
Look at that smile, that body, those legs—perfect.
And how does she move like that in those heels?

But, all the while—on my mental scales—another thought teetered opposite this adoration, a thought that sounded a bit like
BE CAREFUL GODDAMMIT!!!!

He's strumming it too hard!
Don't step on her toes!
Okay, breathe... It's cool, she can handle it. Those are new strings, strong strings...
Hey... What's he doing?
DON'T MESS WITH THE TUNING!!
That guy better back up a few inches. And move his hand up off her waist while he's at it...

But, before you know it...

My guitar sings its last note for the Jeanie.

My girlfriend gets dipped one more time by the guy in the vest who took salsa lessons...

And then the two of us are back again, as we should be—together.

I grabbed my case and walked toward the stage to be reunited with my lady. The Jeanie stepped down and returned her, still warm from their dance.

"Thanks a lot, buddy. I owe you one."

I bent down and laid the guitar to rest. She'd had a long day.

"Sounds like I owe *you* one," I responded. "Did I hear you say it was your birthday up there?"

The Jeanie adjusted his ball cap and nodded. "Yeah," he said. "The big three-oh. Goodbye twenties..."

"The dirty thirty," I looked toward the bar and then back at the Jeanie with a smile. "Well, I hope you like whiskey."

The two of us leaned our cases against the wall and made our way to the bar. I ordered a couple shots and handed one to the birthday boy before lifting mine.

"I'm Jason."

"Dominic," the Jeanie revealed as he raised his shot. "Thanks."

"No problem, Dominic. Cheers."

Clink!

"Happy birthday."

Dominic and I set our empty glasses on the bar as the warm whiskey administered mutual esophageal massages. Dominic shook himself, rolling his lips. "Happy birthday to me," he said.

I laughed. "That getcha?"

"Whiskey kills me every time," Dominic replied. "But turning down a birthday shot is like turning down a handshake."

I smiled and nodded toward Dante, seated across the room. "Wanna come hang with me and my new Portlandian friend?"

Dominic turned his attention to Dante, who was floating in some private void, intensely focused on the current performer and thinking who-knows-what under that frayed fedora.

"Sure," Dominic said. "I'm in. Lemme go get this guy from Boulder I've been sitting with; we'll be over in a minute."

I sat down at the table with Dante, and, after a bit longer than a minute, Dominic and Boulder came to join the festivities, bringing beers and guitar cases along with them. Dante and I were seated with our backs to the bar, facing the brick wall. Dominic and Boulder took the seats across from us. This arrangement allowed each of us a great view of the stage with just a slight turn of the head.

Once situated, we, the Rusty Bucket contingent, went around the table and introduced ourselves.

What an interesting crew we had there.

Boulder was a big man. Not particularly muscular—a little bit of cushion around his edges, but he wasn't a guy I'd want to tangle with. He looked about forty, with a shaved head, reddish face, and blonde eyebrows so light they almost made him look hairless. (His real name was Tyler, but I'm going to continue calling him Boulder because it sounds cool.)

"You guys local?" Boulder asked, nodding toward Dante and me with sleeveless arms folded on the table in front of him.

Something bulged from inside his lower lip.

Dante, seated directly across from Boulder, nodded slowly, a smile tugging at one side of his mouth. "Just drove up from Portland."

"Trail Blazers territory," Boulder said, taking a confident swig of his beer. "Best strip clubs on the West Coast down there." Dante nodded as Boulder nudged Dominic. "Don't even bother with the clubs here in Seattle," he advised. "All they'll give you to drink is a goddamn sodie pop."

Dominic looked at me with raised eyebrows. "Seriously?" he asked.

I nodded. "Yeah. It's illegal for strip clubs to sell alcohol here in Seattle, or to let you *drink* alcohol while you're inside. So once you walk in the door, the bouncer hands you a sixteen-ounce plastic cup and points you to the soda fountain where you get free refills all night long."

Dominic smiled. "Sounds like a party."

Coloring Outside the Lines

Boulder lifted his bottle and pulled the napkin out from underneath. "'Scuse me boys," he said, holding the napkin in his left hand and opening his mouth slightly. He reached up and pulled a huge wad of chewing tobacco from his lower lip, enclosing the dripping mass in the napkin and sucking the residual juices from his fingertips.

Dante recoiled in disgust and voiced the table's shared sentiment. "Aw, c'mon!"

Dominic said "Nasty" as he glanced back and forth between Boulder and Dante with an amused grin.

"You had that in there the whole time?" I asked Boulder, who nodded proudly.

"Yup."

"No spitter?" Dominic asked.

Boulder leaned back in his chair and patted his bulging belly, making a slapping sound through his gray shirt.

"Gut it," he said, happily anticipating the rest of the table's collective disgust, which manifested itself in the form of a three-part groan.

Boulder chuckled hard, hands still resting on that belly of his. He looked, with that jolly red face, like I imagine Santa Claus looked in his forties before he grew a beard and quit his construction job for a life of milk and cookies.

"Yup," Boulder went on, still smiling big. "Can't hold a spitter when you got both hands mixin' concrete."

"Is that what you do?" I asked. "Concrete?"

"If the job calls for it," Boulder said. "I do remodels. Been doin' 'em down there in Colorado for fifteen years, which is about..." Boulder counted on his fingers, deep in mock-thought. "...Fifteen years too long." He laughed and took a sip of his beer. "'Least I can hire guys to do the Sheetrockin' for me now, though."

"Sheetrock?" asked Dante.

Boulder nodded. "Drywall. Can't stand muddin' and tapin' that shit, sandin' all day in a basement with no ventilation, no windows. Then goin' home and my old lady thinks I've been doin' coke for ten hours 'cause I've got white dust trails up under my nostrils."

"Don't you wear some kind of mask?" Dominic asked.

"Oh yeah," Boulder said. "But that dust finds a way in. Hell, some days I'll go take a piss after nine hours a' Sheetrockin' and a big white cloud'll shoot right outta the tip a' my dick!"

The table chuckled as the next act, a male-female duo, took the stage and began their first song. The man played an acoustic guitar and the woman tickled a fiddle. Those two swayed side by side on stage, playing an up-tempo, boot-stompin' little ditty, owning their instruments with practiced precision. As they began to sing, their voices soared simultaneously over the chords with a seasoned grit.

Boulder glanced toward the stage and abruptly stopped laughing. With eyes still locked on the performance, he spoke to himself loud enough for the rest of us to hear. "No shit..."

He looked around the table before nodding toward the players. "Those two up there are from Boulder."

The four of us glanced toward the duo, still blazing through their tune as the crowd clapped to the beat.

"Really..." Dante pondered, stroking his hairless chin, intrigued.

"Sure of it," Boulder replied. "See 'em down on Pearl Street all the time." He took the last sip of his beer and then shook his head. "Small world," he said, standing with empty bottle in hand. "You boys thirsty?"

Boulder pointed a finger around the table.

First to Dominic: "Sure."

Then to me: "Yeah, thanks."

Boulder's finger found a smirking Dante: "Always."

Boulder nodded once. "Three Pabst, comin' right up!"

As he walked toward the bar, Dominic, Dante, and I killed what was left of our drinks.

Dante shook his head. "Funny dude."

"Yeah," I agreed, looking toward Dominic. "You just met him?"

Dominic nodded. "Uh huh. He's been cracking me up for the last hour. One thing's for sure, that guy's got some crazy stories. He told me about some time he spent in San Francisco that made me feel like I haven't even experienced my own city, and I've been there for three years. He was only in town for two weeks."

Wait a second.

"You're from San Francisco?" I asked.

Dominic tapped the red "SF" occupying the center of his black cap.

"Moved there from Chicago three years ago."

"No way..." I said, trailing off as I was sucked into a small-world moment of my own.

The synchronicity hit me like a wet salmon to the face.

My wish list of cities lived in the notebook that sat atop the table; the same table where *I* sat, shooting the shit with traveling musical ambassadors from three of those eight cities...

"Bottoms up!"

My trance was broken by four tall cans hitting the wooden tabletop with a unified thud.

Boulder sat down and slid frosty cans across the table to their final destinations. A collective "thank you" rose from those on the receiving end of Boulder's generosity before we tipped our cans, enjoying the first sips of cold beer.

The open mic host, a man with glasses and a large red beard, walked over and placed a hand on Dante's shoulder. "You're up after this song."

Dante looked at the host and nodded. "Cool."

The nod was returned, and the host quickly ninja'd back across the room to resume his post at the end of the bar. Dante reached into his satchel hanging from the back of his chair and pulled out a stack of about half a dozen white mailing envelopes. He set them on the table and fished a black permanent marker from his pocket.

"Sendin' out a few birthday cards?" Boulder asked.

Appearing annoyed by the interruption, Dante set the marker down and lifted the paper sleeve, opening the flap and reaching inside to reveal a homemade CD inscribed with black ink. Dante showed the disc around the table before sliding it back into the envelope and again picking up the marker.

There was unanimous approval of Dante's innovative packaging.

Those envelopes had been intentionally abused and dirtied, giving them the appearance of having traveled some long distance—perhaps by pony express. I took a peek at the stack that began to form once Dante had finished a few of them, and saw that he had addressed the envelopes "To: You—Wherever you are." The return name was his, Dante Blue, and the address was Dante's website and a "Thank you."

When Dante stepped up on stage to play, his huge form hunched over the microphone and he sang down into it with eyes barely peeking out from under the brim of that hat. He had a great voice—a hint of Bob Dylan blended with some unique edge.

The room fell silent for Dante and his magnetic presence—sucking us into his experience via vibrations from a weathered guitar and throat full of gravel—and his chorus cut through that silence like an arrow, finding a spot to lodge itself deep in my spine, sending chills throughout my entire body.

"So when you're bouncing back and forth between your heart's every desire...

Make sure those paper fantasies don't burn up in the fire."

I scribbled Dante's lyrics into my notebook, which was very happy to have some attention after all the social interaction of the evening.

Dante's song ended to explosive applause.

After a long moment spent processing the room's reaction, Dante reached for the small stack of envelopes that sat atop the chair beside him. He picked one—looking like a little white business card in those big black bear paws—and stretched his arms out in front of him, panning the envelope from left to right as he spoke—an offering to the room, exhibit A.

"If you've enjoyed my music," he said, "I have it for you here..."

Dante then brought the envelope back toward his body and examined it.

"I love it when I receive a piece of mail," he said, as if only to himself. "Writing letters is such a rare thing these days."

He looked back up at the room and held the envelope in front of him with one hand.

"I did this for you because I think that everyone likes to get a piece of mail from time to time—"

A male voice shattered the silence, cutting Dante short. "Not if it's a bill!"

All eyes focused on the offender, seated a few feet from the stage, and Dante's gaze shifted slowly in the man's direction. Then, with one quick flick of his massive wrist, Dante sent the envelope flying toward the man's table like a Frisbee. The package landed squarely at the heckler's feet.

"That's not a bill," Dante assured the stunned spectator.

Dante then took his right hand and held it open in front of him, closing it slowly and speaking calmly. "I've melted ice cubes with my fist...so you can have water to drink."

With that, Dante unplugged his guitar, nodded once, and walked off the stage.

7

"Shit!"

I flailed my hand in an attempt to neutralize the pain. The woman to my right, packing up her display after a day of selling her handwoven scarves, laughed and shook her head.

I'd told myself several times that I needed to let the lights cool down before I unclamped them and wrapped them up for the day. But in my haste to close up shop, I'd forgotten again. The searing sting from an exposed bulb, freshly unplugged after eight hours of burning bright, served as a stern reminder.

I left the lights alone for the time being and began to pack the rest of my table, glancing up every now and then at the few scattered souls who still wandered aimlessly through the market, in search of something that would catch their eye and their cash.

The packing process began with me wrapping six canvassed acrylic paintings in cloth and placing them in a long plastic container. Once I'd secured the lid, I stashed all the vinyl decals into a smaller container before storing the 8x10 prints in another. The T-shirts, which had been hanging on a bungee cord above the table, were folded up and placed into a bin of their own. I made sure to fold them nicely. Zoe, the artist I was selling for, worked the next day and hated unpacking the cart to find wrinkled shirts. Unfortunately, I knew this from experience. (Don't worry. She didn't beat me *too* severely.) Last but not least, as it officially signified the end of my pack, I folded the blue cloth that had been covering my four-foot space and tossed it into the container with the shirts.

After all the product had been packed, I made sure to run to the deli across the street and purchase a piece of candy with a twenty dollar bill so I could leave Zoe with enough small bucks to start her day.

Once I'd done this, I walked back to the craft line, dodging a renegade bicyclist en route, and popped the chocolate into my mouth. When I arrived back at my table—now just cold steel again after the art had been packed—I touched one of the lights above the bare space. It was finally cool. I unclamped that light, wrapped it in its own electrical cord, and placed it in the last plastic container. Then I repeated this process with all four bulbs. Once everything was in its proper place, I stacked the plastic containers on a four-wheeled metal cart, threw a cloth over the top, secured everything with two bungee cords, and began to push the load down the craft line.

As the cart's wheels rattled over arcade tiles, startling a few wayward pigeons in my path, I passed packing crafters to my right and left, closing their tables for the day. It was five o'clock, and most of the folks at Pike Place were usually cleared out by six. Some of the vendors were holding tight, though, waiting for desperate stragglers to impulse-buy something "Seattle" before they rushed to SeaTac for their eight o'clock back to Pittsburgh.

I said goodbye to some of the closing folks as I rolled past—a girl packing her silver jewelry, a guy folding dog leashes made from rock climbing rope. I passed flower farmers to my left, loading unsold bouquets into large white vans with the help of a couple men who were paid a few dollars a day to lend a hand.

As I rattled on, I glanced through small windows to my right that allowed broken glimpses of West Seattle, sitting across the blue of Puget Sound. In the distance, I began to hear Charles banging out a tune on his rollaway piano, which he had set up on the corner of Pike Place and Pine. I remember seeing Charles jamming in that same spot when I was a kid, performing five to seven days a week for nearly thirty years and stashing that little piano in one of the lockers underneath the market. On rainy days, Charles tickles the keys beneath a giant umbrella (like the one stuck through that table on your neighbor's patio). He pushes that little piano up the street each and every set to share his music with the world as it walks by.

Stay in one spot long enough, and it all starts to revolve around you, your image burned into the background.

I rolled past a seafood stand, closing down after another long day of selling salmon to the masses. Several workers in black rubber boots and green rubber aprons yelled jokes to each other as they plucked unsold fish from large, ice-filled containers. The absence of the seafood left pink stains on the frost where those lazy fish had lounged their day away. Breathing the lingering sea-stink, I wheeled my cart down a slight incline where water, originating from a hose blasting clean the glass display case, flowed down the slope beside me. Another rubber-booted worker brandished a broom and pushed excess H_2O into the slits of a rusty sewer grate as I crossed the brick street.

The elevators were tucked in a hallway beside the bakery.
　　I pressed the down button and listened to Charles's tune as I awaited my ride to freedom. The elevator doors slid open, and I was pleasantly surprised when they revealed the girl who worked at the bookstore. She smiled and waved as she walked past.
　　I smiled back and said, "Have a good night," as I pushed the cart through open doors.
There was a faint, "You too," as they slid shut.
　　As the elevator descended, my mind wandered, picturing the conversation that might have taken place if I had packed up three minutes earlier and stepped onto the elevator with bookstore girl and the cart.
　　She looked beautiful that day, always did, usually wearing something purple and a bright smile. Not all girls could pull off dreadlocks, but she made them look great, and her walk was the cherry on top—strutting as though she owned the world. But she didn't rule with an iron fist. No, she was the delicate queen of her realm, moving through it with a confident grace. The two of us threw good looks when we would see each other and had nice

times when we would speak. She was funny, quirky—asked me
one day if I thought drunk clowns would make fucked up balloon
animals.

The elevator doors began to close.

I was already in the basement.

Wait!

I stuck my foot out to block the doors and they slid slowly
open again.

Women on the mind...

I wanted to be careful, though. It wouldn't be wise to get
involved with another market girl. Pike Place was a chatty
community, and word traveled fast down there. Brenna and I both
knew that eventually we'd be moving on and seeing new people,
but I didn't want to rub any potential new relationships in her
face. *Best to keep these curiosities in my head and search for
female companionship elsewhere.*

I wheeled the squeaky cart across the cement floor, between
several rows of large metal cages. These walk-in lockers were
rented out to vendors and stored a majority of the art and crafts
sold at Pike Place. Zoe's locker was 66C, complete with a turn-
dial lock like the one I used to have in gym class—three numbers,
right, left, right. Her lock got stuck sometimes, so even when the
code was correct, I'd really have to give it a good tug to pop it off
the door.

I entered the locker, pulled my guitar out from under a
large tarp, and parked the cart in its place.

Another successful day on the books.

I took my share of the day's money and stuffed it into my wallet
before clanging the metal door shut and clicking the lock closed,
securing the art and the cart for the night.

Freedom!

Now, it was time to go meet the Rusty Bucket crew for their last
night in town.

After the night we'd met, Dante, Dominic, Boulder, and I had
spent the next two evenings playing at a few other spots around
town—Monday at an open mic in Wallingford and Tuesday in

West Seattle. The three travelers were in town until Thursday, and the four of us had figured that, with as much fun as we'd had that first night, we may as well meet up for an open mic every evening until they left Seattle. Both outings following our first night were equally as entertaining, sharing more music, beers, and laughs, and this night was to be the fourth and final stop on the Seattle open-mic tour.

I had no doubt it would be an evening to remember. Little did I know how right I was.

I took a moment to turn around as I hiked the hill from Pike Place to First Avenue.

The sun was just starting to set over Puget Sound, begging me to slow for a moment to appreciate the view of the Olympic Mountains splashed pink and orange across the horizon—smell the air, take it in.

Beauty.

Loading up on natural wonder, I laid my guitar down and gave Dominic a call. We decided to meet downtown where he was hanging with a friend of his from Chicago. The three of us would rendezvous on Blanchard before carpooling to Boulder's motel on Eastlake.

After hanging up the phone, I picked up my guitar and enjoyed one last sip of the sunset cocktail before turning around and starting back up the hill, excited about what the night might bring.

"Long time no see!"

The voice came from behind me. I spun around to investigate.

Bare legs, topped by cut-off jean shorts, stepped from the driver's side of a mid-eighties Mercury Grand Marquis, a beat-up boat of a car, parked diagonally on the hill. The car's navy blue paint job was peppered with a healthy dose of rust and its pilot wore John Lennon glasses with a colored headband.

"Jaclyn, right?"

She tilted her head downward and pulled those sunglasses onto the tip of her nose, revealing green eyes. "Yessir."

"I had a feeling we'd run into each other again," I said.

"I was hoping so." She took a loaded pipe from the pocket of her little jean shorts and held it toward me. "You smoke?"

I did my best to imitate Jaclyn's tone from a moment ago, head tilt and all, pulling imaginary glasses over my nose. "Yes, Ma'am."

Jaclyn laughed and handed me the pipe. "Good, 'cause I don't wanna smoke this alone."

What a lady.

I produced my lighter and put it to work.

"Can you believe this sunset?" Jaclyn asked, holding her arms out toward the open air like she was hugging it. She threw her head back and let out a cry from somewhere deep inside. "Aaaaah!" she screamed. "I wanna eat it."

I laughed.

I have a name for these little outbursts. I call them soulgasms.

Soulgasm: Noun. When an intense amount of goodness builds up deep inside and you have no choice but to release it via some explosive sound or gesture.

I passed the pipe and lighter to Jaclyn. "I love it," I said. "Looks like the sky's on fire."

"That's not the only thing," Jaclyn replied as she sparked the lighter, inhaling and blowing a large cloud toward the sky like some pretty volcano.

After her eruption, Jaclyn looked back at me. "Where are you headed?"

I nodded up the hill. "Going to meet a buddy of mine over near the Green Room. Guy from San Francisco."

Jaclyn took her sunglasses off and placed them atop her head. "Yeah?" she asked. "How do you know him?"

"Just met him the other night," I said. "At an open mic in Ballard."

Jaclyn passed the pipe and lighter back to me. "You ever been?"

"To San Francisco?" I asked.

Jaclyn nodded, and I took a moment to turn my attention toward the exploding sky.

A ferry crept across the crimson water, on its way to Bainbridge.

"No," I said, glancing back at her. "But it's on my list."

A smile sprouted along the corners of Jaclyn's mouth, and she rubbed her chin with ringed fingers, looking at me through sparkling eyes.

"Wanna cross it off?

8

We picked the guy up in the parking garage at the airport, right where he said he would be.

Jaclyn and I caught our first glimpse of him in the rearview mirror as he crossed the concrete to the Marquis: long dirty blonde hair, blue jeans, and a black leather jacket, wearing aviator sunglasses at seven at night.

He strutted up to the Mercury and stuffed his large duffel bag between the two guitars in the trunk.

Jaclyn and I had gotten to know each other a bit better during the half hour waiting for this guy in the Mercury. Even when that car was turned off, it smelled like gasoline, like someone had spilled gallon across the back seat. Jaclyn had spoken to me about her writing, photography, and dreams to travel the world. This would be her first trip down to San Francisco, a place that she'd wanted to visit for a long time.

Jaclyn worked for a company that contracted folks from all over the country to perform duties at various festivals, gatherings, and social events. Because so many of these opportunities popped up outside the state of Washington, Jaclyn's job fit perfectly with her desire to travel.

That particular trip would find Jaclyn at a networking event for hundreds of budding businesses, wo-manning a booth for a company that sold spray-on deodorant. Jaclyn would spend five days handing out free samples of the product and spraying stinky fuckers who waltzed up to her table in the hopes of getting the smell of three-day-old sweat out of their 49ers T-shirt.

Our travel companion slid into the back seat of the car, and Jaclyn

fired up the blue monster, gurgling gas as it roared to life. This
was the first time either Jaclyn or I had met—
     "Blaze," he said, extending a hand over the front seat.
"It's my last name. And considering my line of work, I'd be stupid
not to roll with it."
     Blaze (actually spelled Blaise) was a weed runner, headed
to San Francisco to pick up his truck and the next shipment,
which he would then deliver to various dealers across the country.
Blaze had acquired this ride via an ad that Jaclyn had posted
online earlier that day. She had offered passage to the Bay Area in
exchange for a little gas money and good company.
     "This thing gonna make it to Frisco?" Blaze asked from
the back seat.
     "One way to find out," Jaclyn replied, as the blue beast
lumbered onto the highway. "I bought it for five hundred last
month from my friend's dad. It's beat up, but he says it runs
great."

That car had no division between the passenger and driver's seats.
From the looks of things, Mercury had teamed up with a company
that manufactured couches and dropped two sofas into each
Marquis rolling off the assembly line. Those seats were very cozy,
and roomy enough to fit a third person up front should Jaclyn feel
inclined to maximize the space.
     Blaze leaned over the middle of the front seat to speak.
     "Well, a drive down to Frisco is a hell of a way to test it.
You can do the run in fourteen hours straight if you keep it
between seventy and eighty. But that's if you only stop to piss and
get gas. Maybe eat something." He slapped the front seat. "This
thing's got a V8 in it too. Fuckin' tank!"
     Blaze leaned back into the rear couch which, for the time
being, he had all to himself. The three of us were on our way to
pick up two of Jaclyn's coworkers near Portland. They would be
joining us for the ride to San Francisco, and when they did,
Blaze's space would become much less spacious. He enjoyed
stretching out back there while he could—laid out across all three
seats with hands folded behind his head and boots resting on the
upholstery.

The sky poured heavily that night, and the car's wipers, even at full speed, fought hard to keep up with the amount of rain being dumped onto the mighty windshield.

This was early November, a little over a month since I'd run into Jaclyn climbing that sunset hill.

9

The rest of that September night had been a gradual rise to a furious blur. One of those where all colors blend to black.

The evening had begun when Dominic, a girl named Abby (Dom's friend from Chicago), and I had arrived at Boulder's Eastlake motel. We were pleasantly surprised to find the room stocked with enough beer to fill a bathtub, but Boulder wouldn't allow the four of us to get into those brews until we started on the whiskey.

"No, no, no, kids," he had said, smacking my hand as I reached for one of the beers atop a wooden cabinet. Boulder then walked across the room and pulled a bottle of Jack from the top drawer of his dresser. After twisting the cap, he turned to face me with bottle outstretched.

"Dinner first..." Boulder smiled. "*Then* you can have your dessert."

Boulder and Dominic took seats on the bed as Abby and I made ourselves at home in chairs on either side of the wooden TV cabinet. We sat facing the bed as the bottle of whiskey made its rounds. Boulder took the first pull before passing the bottle to Dominic, who followed suit and passed to Abby, a quiet girl with short, dark hair and electric blue eyes. Abby lounged in her chair with one black-jean-wearing leg slung over the other, wearing a look of constant amusement like some stand-up comedian lived in her ear and told secret jokes all day.

"So I got an idea," Boulder declared, seated on the edge of the bed with a fresh tobacco lump in his lip and red flannel decorating his torso. Dominic and Abby leaned forward, eagerly waiting to hear what Boulder had conjured up in that shiny head of his. I took a drink of the whiskey and handed it back to Boulder, who leaned off the edge of the bed to grab Jack Daniels before resting the bottle on the mattress between Dominic and himself.

"I'm gonna make a million bucks," he said, "and I'ma give you all a piece of the money when I do."

Boulder bobbed slightly on the bed as he spoke, and with each bounce, the bottle of whiskey inched closer to the edge of the mattress. Neither Abby nor I said anything about Jack D. preparing to bungee jump.

I think we both secretly wanted to see the bottle fall.

"This old girlfriend of mine," Boulder said. "I 'member she used to have a calendar hangin' up in her laundry room. Twelve months, twelve men. All in construction clothes and lookin' studly as all hell, carryin' sheets a' plywood shirtless and sweaty, ripped and oiled up. September was a picture taken sideways of a big ol' boy on a ladder, flexin' hard with his hammer in his hand, gettin' ready to pound this nail somethin' fierce with his bulgin' biceps and makin' all the neighborhood girls' panties—NO YOU DON'T!"

Boulder's catlike reflexes stunned the room when he caught the bottle of whiskey as it began a tumble toward the hardwood.

Laughing, Boulder twisted the cap and took a pull.

"If I'm still movin' that quick," he said, "I ain't had enough yet."

Boulder passed the bottle to Dominic, who took a swig as Boulder continued to enlighten us.

"So I've been workin' construction fifteen years and I'll tell ya: I ain't never seen a guy on *any* crew looked like that. Now hear me out, I've known some fit men, but nothin' like what I saw in that calendar. Guy'd have to spend three hours in the gym *after* his ten hours of framin' to get in that kinda shape."

"So you're gonna start some sort of gym for construction workers?" I asked as the whiskey made its way from Abby to me.

Boulder grinned before looking at Dominic, then across the room to Abby.

"Nope," he said, glancing at his feet and leaning forward,

elbows on his knees. He looked up at me and nodded profoundly. "I'm gonna make a calendar of my own"

Abby laughed—actually it was more of a giggle—placing her hand over her mouth as it burst forth. "Yeah?" she asked. "What kind of calendar is that?"

"I'm gonna give the 'Merican people a dose of the real world," Boulder assured as he stood up, grabbed a backpack from the floor, and walked into the bathroom. "Starting with you three."

After Boulder closed the door, Dominic, Abby, and I looked at each other, half-wondering what he was up to and half-terrified of what was about to happen.

"What the heck?" Abby asked, laughing. She looked toward Dominic. "Where did you meet this guy?"

"At a bar in Ballard," he said. "He was jumping up and down because the Broncos just barely beat the Patriots on Sunday night and then he bought shots for everybody sitting near him, including me. After that, he saw my Giants hat and spent the next hour telling me stories about getting drunk around San Francisco..."

The bathroom door opened slowly.

"Lady and gentlemen of The Eastlake Motel." Boulder's voice boomed with exaggerated bass like a boxing announcer. "Live, and coming all the way from Boulder, Colorado... I give you..."

When Boulder stepped out into the room sideways, the first thing I caught a glimpse of were those legs—those damn legs—each one beginning in a dirty construction boot and running big, white, and hairy up to a frayed pair of cut-off jean shorts. Those Daisy Dukes hugged Boulder's butt so tightly that his jolly red ass cheeks spilled out from below the edge of the denim, gasping for air.

Boulder turned to face the three of us, revealing a hammer in his left hand, and took two steps forward before curling his right arm and eyeing that bicep. He then raised the hammer-wielding left above his head and tried hard not to smile as he finished his announcement.

"The 2013... Average Joe... Construction Calendar!"

The top of Boulder's shorts clung tight around his bulging belly, causing love handles to hang over the belt loops like a scoop of pink ice cream sitting atop a light blue sugar cone. Boulder was shirtless, with the exception of an orange and yellow reflective construction vest that was too small for his pudgy body. And if that body was the ice cream, then that would make the little orange hard-hat on Boulder's big head the cherry on top of that middle-aged, beer- and barbeque-flavored, construction sundae.

Boulder strutted casually across the room and grabbed the bottle of whiskey from atop the TV stand. Abby giggled uncontrollably, balled up in her chair. Her fetal hilarity was the by-product of a violent collision between humor and disgust, as she barely managed to squeak, "Eeeeeeewwewewewew!" through red-faced laughter. Boulder intentionally dropped his hammer on the floor in front of me.

"Whoops," he said, smirking. "Silly me."

"AW, MAN!" Dominic yelled as he jumped up from the bed and backed against a nearby wall. Boulder had bent over to pick up his hammer, pointing his big ass—which was most likely devouring that poor pair of shorts—directly at Dominic. Still folded over, Boulder chuckled hard and his orange plastic hat fell off of his head, bouncing once as it hit the hardwood.

I stood up from my chair as Abby bolted for the door. She turned the knob and burst, laughing, into the safety of the outside world, free from construction strippers; Dominic quickly slid outside after her, and I, the last one left inside, was just barely able to ninja past the laughing calendar model, snatching the six-pack of beer from the TV cabinet in the process.

Once in the safety of the open air, I closed the door and looked at Dominic and Abby, seated in two chairs against the brick wall to my left. Abby wiped a tear from her eye.

"Oh...my...god," she said, breathing between each word. "That may have been the worst thing I've ever seen."

"He had to buy all that stuff," Dominic added. "There's

no way he travels with clothes like that…"

I laughed, picturing Boulder bolting down to Goodwill after the
birth of his idea and trying on those clothes—the shorts, the vest,
that hat. Then I pictured him actually *buying* the clothes for the
sole purpose of creating the scene we'd just witnessed in that
motel room.

I shook my head and popped the caps off two bottles with
my lighter, handing a brew each to Dominic and Abby before
opening one for myself. I then took a seat atop the thigh-high
brick ledge across from them. The three of us took long swigs to
wash away the trauma we'd just been exposed to.

After a few moments of peace, the door swung open.

Red-flannelled Boulder and the bottle of Jack came
outside to join us. He sat on the ledge beside me with a grin.

Superman had once again become Clark Kent.

Abby tried not to smile as she looked at Boulder and said
what was on everyone's mind. "That was horrible."

Boulder tilted the whiskey toward some point at the
center of us.

"Million bucks," he said. "And because you all were my
first clients, I won't forget'cha when the big cheddar starts rollin'
in. That calendar'll be the gag gift of the century. Think about it,"
he added. "Twelve months of what you just seen." Boulder held
his hands out in front of him like he was painting some picture for
us. "Average guys—with beer guts, love handles, and hair all over—
posed all model-like for the camera with big drills and
jackhammers, all dead serious, and all dead sexy."

I *did* think about this for a second, as Boulder had
suggested, but I thought I felt my beer trying to climb back out of
my throat, so I stopped.

"Gag gift, indeed," I said.

Abby giggled.

After the shock of seeing Boulder's hairy butt cheeks had faded,
the four of us decided to take a stroll down the hill to visit the
houses that floated on Lake Union. Disregarding a few "No
Trespassing" signs, we walked to the end of a long dock that
connected two rows of the water dwellings. Fourteen houses lined

that section of the floating neighborhood, seven on either side of the dock. Each house possessed a distinct personality—color, size, shape—and I imagined that each must've been inhabited by folks with extremely strong stomachs.

After passing the last of the floating homes, the four of us arrived at the end of the dock where the view of the lake opened up. Boulder, Dominic, Abby, and I watched as the last traces of daylight slipped away behind Queen Anne hill and reflections from lights across the water danced on the its surface like groovy fireflies to the subtle rhythm of the waves.

On our way back up the hill, a song lodged itself in my head. I began to sing it out loud as we walked, not familiar with the words, but knowing the melody well—something from the 70's I'd heard a few times. *Maybe the Bee Gee's?*

Abby didn't know the name of the song either, but she started to sing along anyway. In fact, the four of us discovered that we shared the same relationship to this mystery tune (a melody, but that's about it)—no lyrics, and no clue as to the song's origin beyond our common belief that it was indeed a disco-era ditty. Either way, we sang together, filling in those words we didn't know with "la-de-das" and "doo-de-doos," a choir of buzzed fucks moving toward the next phase of their evening.

After we'd disco'd our way back to the motel, the crew piled into Dominic's rental car and headed to Queen Anne for an open mic. Boulder brought the fifth of Jack, and we each grabbed a few beers from the motel room.

Dominic navigated the maze of one-way downtown streets like a northwest vet and pulled up to the spot with time to spare before sign-up. Abby and I stepped out of the car and hung out in front of the venue while Dominic and Boulder continued to drive around, searching for a place to park. She and I sat on a bench and sipped our beers, talking about life in Chicago, life in Seattle. Throughout our chat, that same 70's song kept creeping into my head, filling cracks between the sentences.

It wasn't long before Boulder and Dominic walked up to join us. Abby and I passed what was left of our beers to them, and they finished them without hesitation, a signal that it was time for us to step inside.

The place was small, well-lit, and full of people. A compact bar sat tucked in the back of the room and a very small stage—looking like it would be a tight fit for anything but a solo act—lived in the center of the right-hand wall. As our group walked into the venue, another group of folks stood up, vacating one of the tables nearest the stage. Our party swooped in accordingly.

Once situated, Dominic, Boulder, and I found the sign-up sheet on a stool near the bar. We secured our performance slots and ordered some drinks. Dante, the traveler from Portland we'd met a few nights back, had great timing. He walked through the door a few minutes after we all sat down and ordered himself a double shot of Seagrams to catch up with the pack.

After Dante sat down, the five of us enjoyed a pleasant blend of gut laughs and good conversation while listening to some very solid performances—talented folks, a handful of songwriters on their acoustic guitars, and a girl with her ukulele who played a cover of "Take on Me."

Over the course of the night, I found myself developing a bit of an attraction for Abby. Something about the way her mind worked really intrigued me, and the fact that she was very beautiful didn't hurt matters either, but she and Dante were hitting it off, and the longer that we all hung out at that table, the clearer it became that she was setting her sights on him. A shame, but that's the way it goes sometimes. I figured I'd just keep doing my thing and maybe she'd swing my direction. If not, though, the night was young—as I would soon be reminded.

After about an hour of drinks, music, and babbling, the host announced that Dominic would be playing next. He stood up and adjusted his jean jacket before walking toward the bar to fetch a fresh beer. When he and that beer came back to the table, they brought a girl with them.

She was stunning—a tall, slender beauty with dirty blonde hair and deep brown eyes, wearing a long green coat with fuzzy fur around the edges of its large hood. Under the coat, the girl wore a sweater, tight-fitting jeans, and large boots—all black. Her name was Kendra, and by way of some strange coincidence, Kendra, like Dominic, was from San Francisco.

That night found Kendra in the middle of a drive back down to the bay area from Vancouver, where she had been visiting a friend.

Once Dominic had wrapped up his set, he and Kendra talked about San Francisco for a while—where they worked, places they liked to hang out, etc. Kendra and Abby also clicked instantly on the subject of Costa Rica, where they had both recently traveled. But, as the evening rolled on, Kendra and I began to notice one another.

Initially, I thought Kendra was very young. She looked like she had maybe just turned twenty-one, but as she spoke, her maturity became apparent. Kendra, who was actually twenty-six, put a lot of thought into everything that came out of her mouth, choosing words wisely and carefully crafting sentences to perfectly express what she had on her mind. She would often stop for seconds at a time to fully articulate what she was about to say, filling these thought-processing silences with an "mmmmmmm" or an "uuuuuuummm" as she looked off in one direction or the other, like the word she sought hung framed on some nearby wall. Once she'd spotted the elusive syntax, Kendra would then snap right back into enthusiastic conversation as though she'd never left.

I had a great time listening to Kendra speak. She was a deep thinker and very smart, charged with some vibrant electricity that radiated from her in short bursts. For the next half hour, we six listened to the live tunes and chattered around our table. But the more Kendra and I spoke to each other, the more the volume of the room seemed to fade out. She and I shared stories, asked questions, gave answers, enjoyed laughs, voiced opinions, traded smiles, reflected memories, heard each other's hopes... Kendra and I scanned for signs—searching each other's faces and bodies, reading biological clues and expressions.

The two of us had stumbled upon some private vortex in the midst of that packed pub.

"What made you come to this place?" I asked Kendra, seated to my right.

She leaned closer to be heard over the music. "It was a choice between here and a place called the Green Room." Kendra answered. "My friend up in Vancouver recommended both to me."

"The Green Room's great," I said. "Why'd you end up choosing this spot?"

Kendra grinned before glancing downward and digging a hand into the pocket of those black jeans, asking, "Heads or tails?" as she produced a coin.

I smiled. "Tails"

Kendra flipped the quarter into the air, watching with concentration as it spun metallic.

The coin landed in the open palm of Kendra's right hand; as she raised her left arm, Kendra slapped the quarter down onto the sleeve of her black sweater. She then looked at me with an eyebrow raised before peeking beneath her palm at the suspenseful coin.

Kendra glanced up at me with a smirk. "Heads," she revealed. "You lose." She stuck her tongue out, retracting it quickly between full lips that still held the form of a smile.

Laughing, I took a look around the room. "Was this place heads or tails?" I asked.

Kendra set the coin on the tabletop. "Heads."

I snatched the quarter, saying, "Let me see that thing," before inspecting it and shooting Kendra a glance of mock suspicion.

"Hmmm..." I turned the coin over and back again. "Seems to be just an ordinary quarter..." I held the coin up to my nose and sniffed it, looking Kendra in the eye. "*Smells* like an ordinary quarter..."

Kendra laughed and pried the coin from my fingers. "Gimme that back," she said, shaking her head. "Weirdo."

Kendra flipped the quarter again, catching it and scooting her chair closer to mine, hand covering the coin. Kendra stared into my eyes with raised brows, waiting for me to call it.

"Tails."

Our gazes fixed, Kendra lifted her right hand, and the two of us looked down at her arm.

George Washington grinned up at us.

"Dammit!" I yelled as Kendra giggled. "That coin is rigged!!"

Clink! Clink! Clink! Clink!

Kendra and I both looked toward the end of the table, as did Dante and Abby (who had been sitting across from us, enjoying a similar void).

Boulder sat smiling, brandishing a bottle in each hand, the pair effective in acquiring the table's collective attention. "Boys and girls!" Boulder announced. "My friend Jack just called—he'd like to have a word with us all outside."

The six of us stood from the table, and I grabbed my guitar case. After spilling from the spot, our group walked the few blocks to Dominic's rental car, where I threw my guitar into the trunk and Boulder rescued Jack Daniels from the loneliness of the back seat. We passed the bottle around, standing in a circle in the middle of the street. The night sky was clear and a fullish moon shone bright. After taking a hearty swig, Dante jumped up onto the trunk of the car to howl at that moon, his arms thrown back in animalistic release.

Dante's soulgasm perfectly captured the way I felt at that moment: washed over by something strong—in my case, waves of gratitude and wonder—marveling at the forces that had brought the six of us together.

I glanced toward Kendra, who stood to my right, staring at the sky with hands in the pockets of her long, green coat.

"You wanna take a walk?" I asked.

Kendra looked at me, serene, as if something in that sky had wiped her mind clean. An audible exhale accompanied a nod. "Yes," she said. "I do."

I looked toward the rest of the group, hanging around the car. Dante and Abby sat talking on the trunk while Dominic and Boulder leaned against the driver's door, passing a cigarette back and forth.

"We'll be back in a bit, guys," I announced.

Four heads looked in our direction, and three voices called out at once.

"Alright."

"Have fun!"

"Come back soon."

Kendra and I had just begun our walk when we heard a "Hey!" from behind us. We spun around to see Boulder running up the street with the bottle of whiskey in his hand and a lit cigarette in his mouth. Boulder held the bottle out in front of him, cigarette bouncing as he spoke.

"One for the road?"

Kendra smiled and grabbed the bottle, tilting it back in the moonlight.

Jack Daniels never looked so good.

She finished her drink and passed the whiskey to me. I took a big swig and put Jack back into the hands of our favorite bad influence.

"Have fun, kiddies," said Boulder, the tip of his cigarette jumping up and down in the darkness like a fiery little basketball. "Don't do anything I wouldn't do."

Boulder then winked and wheeled around, walking back toward the car as Kendra and I resumed our journey, destined for the towering lights of downtown.

10

"Okay, this is it," I announced as we stopped on the sidewalk.

"Here?" Kendra asked, gazing up at the massive building, hands in her coat pockets. "What is this place?"

"You'll see," I said, "if we can get up there."

Kendra walked over to the building's double glass doors and grabbed the long metal handle, giving it a hard yank.

The door wouldn't budge.

"How do we get in?" she asked, peering through the glass.

"No guarantees," I said, "but I've been here once before, and if we wait here for a bit, we may get a tenant either coming or going. Then we just slip inside."

Kendra turned around with a look on her face that said, *that's ridiculous.* "What's inside?" she asked.

I shot an optimistic glance through the glass—no one yet—before looking back at Kendra. "Hopefully you'll get to see."

The two of us chatted to pass the time, hanging a few feet from the doors and looking around hopefully every minute or so to see if anyone was coming our way. It was about 10:30 at this point, and I was thrilled that it didn't take long for someone to come walking across the marble floor of the lobby—a man with both arms wrapped around a large cardboard box. Kendra and I acted as though we were just walking up to the building's entrance when the man turned around to push one of the doors open with his back. I did the neighborly thing and held the door for him as he huffed past the two of us with a nod and a "thank you." After he'd gone, Kendra and I shared a silent, smiling celebration as we ducked through the doors and darted across the lobby to the elevators.

"Going up?" I asked as I pressed the button, picturing

myself as a butler in some fancy mansion.

When the elevator doors slid open, the two of us stepped inside, and I pressed the button for the twenty-seventh floor, all the way at the top.

"I can't believe that worked!" Kendra said as we shot up the shaft in our people-box "That was so perfect the way the—" (I know Kendra said other words here, but I don't remember what they were. Seeing her lips moving, all I could think about was kissing them. Thank god for the *ding!* of the elevator's arrival that snapped me back to reality.)

The doors parted.

Kendra and I stepped out of the elevator and rounded a corner, following glowing green exit signs that led us to a door at the end of the hallway. A chill gripped the two of us as we stepped through that door into a cold, concrete stairway. After shuffling up a few flights of stairs, Kendra and I found ourselves standing before a door marked with large, red letters: ROOF ACCESS.

Kendra looked at me with wide eyes. "No way."

"Shhhhhh," I said, smiling. "Don't jinx it."

I pulled my wallet from my coat pocket and my old driver's license from the wallet. The license was no longer valid and had been saved especially for an occasion such as this.

Kendra looked around nervously, checking for cameras in ceiling corners, while I stuck my floppy license into the small crack between the door and its frame. (The flexibility of a Washington State ID is perfect for carding tricky doors. It bends very easily. Just don't make the mistake of using your current license to do the job; I've seen doors chew a few cards up pretty badly.)

I talked as I fidgeted with the card.

"My old band had a practice space on the south side of town, and we always used to lock ourselves out of our room. Luckily, it was an old building, and we discovered very quickly that the locks were easy to card. Hopefully, I haven't lost m—"

POP!!!!

The door swung open and a rush of cold air filled the already frigid stairwell.

I beamed proudly at Kendra, who wore an expression on

her face like a kid who'd just seen their first birthday cake.
"Ready for this?" I asked.

Kendra grabbed my coat with both hands and shook hard, making a squeaking sound through her huge smile. I laughed and took this soulgasm as a yes.

The two of us stepped outside and were initially enclosed on all sides by ten-foot walls. There was no ceiling there, just the black night sky hanging overhead. Kendra and I began to climb the narrow ladder to our right. Leading our tandem ascent, I heard the *ping!* of Kendra's boots on the metal ladder below. Her left-right rhythm—amplified in the quiet night air—accompanied some excitement that seared inside me, like a razor blade trying to slice its way out of my gut.

I pulled myself up onto the top of the Seattle world, winking at glittering skyscrapers as I turned to extend an arm toward Kendra. She grabbed my hand, and I helped her from the ladder's final rung onto the roof. From my position I had an amazing view of Kendra's jaw hitting her boots as she took in the entire city of Seattle, rolled out for miles in a three hundred and sixty degree spectacle.

"No way!" Kendra exploded as she grabbed my arm and pulled me toward the edge of the roof.

"Oh...my...god," Kendra whispered as she peered over the side. "This is amazing."

Kendra looked slowly left to right across the expanse of that city, living and breathing before our eyes. "What a beautiful place," she said, with eyes distant and glowing, focusing on everything and nothing all at once. After a deep breath, Kendra glanced down at her hand, still clutching the middle of my forearm. I watched, amused, as her brown eyes traced my arm all the way up, meeting my gaze before her lips curled upward with a hint of embarrassment. She released my arm from her kung-fu grip and laughed as she dusted off my sleeve. "Sorry about that."

I smiled and looked back across the city.

For a moment, there was a silence between us as we surveyed the vast landscape, and the collective noise of Seattle filled the evening air with a relentless low rumble like the snoring of some sleeping giant. Kendra spoke over the monster's respiration as she turned slowly to her left, soaking in the full extent of the man-made beauty before her. "This view is incredible..."

Our perch sat near the border of Belltown and Queen Anne, on the north end of downtown. And, as Kendra and I scanned the scene, the city's trademark landmark—the Space Needle—entered our field of vision, glowing like some massive thumbs-up from god just a few blocks away. But this heavenly hitch-hiker, though spectacular, was just one small piece of the immense metropolitan puzzle that surrounded us.

Ferries—looking like little sailing skyscrapers—drifted silently across Puget Sound, while West Seattle and The Olympic Mountains slept soundly on the other side of the water. The lights of Capitol Hill, Belltown, and Queen Anne burned bright as the people there pulsed with life. Downtown Seattle loomed powerful to the south with its massive edifices—the keepers of the city, watching over the hive and protecting the colony.

Seattle streets, even at this hour, were alive, teeming with shuffling feet and pedaling bikes. Sirens screamed at sporadic intervals, echoing through the night as they raced toward some urban trauma. People crowded into busses and zipped around in cars, moving back and forth, to and fro—busy little specks down below, completely unaware that twenty-seven stories above two equally tiny people marveled at their small part in such an intricate picture.

The view was already spectacular, but seeing Kendra devour that scene for the first time made me appreciate it in a whole new way. I was happy to share that moment with her and smiled as she pulled a phone from her coat and walked from one side of the rooftop to the other, snapping pictures as the wind blew her blonde hair around from beneath that fuzzy hood.

Once she'd taken some shots of the city, Kendra and I sat down on the edge of the building and let our legs dangle over the side. We'd found an area of the roof where, if we *were* to fall, it was only a ten- or fifteen-foot drop to another part of that same building. This wouldn't have been a fun ride, but it would've been a hell of a lot better than dropping twenty-seven stories down to Fourth Avenue.

Kendra showed me some of the pictures she'd taken. They were good, but nothing short of being on that roof could've done that view justice. There was an energy to that behemoth before us that no camera could capture.

"I wanna stay up here forever," Kendra said as she repositioned herself, resting her back on the flat rooftop and staring up at the night sky. She kicked her boots up onto the raised edge on which we'd been seated.

I laid beside Kendra in this same fashion, and as I did something popped into my head.

"Have you ever heard this song?" I asked, looking to her on my left. "La de da... Ladada dadeeda... La de da... Ladada dadeeda..."

Kendra laughed. "Can't say that I have."

She was silent for a moment before she said, "Here," and pulled her phone from her coat. When she ran her finger across the screen, the blue light shining upon her face allowed me a nice view of what she would look like as a Smurf.

Kendra held the phone in front of my face. "Sing into this..."

I did as I was told and sang the mystery tune again. "La de da... Ladada dadeeda... La de da..."

After a few more bars of my exquisite performance, Kendra brought the phone back toward her and watched the screen.

"Give it some time," she said, as the pocket computer processed my gibberish. "I can play songs into this app, called Shazam, and it'll tell me who the artist is." She concentrated on the screen for another moment before cracking a smile and holding the phone in front of my face. Apparently, my interpretation of the mystery tune wasn't as dead-on as I'd suspected, and Shazam didn't know what the hell I was singing.

"Dammit!" I yelled.

Kendra laughed. "The search continues."

"Indeed," I said as I kicked my legs back over the

building's edge and sat up, facing the city.

Kendra continued to lie with boots propped up on the ledge beside me. "How'd you know about this place?" she asked.

I spun around to face her, seated on the elevated edge and leaning forward, elbows on my knees.

"On New Year's Eve," I said, "me and a few friends came down here and went to a couple different spots for drinks. We had some sake at a sushi place on First and then went to visit another friend who was bartending a few blocks away. As we were walking to that bar, my buddy Joey stopped us all and pointed up at this building—" I pointed into the distance and did my best impression of Joey, with a bit of stoned drag. "'*Dudes...* Let's go watch the fireworks from up *there...*'" Kendra giggled and I continued. "There were five of us, and we didn't know if we could get up onto the roof, but we were all down to try. There's a huge fireworks display from the Space Needle every New Year and we knew if we could get onto this roof, we'd have the best seat in town."

Kendra propped her torso up with her elbows and listened intently.

"So we got to the front of the building right about the same that time an older couple was coming in through the double doors. We followed them inside, and our five faces probably looked a little *too* happy, because the man stopped us in the lobby and asked who we were. He lived here, and had never seen any of us before. I told him that I lived in the building and the five of us were going up to my apartment, but he didn't believe me. So I reached into my coat pocket to grab my wallet and pull out my ID, show him my address. Apparently, that was proof enough for him. Because right as I was opening my wallet, the guy said never mind, he didn't need to see it. He apologized and told us all to have a good night. I'm glad he didn't call my bluff. That would have blown the whole thing. But he didn't, so after that we rode the elevator up, carded the door, and watched the Space Needle explode from the best seat in town."

I gestured toward the Needle before pointing down at the maze of tiny streets.

"Then we watched the traffic jam afterward as everyone who'd been to the show tried to escape from downtown all at once. The five of us were having a blast up here on our perch atop the world while every car in Seattle sat gridlocked below with backseats full of drunk uncles and cranky kids."

Kendra stood up and walked over to the ledge, taking a seat beside me. "Well," she said, intentionally bumping her shoulder against mine. "I appreciate you sharing your perch with me."

Kendra was close, looking into my eyes.

Her hood was down, allowing strands of hair to blow across her face.

I think they were waving at me, telling me to do it.

So I did.

I brushed Kendra's blonde dancers back; as the two of us stared at each other, a smile tugged at the corners of her mouth—a lovely mouth.

I kissed it.

Soft and slow at first, but with a mounting intensity as we felt something charge through us—two live wires touching each time our lips met. My hand gently caressed Kendra's cheek before sliding toward the back of her head. She placed both hands on my leg, leaning into our electricity—

Then we disappeared.

Only the parts of us that touched existed as we vanished together into a void where even that 70's song couldn't penetrate my thoughts.

11

"Your rhymes are weak... Can't even hold their own,
　　They got no muscle... Nothin' but skin and bone."

Two men stared at each other, eyes locked, standing in the middle of a circle of onlookers.
The first was a tall, white guy, wearing a baggy blue sweatshirt and matching baseball cap. He nodded to the beat, listening with hands behind his back. His opponent was a black man, quite a bit shorter than his sweatshirt-wearing counterpart, but built stocky like a pit bull. The latter barked a controlled and confident stream of poetry over a musical backdrop brought to you by Boulder—kneeling, playing his guitar—and a long-haired kid who pounded out a rhythm on his djembe.
The drum was long, worn, and wooden, and the instrument's master straddled it like a stallion, knees grinding concrete as he rocked back and forth with zeal, beating the defenseless drum trapped between his thighs. The kid wore a huge smile as he swung long hair to the rhythm, continuously grooving on the scene around him while the pit bull unleashed improvised lyrics.

"They're scared and hidin' in a corner while mine are out and on the streets,
　　Your shit is fadin' freezin' man, and mine is hard and blazin' heat."

This spontaneous crowd had gathered in front of a venue where some hip hop show had just wrapped up. Concert-goers had spilled chattering onto the sidewalk, where they were pleasantly surprised to find the music of Boulder and this drummer.

A few of the rappers, still high on showtime adrenaline, had seized this opportunity to keep the performance rolling.

Among those in the human circle were Kendra and I, who had descended from the physical height of our twenty-seven-story spectacle, but still hadn't come down. She and I, along with Dante and Dominic, danced amidst the throng of bodies locked in that late-night happening.

Every now and then a particular lyric would resonate with the mob, and a communal "oooooh!" or "yeeeeaaaahhh!" would erupt. On occasion, an oblivious passerby would pause to watch this impromptu show. A few of these fleeting folks stopped to take pictures on their phones (evidence they would present to friends to prove that they had been there), but these bystanders would only stop for a moment before carrying on.

Not like us.

We movers in that midnight circle were in it for the long haul.

"So go and tell your momma when you're cryin' on the phone,
        That you learned your lesson here, and then the teacher sent you home."

Blue sweatshirt, on the receiving end of this rhyme, looked down at his feet while rocking back and forth. Shaking his head as he spun some sort of comeback beneath that baseball cap.

"'Cuz when you stepped into this circle here to try and battle me,
        I showed you now without a doubt that I'm the best you ever seen."

The pit bull made circles out of his hands and held them up to his eyes like binoculars, causing the crowd to cheer and applaud while the music rolled on with a steady momentum.

A round woman with curly hair and glasses pushed her way into the center of the circle and cleared her throat with exaggerated force. She then took a deep breath, moving smoothly—side to side with eyes closed—and began to sing over the music. She didn't sing words, but rather belted sounds that I imagine a violin might play if one were allowed to soar over Boulder's robust chord progression in simple, flowing melodies.

The challenger, in the blue cap, reached out and gave the woman a hard pat on the shoulder, saying, "Sick!" as he bobbed his head to the beat. He then rubbed his hands together and glanced up at the pit bull, who was still grinning big with self-satisfaction from a well-rapped round.

Boulder strummed his guitar, the drummer continued to pound his djembe, the woman sang violin, the night smiled, and the challenger gestured enthusiastically as he began his rebuttal:

"You're so low to the ground I almost didn't hear what you said,
        Tellin' me to call my mom, but I think I'm callin' yours instead."

A chuckle from the pit bull as the challenger continued:

"I think she might invite me over and put some ham and cheese on bread,
        Then she'd sit me on the couch, make me laugh and give me *HEADS UP!* Look around 'cuz now I'm droppin' my flow,
        You're runnin' round screamin', but you got no place to go."

The challenger moved in close, rapping a few inches from the pit bull, who, at this point, was beginning to look more like a timid Chihuahua who'd just pissed on the new rug.

"Now if you're scared, I'll pick you up and sit you in my brand new Caddy,
        And you can come and take a ride with your new stepdaddy."

The challenger spread his arms in defiant triumph, amplified by the unified "ooooooooh!" that rose from the crowd.

The woman stopped singing and grabbed the challenger's sweatshirt, rocking back and forth in an attempt to shake the guy, but giving up when his feet stayed cemented where they stood, his body shifting only slightly under the influence of three hundred pounds of excitement. Challenger and pit bull then came together with a hybrid handshake-hug before stepping to the side of the circle, laughing and trading comments.

This absence of rappers left only Boulder and the hand drummer in the middle of the mob.

Boulder, sensing an opportunity, shifted his position—from kneeling to sitting cross-legged—before laying his guitar across his lap. The percussionist continued his steady assault, and Boulder, once situated, began to bang along, using the top of his acoustic guitar like a drum head.

As we closed tight around these two, dancing together, a thought crossed my mind.

This beat could use some words...

And I knew just the lyrics for the job.

(Well, sounds rather.)

I began to sing.

"La de da... Ladada... Dadeeda..."

Boulder, recognizing the 70's tune, looked up at me and nodded, continuing to pound on that poor guitar. He began to sing along, the two of us spouting bursts of harmonized gibberish over the tribal backbeat. Our noise caught the attention of Dante and Dominic, dancing to my left, who contributed their voices as well, along with Kendra and her giant smile, who joined in while grooving to my right. A few of the nameless faces followed suit, and soon the whole group started singing the 70's melody that had somehow become the theme of the evening.

"La de da.... Ladada... Dadeeda..."

"La de da.... Ladada... Dadeeda..."

And that's when it happened.

Locked in some trance of togetherness on that downtown dance floor, I began to hear them, words filling in the "La's" and "Da's" of the elusive tune—voices at the edge of our dancing mass.

Could it be that someone actually knows the song?

I listened intently.

93

"La de da... Say do you remember?
La de da... Dancing in September,
La de da... Never was a cloudy
daaaaaaaaaaaaayyyy..."

Yes! The words!!
They existed.
And by the grace of some holy coincidence, they could not have been more perfect for that evening on the cusp of October as we all followed suit, singing proper lyrics to the disco hit and grooving on that Seattle street corner.

"La de da... Say do you remember?
La de da... Dancing in September,
La de da... Golden dreams were shiny
daaaaaaaaaaayyyyysssss...
"La de da... Say do you remember?
La de da... Dancing in September."

Yes, "Earth, Wind, and Fire."
I do.

12

"Almost there..."

Her voice called to me from the end of the hallway. I knew the sound of it well, but her name escaped me. Floorboards creaked beneath blood-red carpet as I crept curiously forward.

"Jason..."

Several candles, flickering from ruby walls, gave life to my shadow as it lurked beside me—a dark projection of myself sneaking slowly along the edge of my vision.

"Up here..."

The strange whisper seemed to come from all around me.

A dozen worn, wooden doors lined that hall, but somehow I knew she'd be waiting behind the one at the very end—white and luminous against the crimson of the carpet and wallpaper. I approached the door and peered down at its faded golden knob, turned many times by who knows how many hands. After placing my own palm upon the antique orb, I added one more name to the phantom list, twisting it slowly.

A chill ran down my spine as the door creaked wide, a flood of white light washed over me, and the horn from an eighteen-wheeler blared loud, rolling by lonely in the I-5 night.

My eyes shot open.

Awake again.

Goddamn.

It was going to be a long night. Already had been.

I didn't check my phone, but assumed it was somewhere

around five in the morning. I couldn't have been asleep for more than an hour and, looking around the car, noticed that I was the only one stirring out of the five people packed into the Grand Marquis at that restless Oregon rest stop.

My inability to stay asleep may have had something to do with my body being pressed up against the steering wheel of the blue beast, unable to recline because of the folks passed out in the back. It also may have had something to do with the fact that every time a truck drove by going north on Interstate 5, I was drowned in a sea of white headlight.

No matter the cause for my insomnia, I seemed to be the only one having this trouble.

Blaze was flopped out beside me, his ass in the passenger seat and the top of his body folded over onto the Marquis's front couch. He was using his boots as a pillow. At that point, I couldn't tell whose foot odor was whose. Three of the five in our group had decided to remove their shoes before sleeping in that tight space, turning that mid-eighties sedan into a steamy, stinky sauna. My finger made a squeaking sound as I dragged it across condensation coating the driver's side window.

I drew a sad face.

After watching a few sets of passing headlights illuminate my work, I turned and looked into the back seat. Jaclyn slept in the middle, leaning straight back and snoring softly with mouth wide open. Her little colored band had found its way from her hair down to her brow; on either shoulder, she supported the head of one of her sleeping coworkers. Those three in the back seat had been smoking pretty steadily since we'd swooped the guys up near Portland. The pot had knocked them out quickly.

Blaze and I had been the only ones awake for the last few hours of the drive—jabbering back and forth in the front seat and stopping every now and then to share a tall can by the side of the road. I knew the weed would put me out, but the beer seemed to keep me going. After a while, though, despite the intermittent Pabst injections, the white line hypnosis worked its magic, and I decided to pull the car over before I fell asleep and put us all in some central Oregon ditch.

I pulled my green beanie over my eyes and rested against a sweatshirt that I'd placed between my head and the window. It took me a while, but I eventually began to tiptoe that tightrope between waking and sleeping consciousness, where dreams and thoughts begin to blend...

VROOOOMUMUMUMUMUM!

My eyes snapped open.
"What the hell?!"
I said it out loud, looking around and hoping I didn't wake the others. But it didn't matter. They'd heard the noise too.
Jaclyn leaned forward and slowly scanned the scene, grumbling, half-asleep. "What *is* that?"
MUMUMUMUMUMUMUMUMUM!
The noise seemed to shake the car, a low and rumbling sound. *An engine?*
The guys in the back shuffled slightly and leaned against their respective windows, but didn't awaken. Blaze groaned and pulled the leather jacket over his head.
MUMUMUMUMUMUMUMUMUMUM!
I opened my door and stepped out onto the concrete. The night was freezing in contrast to the Mercury's warm, sweaty swamp. Cold air stung my face, and I exhaled visible breaths walking toward the old pickup idling in the parking space beside ours—a beat up, rusty pile with a big camper mounted on the back.
No one inside the cab...
BangBangBangBang!

I pounded hard on the camper's back door. The vehicle rocked back and forth a few times before the door swung inward, revealing a living version of Yosemite Sam wearing sweat-stained long underwear.

"Yeah?" the man barked from beneath a large mustache.

"Hey," I began. "My friends and I have been driving all night and are trying to get some sleep over here. Are you gonna be taking off sometime soon?"

The man stared at me with beady eyes through round glasses.

"Yeeep... Jussis' soonis' I finish mah breakfist."

"Well, would you mind turning your truck off until you do? This thing's shaking the car over there." I pointed to the Marquis a few feet away.

The man looked in the car's direction—even though he couldn't see it from where he stood inside the camper—and then glanced back at me, opening his mouth as if just about to speak.

Then he slammed the door shut.

"Goddammit!" I yelled. "Hey!"

BangBangBangBang!

I pounded on the camper again, harder this time. No answer, just the steady MUMUMUMUMUMUMUMUM of an idling old engine, probably drowning out my knocks and allowing Yosemite Sam to eat his Wheaties in peace.

"Son of a bitch," I muttered.

BangBangBangBangBang!

Nothing.

I kicked the Tennessee plate and punched the camper door. The cold surface stung my knuckles as the engine laughed at my pain.

MUMUMUMUMUMUMUMUMUMUMUM!

I sulked, grumbling, back to the Marquis and slid defeated into the driver's seat, where our neighbor's gasoline symphony was only slightly muffled by the closing of my door.

Jaclyn and Blaze were both awake.

"What's up with that?" Blaze asked, sunglasses crooked across his face as he sat up and looked toward the noise.

"Asshole shut his camper door on me when I asked him to turn the truck off. Said he'd leave after he ate his breakfast."

Blaze grabbed his boots from the seat between us and began to slip them on.

"You gonna go give it a shot?" I asked.

"No," Blaze replied. "I'm gonna go throw a fuckin' rock through his windshield."

I laughed.

Blaze didn't.

"Well," I said, thinking for a moment. "Alright."

I turned the key, starting a petroleum rumble of our own.

"Guys, no..." Jaclyn insisted from the back seat.

I had a flashback of my mother telling me not to squirt ketchup on my little brother as a surge of adrenaline shot through my body, preparing me to play getaway driver.

Blaze finished tying his boots and smiled as he grabbed his door handle.

"Blaze, seriously!" Jaclyn yelled as he stepped from the car. She tried frantically to open the back doors, but was blocked by the bodies of her coworkers, who were somehow still sleeping through all of this.

MUMUMUMUMuMuMuMuMuMuMuMumumumumumum...

I squinted as headlights washed over the Marquis and a faint laughter echoed from outside. Blaze hadn't even had a chance to walk a few feet before the truck, camper, and Yosemite Sam had all sailed sputtering into the night.

He must've finally finished his morning meal.

Blaze climbed back into the car and glanced at Jaclyn, who was shaking her head and trying not to smile.

"Well," Blaze said. "I don't know about you guys, but I'm awake." He looked at me, straightened his sunglasses, and nodded toward the wheel. "Want me to drive?"

13

The sun climbed a stratus ladder as the Marquis rolled down the I-5 hill into California.

Even taken in through a dreary mind and sleepy eyes, the beauty of that mountainous landscape soaked in sunrise was a sort of heaven. It made me smile to think that it looked like that every morning—bathed in purple light—and that to see it, all we needed to do was get there.

The car cruised along as its occupants marveled at the passing landscape and threw words around their shared space, waking for a bit, sleeping for a bit—drifting in and out of dreams and reality that, at this point, all bled together into one long and beautiful experience.

Sitting there in the passenger seat, I took comfort in knowing that even if I wasn't paying attention to the road, we were still moving forward—comfort in the freedom to traverse between two states of consciousness and still reach our destination. I didn't want to miss a bit of the spectacle that rolled by outside my window, so I tried my best to stay awake, but I did obey every now and then when my eyes told me it was time to rest.

The group decided to stop for breakfast at a restaurant in Yreka called Grandma's House, which was decorated head to toe with every type of antique, artwork, and knickknack you could image.

All of these were items that any grandma would be proud to clutter her home with, and all were for sale. I considered buying a painting of a bison that hung above one of the tables, because the acrylic creature's eyes would follow me around the room. The only problem with this purchase (besides it being a complete waste of my already scare funds) was that I couldn't think of a place to hang the painting, seeing as I didn't really have a home at the time.

Maybe I could mount it to the ceiling of the Maxima?

Our fivesome sat down at a booth; after we ordered, the waitress (no doubt handpicked by Grandma herself) loaded our table with plates full of delicious goodies: eggs, hash browns, bacon, sausage, muffins, toast, pancakes, waffles, jam, butter, syrup, jelly, juice (well, the juice was poured into *glasses*, but it was an integral piece of the grub puzzle). We swapped food around the table—a sausage here, a bite of pancake there—each one of us customizing our perfect breakfast after twelve long hours in the car.

Our eclectic cast then dug into the morning feast as we talked around the table.

Jaclyn, age twenty-three—the writer, photographer and traveler straight out of 1967—was energetic, enthusiastic, and curious about everything. Many times she was the leader of group discussions, encouraging all of us to dig in and get to know each other better.

In fact, our ride out of Portland the night before, after picking up her coworkers, had begun with Jaclyn asking, "Okay, so what's one thing that most people don't know about you?"

Jaclyn's first coworker, an upbeat little Mexican dude of twenty-two, had gladly answered this question from the back seat as he loaded a pipe to smoke his first pot before we'd even left his neighborhood. "Hi, guys! My name is Jaime, and I'm an alcoholic." He took a hit and tried unsuccessfully to hold back a mixture of coughing and laughter as he burst, sending a cloud of smoke shooting from his lungs that hung, hazy, around the Marquis.

Jaclyn laughed as she rolled down her window to ventilate the vehicle.

"I'm just kidding," Jaime added. "But I *am* a weedaholic..."

He took another hit.

"...and that's a fact."

Jaime exhaled, passing the pipe and lighter to the coworker with short, black hair sitting to his left.

"I'm Derek," he said, as he took his turn in the smoky rotation, "and, uh, I can't whistle."

"He's also a male model!" Jaime blurted, pinching Derek's right nipple through his white T-shirt.

Derek swatted Jaime's hand and gave him a sturdy elbow to the ribs. "Yeah," Derek reluctantly confirmed. "That too, I'm flying out of San Francisco on Wednesday for a shoot in New York."

Jaime chimed in. "And he's taking me with him!"

Derek looked toward Jaime as he passed the pipe to Blaze, on his left. "Maybe if I stuff you in my luggage."

Blaze, the oldest of the group at thirty-two, stared out the window and took his turn, exhaling completely before speaking.

"Name's Blaze," he said, turning his sunglassed attention toward us. "It's my last name, but—"

Jaclyn interrupted. "But considering his line of work, he'd be stupid not to roll with it." She smirked and glanced at Blaze in the rearview mirror.

Blaze nodded slowly. "Something like that..." He adjusted his leather jacket and continued. "Headin' down to Frisco for the fifth time this year to do another cross-country, white-knuckle duffle shuffle."

After a short silence, Jaime leaned forward in his seat and looked across the car at Blaze. "And what in the hell is *that*?"

Blaze focused on Jaime, but spoke to all of us. "Got a buddy in Frisco who grows weed. I fill some duffle bags with said weed, throw 'em in my truck, and drive 'em across the country to sell the stuff—Frisco to New York." Blaze nudged Derek. "Might even see you over there."

Blaze passed the pipe and lighter over the driver's seat to Jaclyn, and I reached over to hold the steering wheel as she took her turn.

"Aw, thanks," she said. "What a gentleman." Jaclyn exhaled smoke that was sucked into the highway air through a cracked window. "I am Jaclyn, and I..." She thought for a second. "I want to see the world."

After this declaration, Jaclyn stared silently ahead, possibly hypnotized by a montage of fantasy travel destinations.

She soon snapped back to reality and passed the torch to me.

I was prepared.

As everyone had been introducing themselves, I'd been listening and simultaneously searching for a song on my iPod—a song that I felt was necessary for the beginning of our journey.

"I'm Jason." I connected the iPod to a mini boom box that sat on the dashboard. "And I love *Rocky*."

Pressing play sent the theme from Sylvester Stallone's '76 flick trumpeting through tiny speakers to unanimous approval from the Marquis crew. Jaclyn turned the volume up full blast, and the five of us rolled down the nighttime highway at eighty-five (top speed for the beast), punching imaginary slabs of meat that dangled before our faces.

The meat on grandma's table however, was not imaginary; it was delicious, and the five of us had eaten every last morsel. We'd descended on that morning feast like famished beasts, not leaving so much as a muffin crumb or drop of orange juice undevoured. Stomachs satisfied, the group paid the check, filed outside, and piled into the Marquis.

Once settled into the back seat, I opened my wallet to evaluate my financial situation.

My intention with this trip was to bring only enough money for the rides to the Bay and back, leaving myself in a voluntary "sink-or-swim" situation that would force me to play my way to prosperity. Due to the slow days I'd been having at Pike Place, and the fact that I was paying a few hundred bucks a month to sleep on my friend's couch in West Seattle, my funds had been consistently low for a few months, and I figured the Frisco trip would be a great way to inspire some busking evolution.

I had no credit card, and nothing in my bank account.

In my wallet there were three twenties and some change.

In my backpack: peanut butter (chunky), honey, bread, and a few cereal bars, along with some clothes and a toothbrush.

My mom thought I was crazy (in fact, I think many people close to me shared this sentiment), but I didn't care. I felt alive, taking a walk down some staircase in the dark, unsure whether the next step would be there or not.

From Yreka we headed south, talking, laughing, blasting songs—a carful of travelers singing "What is Love?" from the movie *Night at the Roxbury* at the top of our lungs, blazing by in a blue blur. We shared stories, drank beers, smoked some pot (mandatory for everyone as we passed through a city called Weed). The California landscape flew by; and as we started to see numbers on the signs shrink—San Francisco: 150 miles... 100 miles... 50 miles—I noticed that my stomach started to do funny things.

I was excited to be in that rusty rocket with those folks—living, making progress, diving into some new city with no plan whatsoever. Five weeks prior, San Francisco was just an idea on a piece of paper, a hopeful thought.

Now, we were barreling toward it, and that thought was coming to life.

If the nerves tickling my tummy were some sort of cocktail, this unknown metropolis speeding closer with every second was the main ingredient. But there was something else bubbling in the recipe.

After the night Kendra and I had met in Seattle, she and I had stayed in touch. And, once I crossed that bridge, the two of us had plans to see each other again.

14

Flashback to that September morning in Seattle—after the lake houses, Boulder's butt cheeks, Kendra, the rooftop view, the sidewalk dance party, and more alcohol than I'd like to admit.

That September morning, I woke in a fleeting panic, not knowing where the hell I was.

Shooting upright in bed, atop a blanket I'd not bothered to sleep beneath, I looked around the room. The blood swishing inside my head made me dizzy—a one-two punch when combined with the light shining through the drapes that burned my eyeballs. I turned from the window to see an empty case of beer sitting atop a long wooden cabinet, home to a TV that was surrounded by countless bottles and cans. Next to the cabinet, two guitar cases leaned up against the wall, and to my right: Boulder, passed out and fully clothed in the bed next to mine.

The motel. Right.

I rubbed my eyes, shook my head, and took a deep breath.

My notebook lay open beside me. I picked it up to take a look at what I'd written before I passed out the previous evening ("written" is the wrong word here, let's instead say "scribbled"). It took me a while to decipher the chicken scratch on those pages, but here's what I got:

I love it.

What a beautiful day, week, life. An amazing existence.

Let's keep 'er rollin'.
Yeah. That ride.
Get it going the right way...but no control once it has left my
sphere.
Like throwing a baseball.
Focus. Attention. Intention...
And then flow and receive.
Interpret and act and enjoy.
Yes, beauty.
Beautiful girl, beautiful life,
beautiful people.
Dive in.

There was a line drawn under this mess and a new thought below,
also scribbled—possibly frantically.

Time is short. Create.
We are dying. Create.
Burning alive inside and out. Ticking clocks.

It's always a nice surprise when nocturnal-me leaves morning-me
little notes like this. Sometimes the writing triggers memories of
the evening before, and sometimes it just leaves me to wonder
where the hell my mind was at and what was going through it.
Either way, the words are recorded. A snapshot of a psyche
floating somewhere, connected to an arm with a pen—my anchor
to the physical world.

The rest of that morning was painful.
Boulder woke up, and, over breakfast at a café down the
street, the two of us pieced together the events of the previous
evening, following the sidewalk dance fest.

Memories of that night had become fuzzy as we'd crossed into the

AM hours.

I remembered saying goodbye to Kendra after the music on the street. She had a room at the hostel on First and had decided to catch a cab back that way. The two of us walked a few blocks from the sidewalk festivities, and she hailed one of the yellow boys.

"Thank you for a great night," Kendra said, smiling and brown-eyeing me as the cab driver waited patiently.

"You're welcome," I replied. "I'm glad you stopped here in town. Glad I got to meet you."

"Me too," Kendra agreed. "See you when you make it down my way."

Kendra and I gave each other a hug and, to quote my notebook—

the kiss that felt like sex...

After this, the two of us said good night, and Kendra slid into her yellow chariot. I took a deep breath and smiled to myself as I watched the taxi whisk her downtown.

"What an angel," I said aloud, with no one to hear. I kept noticing myself using that word for her, in my notes and in my head. It seemed to fit: the San Fran angel (*the San Frangel?*).

Once she flew away, I walked back to the group, and the dogs were unchained.

With no more Kendra to impress, the boys and I carried ahead full steam. Left with only a few precious hours of bar time, Boulder, Dominic, Dante, and I became a drunken whirlwind, bouncing from bar to bar and sucking up all the whiskey and beer we could get our hands on (much of it on Boulder's dime because he was having an extremely successful year and had decided to share the wealth.)

Shots, food, beer...

Sidewalk, weed, streetlight...
Next bar... Neon, table, laugh, talk, cocktails...
People! ...howareya, metoo, youdontsay,
onlyonceandihatedit...
Next bar... Whiskey, jukebox, guys, girls...

"Last Call!"

Dante, Boulder, Dominic, myself, some guy we'd just met who
insisted on joining us...
Sidewalk... Stumble, try to trip Dante, he throws a garbage
can at me...
Dante and I try to knock a stop sign over...
No luck. But a great bonding experience.

Dante in a cab... Dominic in a cab... Goodbye!... Goodnight!... It's
been great... Thank you... No, thank *you!*... see you in Portland!...
See you in Frisco!... Vrooooooooooom!
Boulder, the new guy, and I: howling at the cabs like
werewolves (imitating Dante) as they roll away...
Then the three of us pile into this newcomer's car and he
swoops us safely back to Boulder's motel.

A night out, indeed—and I was paying for it that next morning.

As we crossed the bridge to West Seattle, the movements of
Boulder's car made my stomach angry and I leaned out the
passenger window on a few occasions thinking I might lose my
breakfast. Luckily, that didn't happen, and the cool air blowing by
at fifty miles an hour felt good on my face.
The city sat across Puget Sound, arms folded, shaking her
loving head at me.

When Boulder and I arrived at the apartment where I'd been

staying, we stepped out of his little rental car and shook hands.

"Great times, this week," Boulder said with an invincible enthusiasm, wearing the same red flannel from the day before and appearing unaffected by the night's activities. He even looked like he could go another round—a seasoned pro.

"You too, man," I replied. "Thanks for the ride. And the hangover."

I grinned, and it hurt a bit.

Boulder chuckled and placed a hand on each of my shoulders, shaking me like a dickhead. "That Jack D. is a reeeeeal asshole isn't he!?"

Laughing, I smacked his hands down. "Fuck off!"

Boulder held up his paws in a gesture of surrender, eyebrows raised with his mouth in the shape of an "O" like a kid who'd been caught coloring on the wall with his mom's lipstick.

"Seriously, though," I added, "thanks." I tilted my head back and felt the sun on my face before looking again at Boulder. "A bus ride would have sucked today."

"Don't mention it," he said. "Thanks for showin' me 'round the city. Too bad I gotta get back to the real world."

I nodded. "No problem. Have a good trip, man. I'll hit you up when I make it down that way."

"You'd better," Boulder said, pointing a finger before walking around to the driver's door and sliding inside.

I stood there and watched as he pulled into traffic, forcing a car coming from his left to slam on its brakes. Boulder didn't seem to notice, or if he did, he didn't care. He just kept cruising, windows down, giving me a honk and a wave as he sped out of sight.

15

"I see a trip ahead in your near future and a great deal of money. Your life may take you to many distant lands, but you will always return safely again. I see much adventure for you! There will be a special letter awaiting you in the mail. Your future looks bright and promising. A bald man brings you luck, but beware of a young woman in a red sports car. Wearing a green stone will bring you peace of mind.

"Play again and I will tell you more!

"Lucky numbers: 2, 3, 16, 18, 22, 37."

I had glanced down at the little card a few times during my Starbucks set on that October afternoon. People walked over it, strollers rolled past it. I don't know why I picked it up, seeing as I don't normally collect random pieces of paper that litter the ground at Pike Place Market, but I'm glad I did.

It was a white three-by-five card with the image of a crystal ball decorating its upper portion. I recognized the fortune instantly, dispensed from a machine at the market's magic shop.

Maybe someone had been unhappy with their future and tossed the card onto the sidewalk?

How it ended up there didn't matter, but the fact that the card found its way to me in that moment was serendipitous, and looking back at its message in retrospect is interesting.

I don't know who the bald man is (maybe the cop who pulled me over later that week for having expired tabs and talking on my phone, only to let me go with a warning). I also don't know what to make of the woman in the red sports car, and have yet to see that great deal of money. But that year was definitely full of adventure, and there was indeed a special letter waiting for me when I stepped off the bus in West Seattle after that day of Pike Place busking.

I felt a surge of electricity when I saw the return address:

Kendra Sorenson
2564 Golden Gate Ave.
San Francisco, CA

It had been a few weeks since I'd mailed Kendra a copy of my CD and a postcard soaked with my ramblings. I hadn't heard anything back, and had given her a call at one point to see if she'd received the package, but there had been no response. I figured she'd gotten wrapped up in life, and that was that.

I ascended the stairs and entered my friend's apartment—where I was staying at the time—and, upon opening the door, was greeted by her dog, Tonic. Tonic was a German shepherd who would run excited laps around the island in the kitchen whenever I would come home. After his puppy marathon, he would grab his rope chew toy and shake it ferociously for a few seconds. He'd then lie down on the floor with tongue hanging from a huge canine smile, waiting for me to make the next move. No matter what kind of day I'd had at the market, Tonic's greeting always put me in a good mood.

I sat down on my bed (the couch) and opened the manila envelope. After dumping its contents onto the blue cushions, I was surprised to find Galileo's image adorning a black and white picture that had been glued to a piece of gray construction paper. The paper was frayed along its edges. In the picture, Galileo stood beside a telescope, pointing at the sky while standing behind another man who looked eagerly through the lens and into the heavens. Inside a whitish margin running along the bottom of the picture were the words *"First the Dream, Then the Deed."*

I wondered where this image had come from. The yellowing of the paper, which had clearly been white at one point, made me think the image was fairly old. I flipped the construction paper and began to read blue ink on the back. As I did, Kendra's voice spoke sweetly in my head:

Jason,

Opening my mailbox to find your postcard and CD was such a nice surprise! Thank you for sending both. It was great to hear your voice in the music and in the story you told me about your time in San Diego. My drive down there was gorgeous. I stopped at many beautiful beaches and towns along the way— Monterey, Big Sur. The drive took me five days, but I could have easily spent two weeks exploring the coast.

At one point during my trip, I managed to lose my phone, and your number along with it! I'm pretty sure it's buried somewhere in the sand near Santa Cruz. At first I was upset about this, but, to be honest, as time passed, I found it nice to disconnect and decided to see how long I could live without it.

My visit with the parents was great, and so was the drive back up to San Francisco, but once I returned to reality I realized I needed to buy a new phone. I'm now connected again, but would strongly encourage you to try the seven-day no-phone challenge. As a matter of fact, I dare you!

I think you'll find it enlightening.

I hope you like the picture. I thought of you when I came across it in an old magazine in my parents' basement. I've also

included a pin that I found at the Beat Museum near my office.
You'll have to explore that place when you get to San Francisco.
It's right near the City Lights bookstore.

By the way, did you finish On the Road*?*
What did you think of it?
When you're done with Kerouac, you should find some
Tom Robbins. He's another must-read.

Thank you again for your package. It really was great to
hear from you, and I'm looking forward to seeing you again in
November. I hope you're well, and trust that you are. Also, you'll
be thrilled to hear that I'm still having dreams about that view—
and that stupid song!

Let me know when you make it to San Francisco. I'm
already planning my payback.

Take care,

Kendra

I set the letter down on the couch before exhaling deeply, sinking into the cushions, and looking at Tonic, who was lying on the beige carpet with head resting between his paws. Tonic's eyes met mine and he sat up with a surge of doggy energy, smiling with tongue out as I picked up the phone and called Kendra.

"You like it?" she asked.

"Yeah," I replied. "Very cool. I love that Galileo picture."

"I thought you might be into that."

"You know what's really strange?" I asked. "While I was playing at the market today, I found a little card lying on the sidewalk with a fortune on it. It told me there was a special letter waiting for me in the mail, and sure enough, I came home to find your package"

"No way," Kendra said. "Really?"

"Yeah, I'll take a picture and send it to you."

"You should," she urged. "I love it when those kinds of

things happen." There was a short pause. "Actually!" Kendra's burst of excitement made me smile. "I had something like that happen to me earlier this week. I was taking a break at work and reading on a bench outside, *The Electric Kool-Aid Acid Test*—"

"The what?" I asked.

"*The Electric Kool-Aid Acid Test*," she repeated. "You *have* to read it. It's about the hippie culture of the sixties. You know Ken Kesey? The author of *One Flew over the Cuckoo's Nest*? Well, he and a small group of like-minded hippies called themselves 'The Merry Pranksters' and decorated a school bus in Day-Glo paint. Then they drove across the country drinking LSD-laced Kool-Aid and promoting the expansion of consciousness through the drug. And guess who drove the bus?"

"Santa Claus?"

"Yes! Great guess!" Kendra laughed. "Even better, though: it was Neal Cassady."

"Yeah?" I replied, surprised that this man had found a way to infiltrate a second consecutive decade of counterculture history. "That sounds really interesting."

"It is," Kendra said. "And a big theme in the book is the concept of synchronicity, things lining up coincidentally—like you finding that card and then coming home to find my letter." Tonic climbed onto the couch and sat beside me. "So in the chapter I was reading, Ken Kesey and the Pranksters go to a Beatles concert—on acid, of course. They're all sitting up in the stands, looking down on the crowd in the arena and, in that state of mind, see the crowd as one giant being instead of thousands of individual people. So, with each band that comes onto the stage, this thing becomes more and more energized. The opening band comes on and the crowd starts to stir, then the next band comes on and the energy goes up a notch. And then there's this third band that makes the people in the arena even more excited. So, after this act wraps up, the crowd of people, in front of the stage, look like they're about to burst with excitement, and the announcer walks out to introduce the fab four. So I read the words, '*Ladies and Gentlemen, I give you...The Beatles!* And I'm not kidding you, Jason, right as I read that, a car pulled up to the stop sign in front of me with its windows down, blaring 'Nowhere Man.'"

I looked at Tonic, beaming beside me on the couch, and rubbed his head as I grew a grin of my own. "That's awesome."

"I know!" Kendra said. "I love it when those things happen. It always makes me feel like I'm in the right place at the right time, kind of like how we met."

"Yeah," I replied. "Crazy how things work out sometimes."

There was a short silence before Kendra said, "Hey!" with an enthusiastic blast. "Where are you staying when you get down here?"

"I'm not sure," I replied, realizing this was something I should probably put some thought into.

"Well," Kendra said, "I have a guest bedroom at my place near the Haight. I'll talk to my roommate and see if you can just stay here so I can show you around the city."

"That sounds great," I said, picturing the possibilities.

"Cool," said Kendra. "Let's keep in touch, and I'll plan on seeing you in a few weeks."

"Perfect. Great to hear your voice. And thanks again for the letter. It made my day."

"I'm glad. Remember, *Electric...Kool-Aid...Acid Test.* It's by Tom Wolfe."

"*Electric...Orange juice...*"

Kendra laughed from eight hundred miles away

"Good night, Jason."

"Good night."

117

As I slept that evening, visions of the approaching journey flashed through my mind—playing San Francisco streets by day and coming home to Kendra at night—seven days of passion and progress...

The next morning, when I set up on the Starbucks sidewalk, I hung Galileo and his message inside the open case for the passing world to see.

First the Dream, Then the Deed

I began that set with a happy song.

16

"There she is, boys and girls!"

Blaze lifted his right hand from the steering wheel and pointed out the passenger window. Jaclyn, her coworkers, and I looked out across the water. Mid-afternoon on a perfect November day, clear blue skies—great conditions to look upon her for the first time. And damn, did she look good. The city I'd read about, seen in movies, dreamt about—there she was, sending vibrations through my retinas and into my brain, where they were then cocked and shot straight into a quivering stomach.

Seeing San Francisco for the first time had the same effect on me as pulling up to a girl's house to pick her up for our first date: a sharp jolt to the core, sending waves of anticipation rippling through every cell. The Bay Bridge, the Transamerica tower, boats in the bay, the Golden Gate—there, across the water, a collection of colorful universes pulsated together on an electric (Kool-Aid?) peninsula. The Marquis crew celebrated our arrival and took in the sight of that not-so-distant city as Blaze navigated the exit off I-80 toward the Bay Bridge.

Jaclyn, sitting in the passenger seat, turned to face me with her palm out, I high-fived it hard and said, "Thelma made it!" (Earlier that day, Jaclyn had chosen this name for her car, out of the blue. When I had asked her, "Why Thelma?" she'd simply replied, "Because that's her name.")

"Hell yeah, she did!" Jaclyn said, turning back around and

smacking the dashboard with both hands. She then unbuckled her seat belt, rolled down her window, and stuck her body outside, shouting, "Whooooohooooo!" against the roaring wind and road.

Jaclyn resumed her seated position as we passed through the Yerba Buena tunnel and onto the second section of the Bay Bridge. Seeing this concrete monster in person, with its massive suspension tentacles, was a surreal experience. I couldn't help but think about what kind of process would be necessary to build something so ambitious.

As Thelma and her five passengers rolled on, the city grew larger every second and began to look like its own breed of beast—living, breathing, and crackling with energy—contained by the blue waters of the bay.

Thelma roared into the city, swooping through streets that led us toward the hotel where Jaclyn and her coworkers would be staying for the week. It was only four o'clock at that point, though, and the three of them didn't need to be in the lobby to check in until five. With a bit of time to spare, Thelma weaved between massive buildings—towering over us with metropolitan authority—which, minutes ago, were just small shapes on the horizon. Rolling the windows down, we soaked in rush hour sensations. Every type of person you could imagine jetted back and forth across city streets to the sounds of a buzzing hive clocking out for the day: horns, voices, engines. Somewhere beneath this cacophony lived a constant low reverberation—the breathing of the beast (similar to Seattle's slumber rumble—*perhaps the two cities are of the same genus?*).

Thelma powered up and over steep hills, cresting tall and dipping quickly at angles that made my stomach jump into my throat like coming over the top of some large rollercoaster. At times, these hills were so steep that I felt the car's brakes wouldn't be able to stop us before we careened through busy intersections at the bottom. From atop these streets, the five of us took in various views of the area's vast majesty. The Golden Gate Bridge rolled out to Marin County, across the waters to the north, Mount Tamalpais looming massive beyond. The Bay Bridge connected San Francisco to Berkeley, Oakland, and the rest of the East Bay. And poor little Alcatraz floated out there all by itself—the lonely island that nobody wanted to play with.

Every now and then, Thelma would shoot over the top of a hill, and the car would be wrapped in a blanket of sea air, smothering us with saltwater scent as we gazed down at buildings that lined the streets in neat little rows. Most of the architecture in San Francisco sat very closely together, and much of it flaunted a Victorian style: houses, condos, shops, bars, restaurants—buildings of all different sizes, shapes, and colors, each one a unique brush stroke on a forty-seven square mile canvas.

Blaze guided Thelma through a section of town called the Tenderloin en route to the hotel. The energy there was dark and heavy. Folks sprawled out across sidewalks in sleeping bags or on cardboard beds as bearded zombies staggered down alleyways heading toward, or away from, who knows what. Windows were covered with bars, sirens screamed in the distance, and random smoke seemed to hang all over (maybe this effect was just in my head?). Idling at an intersection, I peeked out my window to see a man dressed head-to-toe in a purple pimp suit. He strutted up the sidewalk using a golf club as a cane, with his free hand wrapped around the waist of a skeleton in a mini skirt. I dubbed these two the mascots for this interesting part of the city where I would find myself spending some quality time in the very near future.

We rounded one last corner, and the car arrived at her resting place: the Weiss Hotel. There, we found a parking spot where

Thelma could cool her exhausted engine, hot from a full day's drive and subsequent tour of the city that had her hauling five adults and all their shit up several steep slopes.

It was amazing how quiet things became once we turned that car off.

The group released a collective breath.

We had made it.

Thelma's doors swung open and ten legs hit the concrete, followed by ten arms stretching, five backs cracking, and a million possibilities whizzing around inside my head like some hopeful hurricane. Blaze and I grabbed our things from the trunk and said our goodbyes to the working crew, who had only minutes before they needed to jump into their orientation. Blaze wouldn't be seeing these three again, but I'd be riding back up to Seattle with Jaclyn and her coworker Jaime at the end of the week.

"Thanks, Jacks," Blaze said, reaching into his pocket. "Here's my share of the gas."

Blaze handed Jaclyn a twenty, which she gladly accepted.

"Sweet," Jaclyn said as she stuffed the money into her jean shorts. "Glad you came with us, Blaze! It was a blast." She pulled her phone from her back pocket. "What's your Facebook?" she asked. "I'll send you some pictures of the trip."

Blaze and Jaclyn exchanged information as I shook hands with her coworkers. "Have a good week, guys," I said. "Nice riding with you, Jaime, hope the job treats you well. And Derek, have fun in New York."

"Thanks, bro," Derek said with a nod. "Take it easy."

"Great riding with *you*, Jason!" Jaime said, full of energy as always. "I hope you get rich playing down here!"

"Me too," I replied.

It's crazy how quickly you can bond with people when you're packed into an eighty-five mile an hour hunk of metal with them for twenty-four hours.

I was going to miss that crew.

I glanced at Jaclyn, who had been watching my goodbye through sunglasses. She waved at me when our eyes met. I thought maybe she was thinking the same thing I was—about the day we'd met at Pike Place two months prior that had led to this eight-hundred-mile trek, or the chance sunset meeting that solidified it. Either way, there we were, alive in some simultaneous dream-turned-reality and ready to be turned loose in that new world.

I walked over to Jaclyn and gave her a hug. Then, leaning back and keeping my hands on her shoulders, I looked at her and smiled, speaking the single syllable that said it all:

"Check."

17

Blaze and I stepped through the back door of the bar and descended wooden stairs onto a large dirt patio full of people and alive with conversation. Several packed picnic tables populated the fenced area, only one showing any space unoccupied by human asses. The two of us set our sights on those open seats and made our way through the dense crowd to set our things down at a table where a couple guys were having a good laugh about something.

It was nice to relieve myself of the weight of my guitar case and remove the metal stand from my left shoulder. I was also wearing my backpack. When I slid its straps from my shoulders, my back was moist with the sweat that our walk had conjured up.

After saying goodbye to Jaclyn and Co., Blaze and I had hiked eight blocks to Market Street and caught the bus to Valencia in the Mission District. We then trekked a few more blocks and landed at this bar.

Blaze had negotiated the San Francisco streets with ease as a result of his many journeys to the area, and the first pitcher was on me, a token of my appreciation for his navigation. Part of the reason that Blaze had insisted we visit this establishment (called Sable) was to show me "the best burger in the city, maybe even the West Coast." The first thing we'd done after walking through the door was have the cook throw two patties on the grill and drop a basket of fries into the oil. We hadn't eaten since Yreka that morning (unless you count the afternoon beers in the gas station parking lot) and were very hungry.

Once we'd claimed our table, I went inside to procure a pitcher. As I made my way to the bar, I took in every detail of the place. A collection of old street signs decorated the wooden walls—Stop, Larch Lane, Allman Avenue, Yield, Caution. Heavy metal blared through ceiling-mounted speakers, snare drum hits sporadically accented by shattered racks of pool balls, broken by figures in black bearing numerous tattoos.

I paid for the beer, walked back outside, and sat down at the table beside Blaze, who was smoking a cigarette while chatting with the two guys seated across from him. It was seven o'clock at that point, and had to be about twenty degrees warmer than any November night I'd ever experienced in Seattle. I was happy to peel my coat off and drink a beer in my T-shirt this close to winter.

I checked my phone.

Earlier, while riding the bus with Blaze, I'd called Kendra to let her know that we'd made it into town. She hadn't answered and, so far, hadn't called back. Beyond Kendra's guest bedroom offer, I hadn't made any arrangements for a spot to sleep that evening. I was beginning to think that this may have been a dumb move, but I'd spoken with her when I'd left Seattle the night before, and everything seemed to be a go. Hopefully she wasn't backing out...

But what if she...?

...Stop.

The voice in my head was right—one of them at least. There was beer to be attended to.

I filled a glass and slid it toward Blaze before pouring one for myself and shaking hands with our new amigos, seated across the table. "What's up, guys? I'm Jason."

"Jason, huh?" asked the guy with slicked-back hair. "That's my brother's name." The two of us shook hands. "Miguel."

"Good to meet you, Miguel." I looked toward the man seated on Miguel's right. He wore a red bandana and a look of stern intensity.

"Raul," the man said, as he shook my hand firmly.

"Good to meet you both, cheers."

Clink, clink, clink, clink!

Blaze glanced at me and tipped his beer toward the duo. "These guys just moved up here from Puerto Vallarta."

"Yeah?" I said, looking across the table.

"Bucerias," Raul corrected. "But we say Puerto Vallarta 'cause everybody knows there. It's half hour away."

Blaze took a quick sip of his beer. "Dude," he said as his glass hit the table, "I was *just* down there last January; it was rad. Mid-seventies the whole time."

Miguel nodded. "Yeah, that's for sure the time to go. Summer here is the rainy time down there, and winter here is reeeeeal nice there. Me and Raul lived a year in Bucerias. Mexico City before that."

"So you guys are buddies, then?" I asked.

"Buddies?" Miguel said, looking puzzled. "What do you mean?"

Raul took a sip of his beer and leaned forward, resting his elbows on the table and staring at me. "What," he said. "You think we're boyfriends or something?"

Raul looked at Miguel, then slowly back across the table, burning me with his eyes.

Shit... Make a joke... Something good...

A smile crept across Raul's face and he leaned back to smack

Miguel on the shoulder. "I'd be the pitcher for sure!"

Miguel snickered and shook his head. "You wish, *puto.*"

I clarified, relieved. "I mean did you guys grow up together or something? You coworkers?"

"Yeah," Raul replied. "Knew Miguel for thirty years. We were like brothers growing up in Cancún." Raul glanced at Miguel and shook his head. "And now I'm stuck with him."

"So what do you guys do for work?" I asked.

"Oh man," Miguel said. "Construction, kitchen, landscape—little this, little that—we do it all. Someone needs a worker? Poof! There we come."

"Keeps us free," Raul added. "Tied to nothing. We can go anywhere, do anything. Just need to know how to learn, and need to work hard. That's it, everything else comes easy." He paused to take a long sip of his beer and wiped his mouth with the back of his hand. "I wake up and say, 'Hey Miguel, let's go to Bucerias!' and there we go."

Miguel nodded and continued, "Then one day l maybe come home and I say, 'Raul, let's go see San Francisco!' and then we are here, having beer with you."

"Who knows," Raul added. "Next week we could be in Hawaii."

Miguel raised an eyebrow and turned toward Raul. "Now that's a nice idea..."

"Two cheeseburgers!"

Slam! Slam!

Plates hit the picnic table, sending the smell of freshly grilled beef floating into my nostrils, where it found a faucet at the back of my tongue and cranked that thing on full blast. I had completely forgotten that we'd ordered those burgers, and couldn't have been happier that we did.

Blaze and I chowed down the greasy treats, chasing them with delicious beer.

Between bites, Blaze told a story.

"So on like, my second day in Bucerias, I was surfin', havin' a great time—weather was great, girls were hot, all was right with the world. But I needed to get my hands on some weed—*mota.*" Blaze grinned and pointed toward Miguel, proud that he knew the Spanish slang for pot. Miguel looked at Raul before digging his hand into his jacket pocket. Blaze continued. "I didn't know where to start, so I went askin' around to a few other surfers, but nobody knew shit. So I let it go for the day and forgot about it—hit the waves, and, after a few hours, I took a little break and headed to the bar to grab a cold one. So as I'm walking into this bar by the beach, there's a little dude standing right next to the front door of the place, selling handmade bracelets with names on 'em. They're all mounted to this big folding piece of wood that he's holding open, like a book, with both hands."

Blaze held his hands out in front of him to demonstrate.

"This dude's totally ready for the tourists. He's got all the American names ready to go—bracelet for Ashley, bracelet for Bobby, Chris, Debra—all the way down the alphabet. He's got everybody. So I start to walk into the bar and the little dude says, '*Amigo,*' as he taps on this big piece of wood with one finger, tappin' right on one of these bracelets."

Miguel was working on something in his lap. I couldn't see what it was, but he alternated between glancing down at what he was doing, and looking up at Blaze, who continued to tell his story.

"I'm like, just about to step in the door of this place, so I wave the guy off. But then the little dude gets all stern with me and says it again, hard, like, '*AMIGO!*' So I stop and I look at him like, 'What the fuck do you want?' You know? I look at his eyes but he's still tappin' his finger on one of these bracelets. So I look at the bracelet he's tappin' on, and, dude... I couldn't believe it.

Right in between 'Wendy' and 'Whitney,' this guy had a little green bracelet that just said..."

Blaze held a hand out in front of his face, sliding it left to right.

"...WEED."

As if on cue, Miguel presented a freshly rolled joint, placing it between his lips and lighting the tip. He took a long drag and, after exhaling, nodded slowly and said, "Those guys run that beach."

"No shit!" Blaze replied. "Soon as I saw what he was tappin' on, I looked up at him and said, '*Si*,' and, no kidding, in about four seconds flat, *his* amigo is standing in front of me with a backpack unzipped and a fuckin' ounce of pot in his hand." Blaze held up his right hand and spaced his thumb and index finger about an inch apart. "I told 'em I only needed '*pequeno*' and the dude pulls out a dub and tells me it's forty bucks!" Blaze shook his head. "I told 'em both, '*No bueno*,' and started walking away, but then the dude chases me down and says, 'Thirty dollars!' So me and this dude sit down on a couple beach chairs, and I pull out two hundred and seventy pesos—'bout twenty bucks. I lay the pesos on the end of dude's chair and take two beers out of my backpack. I set one on the chair next to my money."

Blaze took a bite of his burger, speaking as he chewed.

"The guy looked at me for a sec, and then he grabbed that beer and cracked it. He took those pesos, handed me the bag of *mota*, and said, '*Salud!*'"

Blaze raised his beer, and Miguel and Raul said, "*Salud!*" in unison, raising theirs.

The four of us banged glasses together.

"Nice work, my friend," Miguel complimented as he passed the joint to Raul, who took his turn before holding it toward Blaze.

"*Mota?*" Raul offered, smirking.

Blaze accepted with a, "*Gracias.*"

"Tourists will pay that kind of money," Miguel said. "They wanna get in and out real quick. Those beach boys probably like your style."

"Yeah," Raul agreed. "There's five of them down there with the bracelets. That's their cover. The cops know about it, too. The police and those guys, they look out for each other."

Miguel chimed in. "The cops don't bust them. But the trade is that those guys tell the cops when a rich-looking tourist buys grass from them. You know, *It's the white guy in the red shirt with the nice sunglasses. His girlfriend has a fat ass.*' Then the cops track the tourist down and scare them. They say they saw the tourist buying the drugs and now the tourist has to give the cops money; cops say they are going to the jail if they don't."

Raul traced a line down his cheek with an index finger. "That's when the girl starts to cry all the over the street and the man opens his wallet."

"That's crazy," I said, taking my turn in the rotation before passing the joint back to Miguel. The end of the paper burned bright red as Miguel took another long drag, held his breath, and let the smoke creep from his cracked mouth. Miguel then studied the rolled *mota* and glanced back across the table, twisting the joint between his fingertips and adding, "Being a cop pays good money in Bucerias."

18

"So what's up with this girl?" Blaze asked as the two of us trekked between dozing houses. I pulled the phone from my pocket: 9 o'clock.

"Still nothing."

"Bummer," Blaze said. "Well, if you want, I'm gonna be parking by the beach tonight. You're welcome to sleep in the back of the truck."

"I appreciate that, man. May take you up on it."

I tried to take my mind off the fact that I hadn't heard from Kendra. The air smelled musty, a new scent in a new city, and I still couldn't believe how warm it was for a November night—a good night to be rambling somewhere on the south side of San Francisco. The neighborhood was very quiet except for the steady footsteps of Blaze and me as we hiked to the top of the street and took a left.

"There's my baby!" Blaze said, as he ran up to a big beige Toyota pickup with a canopy. He smacked the tailgate and pulled a set of keys from his jeans. Then he unlocked the driver's side door, opened it, and threw his backpack across the cab.

"Oh," he barked, circling around to the front of the truck. "What the fuck!?" He snatched a small, white envelope from beneath the windshield wiper. "I told Travis to move the truck for street cleaning!"

Blaze held the envelope up for me to see "That dumbass is payin' for this!"

"Street cleaning?" I asked.

"Yeah, that's how San Francisco makes their money, dude." Blaze opened the envelope and pulled out a small strip of paper. "These little guys are sixty-five bucks a pop. Once a week the city comes by and cleans the streets, and if your car's in the way of the sweeper, boom! Fat ticket."

"Shitty."

"Yeah, super shitty. And I told my buddy to move my truck on Wednesday when they came through, and guess what? He didn't. So now he's payin' for it." Blaze shook his head and stuffed the envelope into his back pocket. "I'll be right back."

Blaze walked up to a nearby house and let himself in. As he did, I relieved my metal stand of its shoulder duties and set my guitar on the curb. It was nice to be there, in that moment, on the edge of whatever was next, even if I hadn't heard from Kend— *Hey...*

What about Dominic?

I had spoken with Dominic a few days before I'd left Seattle, but I hadn't talked to him since I'd been in San Francisco. He and I had kept in steady contact since our nights playing together, and I felt it'd be good to see him again. I wondered what he was up to, so I called him to find out.

"What's up, buuuuuuddy?" Dominic greeted as he answered the phone.

"Hey, man! Just got into town a couple hours ago and grabbed a few beers with this guy from the ride down. Now, no plans; what are you up to tonight?"

"Where you guys at?" Dominic asked.

"Well..." I thought for a second. "We were just on Valencia Street..." I looked around for a sign. "And I'm on Twenty-fifth now."

"Nice!" Dominic said. "I'm literally two minutes away. Meet me on Valencia; we're going to a show at the Moab."

"The Moab?" I asked

"Yup. Race ya." Dominic hung up.

I chuckled to myself before standing and slinging the stand over my shoulder. Just as I bent down to grab my guitar, Blaze burst from the house and strutted down to the sidewalk.

"He's gonna pay it," Blaze announced with a proud grin.

"Nice work," I said as he nodded, satisfied. "Hey, man, I really appreciate the offer to crash in the truck but—"

"She called you?"

I smiled. "No, but I got a hold of a friend who's heading to a show at some venue across town. I'm gonna go check that out with him."

"Solid."

"You wanna come with?" I asked.

"I would," Blaze said, "but I'm beat. All I want to do right now is to park down by the beach, rub one out, and *pass* out. Been a long couple days. And got a long week ahead."

"I feel you, man," I said, realizing that my momentum was fading as well. "Well, have a good night, then. Great riding with you."

"You too, Jason. You're a cool cat."

I pointed toward the truck. "Have a good duffle shuffle."

Blaze grinned as he patted his pickup. "You know it. Rollin' out bright and early on Tuesday." He opened the driver's side door, saluting me as he climbed inside. "Later, dude."

I saluted back before turning to begin my journey down the sleeping hill. After a few steps, Blaze's beige brute roared to life and he revved the engine hard, clearing the truck's smoky throat before rumbling into the Frisco night, waking babies the entire way.

19

Clothes spun in beat-up machines as an old Mexican woman sat in her chair, reading a tattered magazine. A few folks folded shirts, pants, and underwear, while other late-night patrons loaded and unloaded washers and dryers. A single sock dangled from a young woman's hand as she stuck her entire head into the open mouth of a dryer that had apparently swallowed the sock's counterpart.

I looked from the laundromat back to the sidewalk as I strolled past an old man. He was fishing aluminum cans out of a garbage bin and adding them to the growing stockpile he dragged around in a large plastic bag.

Valencia: a main thoroughfare in the Mission district, and a very quiet one on that Sunday evening. San Francisco seemed to be asleep, recharging its batteries and preparing to spring into action for a new work week. Most of the establishments I ambled past were closed (with the exception of the laundromat and a few bars). I came upon a tiny Irish spot and took a look inside—a small, dark room inhabited by a few barstools and even fewer people, low music. The bartender glanced my way. I gave him a nod and kept on walking.

"Hey baby! How much?"

A ruby red station wagon sat idling in the middle of the road. The pilot's window had been rolled down, revealing a large smile framed by a well-manicured goatee.

"Two minutes, my ass!" I yelled as I walked toward the vehicle.

Dominic popped the wagon's back hatch, and I threw my guitar, stand, and backpack inside before circling around, opening the passenger door, and jumping in.

"What's up, Dom?"

Dominic looked exactly the same as when I'd last seen him in Seattle: blue jeans, jean jacket, and the Giants cap.

"Welcome to San Francisco!" he greeted, slamming the gas. We swooped a U-turn and gunned it up the empty street.

"Good to be here, man. How you been?"

"Great," he said. "Greeeaaaat, and about to be even better"

Dominic turned up the stereo: Pearl Jam. (Unless I say otherwise, any time I'm taking a ride in Dominic's car, Pearl Jam is playing. To say that the guy is a fanatic would be an understatement. He follows that band on tour like folks used to follow the Dead.)

"What's this place we're going to?" I asked.

"The Moab," he said. "One of my favorite venues in town. You'll love it. My friend's band is playing and there are a bunch of people at the show that I want you to meet."

Meet?

People?

Fuck.

If I was to be doing any socializing, I'd need at least a shot or two to stay awake. After a long night of I-5 driving, three hours of rest-stop sleep, another whole day of the road, and what had already been an eventful evening, I was starting to lose a bit of steam. Even the idea of a nap on one of the passing sidewalks was starting to trigger the same smiling shivers as a full body massage atop the fluffiest cloud.

Dominic parked Ruby along a curb, across from the venue. (I'm realizing now that I may only associate with people who name their cars.)

"Is my stuff gonna be good in here?" I asked as the two of us stepped onto the sidewalk. Looking around the unfamiliar city, I saw imaginary burglars lurking behind every telephone pole.

"Here," Dominic said, opening the back door and grabbing a blanket off the seat. He handed the blanket to me and popped the rear hatch. I walked around to Ruby's booty, threw the blanket over the top of my things, and prayed to the gods of good karma, hoping that I had enough cosmic currency stored up for them to watch over my guitar for the night.

That instrument was my only source of income for the next week. If I lost it, I'd have to go back to stripping, and I hadn't kept up on my pole dancing.

Dominic and I had just started to cross the street when my phone rang.

My stomach jumped as I looked at the screen.

"Well, hello there," I answered, motioning to Dominic that I'd meet him inside.

"Hey you, welcome to San Francisco." Kendra's voice tickled my right ear.

"Why, thank you. Glad to be here. Just got in a few hours ago."

"Do you love it so far?" she asked.

"It's great," I said. "This guy from the ride down showed me a spot called Sable. We hung there for a bit before he took off to go sleep by the beach. Then I called up Dominic, from the night we met, and now the two of us are heading over to the Moab for a show."

"Look at you, hitting all the local spots," Kendra teased.

"You staying in for the evening?"

"Yes," Kendra replied. "I work at seven. What are your plans for tomorrow, though?"

"I'm gonna play somewhere during the day, heard about this place called Fisherman's Wharf, so I'll be checking that out.

After that, though, no plans. Want me to call you when I'm done busking down there?"

"Busking?"

"Street performing," I clarified.

"Oh, right," Kendra said. "Yeah, that's perfect. I'm off at four."

"Great. I'll call you around then."

"Cool. Have a wonderful evening."

"You too."

Click... Click...

It was probably best that I didn't see Kendra that night.

I was a bit too foggy to be in the company of a lively creature such as herself; I wanted my mind sharp and my body full of energy for our time together.

Taking a deep breath of warm air, a million little scenarios involving Kendra never calling melted from my mind, and I was left with the night ahead, worry free.

I try not to be like that, worrying about things so much, but I have a habit of getting ahead of myself, of creating scenarios that may or may not happen, for better or for worse, some side effect of an overactive imagination. I tell myself to stay in the moment, that now is the key. Sometimes this is easier said than done, but I tell myself to do it anyways.

There *was* one thing I couldn't help but notice about our conversation, though: Kendra had made no mention of the guest bedroom at her place. *Maybe her roommate had vetoed the idea?* I scratched my head over this, but had decided not to ask her about it.

If Kendra wanted to bring it up, she would.

I knew I'd have to find somewhere to stay for the evening; after my share of Thelma's gas expenses, and the money I'd spent hanging with Blaze, I was down to eighteen dollars. This could probably buy me a pretty spacious cardboard box, but it wasn't enough for any room in the city.

I'm sure there's a park nearby, some cozy patch of grass...

I shrugged off these thoughts for the time being and decided to worry about my sleeping situation after the show.

Through its large windows, I could see the Moab's lively insides. A long bar packed with people—animated people, laughing and gesturing and smacking each other on the shoulder and standing up to make the story more potent. On my way to the door, I tried to imagine what it sounded like in there. It looked loud—and it was.

Stepping into the venue, I was hit with a wall of noise: the force of fifty conversations piggybacking upon sonic waves that crashed forth from the live band playing inside.

I looked toward two sets of stairs on my right. One descended to a cramped room that was packed with sweating people moving to the rock band that played atop a small stage. This three-piece's energetic performance was framed by crimson curtains that cascaded from a bleeding ceiling. The second set of stairs ascended to a balcony that housed a tiny bar and some seats that looked over the room below. I glanced toward the main bar on my left, where Dominic stood near the middle of the line, waving me over. I walked toward Dominic, and he introduced me to his friend, seated on a barstool—a young, curly-haired songwriter who would be playing that night. Curly reached onto the bar behind him and handed me a shot of whiskey. I took the drink like a good soldier and, remembering that I had some pot in my pocket, decided to share some of this in return.

"Really?" Curly asked excitedly as I presented him with a small nugget from my stash.

"Yeah, really," I said. "'Preciate the shot. It's been a long couple days and I definitely needed that. I figure, you're lifting me now with the whiskey, I'll lift you later with this."

Curly accepted my gift and raised a glass of amber goodness.

"Up we go," he said as he took the shot. He spun around to set his glass down on the bar before turning back around and pointing at Dominic.

"What was her name, again?" Curly asked with a grin.

Dominic smirked through his goatee and tilted his head back slightly as he answered. "Nayara"

Curly shook his head as he repeated the name. "Naaaaayara." He looked at me. "Jason, you should have seen this girl." Curly pointed at Dominic. "I don't know how the hell *this* guy ended up with her, but she was drop-dead gorgeous, maybe one of the finest I've ever seen. Young, couldn't have been more than twenty-two. Beautiful face, perfect ass, great tits, tan skin with a couple tattoos..."

I glanced at Dominic, whose facial expression teetered somewhere between blushing and beaming. He nodded and simply said, "Brazilian"

"Braaaaazillian," Curly repeated, his hair bouncing with each syllable. "Naaaaayaaara from Braaaaazill... And Dominic *fucked* her," Curly stuck a thumb over his shoulder, "in the baaaaaathroooom."

Dominic laughed and shook his head as I looked to him for conformation. His chuckle cooled to a full-toothed smile before he nodded. "Yeah... Yeah..."

"Here?" I asked.

"I've never seen a bigger grin on his face than that night," Curly interrupted, "and I'm sure I'll never see another like it again."

"Yeah," Dominic continued. "That was probably the finest girl I'll ever be with. I still don't know how that happened."

"You and me both!" Curly yelled.

Dominic laughed. "I think she had a thing for musicians—and I fit the criteria."

"Except you can't play!" Curly blurted as he shoved Dominic's shoulder. "This girl came up to *him* and asked for *his* number. I've never seen anything like it. You would swear he was Brad Pitt or something."

"Or George Harrison," I said.

Curly grinned, turning to Dominic and pointing. "See, I *told* you."

Dominic tilted his head to the side. "Okay, maybe I do look like him a *little* bit..."

"So was this just a one-night thing?" I asked Dominic.

"No," he said. "She was staying here for about another month after I met her, an au pair. She lived with a family up in Dolores Heights and watched their kids. The two of us saw each other a few times a week until she flew back to Brazil." Dominic shook his head. "Nayara..." He let out a long breath before continuing. "One weekend, the family went down to Carmel, and Nayara called me. She had the whole place to herself and wanted to have a sleepover. That family had some serious money, and a *nice* house. I showed up there with a bottle of wine, she had rolled a few joints..."

Curly and I listened intently, living vicariously.

Dominic paused for a moment before nodding to himself. "Let's just put it this way," he continued. "If I died right now, and got to heaven, and it was anything besides wine, weed, good conversation, and sex with a beautiful Brazilian woman, I'd ask to speak to god himself and demand a transfer."

Curly chuckled.

"She and I spent the whole night like that," Dominic reminisced. "Heaven. We even had a little dance party at one point—listened to music and spun around naked in her tiny room..."

"You're a bastard," Curly said, shaking his head as he stood from his stool and glanced at me. "As much as I'd love to sit here and let Dominic give me a raging hard-on, I've got to go tune up, we're playing soon." Curly patted Dominic and me on the shoulders. "See you guys in a bit."

Curly's hair bounced as he walked the crowded bar and descended into the music room. When I looked back at Dominic, he just nodded and said, "Nayara," again with some distant look in his eye.

Dominic and I talked there for a while, but he soon encouraged me to come meet someone else at the other end of the room, a girl who played ukulele in some local duo. After the three of us chatted for a bit, it was time to meet someone *else* upstairs: Dominic's old roommate. And then another new face, and another, and another...

"Oh! You've gotta meet this person!"

"Hey! Come here for a second."

"Guys, this is," (Dominic always introduced me proudly as) "Jason, my friend from Seattle."

Dominic seemed to know half of the folks in that place; after the first few hours I'd been there, at least a dozen new names and faces had burned their way into my foggy brain.

I opened my eyes as Dominic pulled up in front of Curly's house.

I'd fallen asleep in the back seat. Curly slurred goodbye as he stumbled into the darkness, and Ruby rocketed off, sailing through silent streets toward Dominic's place. His spot was the bottom floor of a quiet duplex in San Francisco's Outer Sunset neighborhood. The air was fresh as the two of us stepped from the car, different from the musty air of earlier that evening. The entrance to the apartment sat around the building's rear. Dominic and I passed through a squeaky wooden gate and opened a door that lurked beneath the upstairs neighbor's porch. This door opened into a very small kitchen that was just big enough to fit a refrigerator, table, and some chairs. Dominic and I squeezed past those chairs into a hardwood hallway that led to three small rooms—Dominic's room on the right, his roommate's chambers on the left, and the bathroom straight ahead.

The apartment was small, but there was plenty of potential sleeping space on the floor. Dominic handed me a pillow and blanket, telling me that I could crash in the kitchen if I wanted to. It was a tight squeeze, but there was just enough room for me to stretch out completely. I thanked Dominic for the hospitality and said goodnight as he closed the door to his bedroom. He had to work in four hours—*what a trooper.* Luckily, it was at a café where he had access to vast quantities of coffee—and beer, if he felt so inclined.

I shuffled into the bathroom and brushed my teeth before changing into sweatpants. Then, spreading the blanket onto the tile floor, I created a soft surface—my own private nest—where I proceeded to lay my tired body and experience one of the greatest nights of sleep I've ever had.

20

I thought I was in my locker at Pike Place Market when I woke up.

I'd slept on the concrete floor of that locker, using a tarp for a pillow, several times when I'd needed a little boost of energy between sets. For some reason, this is where my mind placed my body when Dominic stepped over me to leave for work at six AM. He must've heard me shift positions as he navigated the dim kitchen.

"Hey, buddy," he whispered. "Feel free to sleep in my bed if you want."

I shot upright, yanked to life when the word 'bed' triggered adrenal glands and sent a healthy dose of the hormone coursing through my veins.

"Thanks, man," I mumbled, gathering my makeshift nest. "I can't believe you're heading to work right now."

"It's only six hours," Dominic said. "Then, I'm coming home and you better be out of that bed, 'cause I'm jumping right back into it."

I shuffled down the hallway, clutching my pillow and dragging my blanket on the hardwood behind me. Without turning around, I asked, "If I'm not, can we cuddle?"

Dominic laughed and said, "Maybe," as he shut the door.

After a night on the tile floor, preceded by an evening in the sweaty sedan—which itself was preceded by countless nights on random couches—the sensation of sleeping in a bed was miraculous. I fell asleep for another four hours wrapped in Dominic's blankets, a man-baby cradled in the loving arms of mother mattress.

When I finally woke, I took a much-needed shower and changed into some clothes that I hadn't slept in. This all felt amazing (nothing like being grimy and sleep-deprived to make you appreciate the simple things).

Clean, well-rested, and ready to explore a new city, I grabbed my guitar and stand (nice to be traveling without the extra weight of the backpack), and stuffed a few cereal bars in my pocket to keep me fed throughout the day. My first mission was to check out the Fisherman's Wharf on the Embarcadero (the road that runs along the port of San Francisco). I'd heard about playing at the Wharf from a few Pike Place buskers who'd spent some time there. That waterfront sounded like as good a place as any to start my quest for cash in the city.

I opened the duplex door to sunshine on that warm November morning, noticing that the AM air had the same fresh quality as the night before. I passed through the squeaky wooden gate, walking down the driveway and onto the sidewalk, where I could now see the neighborhood clearly for the first time, mostly small houses and apartments with the exception of a few businesses. All of these buildings were either one or two stories and had been painted many different colors, some of them very bright pastels—pinks and oranges. Lining the sidewalks, every other driveway or so, tall palms shaded their designated sections of the neighborhood.

Directly across the street from the duplex lived a lumberyard, where workers wearing orange helmets hauled sheets of plywood and various beams back and forth behind a chain-link fence. A large sign running along the top of the building read

"Sunset Supply," and underneath, in smaller, red letters, something was written in Chinese. The lumberyard workers spoke Chinese; with the exception of them chattering back and forth about who-knows-what, the neighborhood was very quiet.

The night before, Dominic had told me that I could catch a train on Taraval Street and ride that all the way up to the Embarcadero. I hauled my guitar and stand toward a road up ahead where a steady stream of cars zipped one way or the other. As I approached this busy street, I noticed a man walking toward me on the same sidewalk.

"'Scuse me," I said, a few paces before the two of us crossed paths.

The man stopped walking and looked at me with eyebrows raised.

"How do I get to Taraval Street from here?"

The man turned and pointed at the busy street. "Go up to Sunset here, turn right, and go up two blocks. It's the street with the tracks running along it—can't miss it."

"Thanks," I said.

The man nodded, and we both continued on.

I hiked the few blocks up to the intersection of Sunset and Taraval, noticing metal rails running along the middle of the street. Following the tracks, I crossed Sunset and found a concrete platform where a few folks stood waiting for the train. I set my things down and joined them.

As I stood there, I scanned the scene, taking everything in. I watched the people of San Francisco go about their daily routines—maybe to a job they'd worked for twenty years or to go buy some groceries; maybe they were on some top-secret spy mission, using that new Benz as a cover. Whatever the destination, these were their lives, and I was a tourist moving amongst them—a part of their world.

I glanced casually to my left and was surprised by what I saw. Excited, I turned to a woman waiting near me.

"'Scuse me..."

The woman faced me with wary eyes as I pointed down Taraval's long incline.

"Is that the ocean there?"

The woman nodded slowly with furrowed brows.

Dominic hadn't mentioned how close he lived to the beach!

This Pacific proximity explained the fresh air in that part of town. I wanted to get to the Wharf and work, but it looked like it was only about a half mile to the water. I threw the stand over my shoulder, picked up my guitar case, and started down the street—determined to warm up my vocal chords by playing some songs for the Northern California coast.

I cruised the Taraval sidewalk, passing apartment buildings with painted steel gates, the open garage of a mechanic shop with random oily parts scattered across a stained floor, and a small market where various fruits cooked in the sun atop a rickety wooden stand, rows of basted ducks dangling in the window. I walked past old Chinese folks, or they walked past me, going wherever they needed to go at a snail's pace. Every few blocks, the lactic acid building in my guitar-carrying arm would tell me that it was time to switch hands, giving both my right and left an equal workout (I'd be interested to know how many calories one burns while walking across a city with a guitar case.)

I could hear it as I inched closer, the roar of the mighty Pacific, welcoming me to the edge of the western world. The smell of saltwater struck my nostrils as sea air filled my lungs, tasting clean. I stopped at a crosswalk that spanned a four-lane road called the Great Highway—San Francisco's westernmost stretch of concrete and the last barrier between me and the beach. After crossing the great highway, I sank into the sand and made my way closer to the water, which was now framed by large dunes looming to my right and left. Tall grass blew carelessly in the cool breeze, and a man walked toward me, carrying a large plastic bag and sporting a serious tan. The man wore board shorts and a T-shirt. The hair on his head had been bleached by the sun.

Looks like a surfer...

The two of us nodded as we passed.

"Hey, bro..."

I turned to face the man. Cars on the great highway appeared to drive through his body as he spoke.

"Just to let you know, I'm spearheading a beach beautification project today. So, if you grab even just *one* piece of trash, and take it with you on your way out of here, it'd be much appreciated."

I glanced down at the plastic bag in his right hand. "That's great," I said. "I'll do that." I held out my left hand to shake his. "I'm Jason, just got into town from Seattle."

Tan Man smiled, and we shook. "Well, Jason," he said. "One more thing you gotta know about this beach." Tan Man set his bag down and reached into the pocket of his shorts. "Before you can enter..."

He pulled out a small glass pipe and a film canister.

"...you gotta smoke some marijuana."

Tan Man began to twist the lid off the black canister. "There's a little hash in here too; you cool with that?"

I chuckled as sun rays massaged my face. San Francisco must've really liked me. Maybe the city wanted to make a good first impression? I'd only been roaming for a total of about thirty-five minutes, and somebody was already offering to share.

"Yes, sir."

Tan Man and I hiked to the top of a tall dune and plopped our asses down in the soft sand to an amazing view. To the North, the trees of Golden Gate Park waved a breezy greeting, and beyond them Marin County peeked around the city to say "good morning" from across the bay. To the south, the coast rolled mistily until it disappeared on the horizon, and, laid out, vast and blue before us, was the mighty monster itself, running from there to Tokyo and peppered with surfers chasing waves in the morning sun.

21

I stood up from my seat to give the man a hand, but he made it up the stairs just fine on his own. He paid the fare and then, as the train began to move, dragged an enormous bag of aluminum cans to a nearby seat. He plopped down and rested his stash in front of him.

That bag looked like it weighed about as much as he did.

The guy had to be close to eighty years old—Chinese, wearing a sweater, sweatpants, and a visor, all gray. He sat with shoulders slumped forward and mouth hanging open, staring out the window across from him and blinking occasionally.

I looked out the window too—lots to see, and all of it for the first time.

Mid-afternoon.

As Taraval Street crept by, I thought about my morning and how interesting it had been. I thought about the tan man from the beach, about how he'd told me that he'd just moved up to the bay from San Diego, where he'd been a dirt bike salesman for a number of years. He said he had been making six figures selling those bikes until he got cut from the force one day. He was now homeless by choice, taking his misfortune as a sign from the universe and deciding to sell his possessions—house and all—and come up to San Francisco to win back his ex-wife. They had two kids together; both were tattooed on his upper arm in the form of lifelike portraits. Tan Man was on a mission to put his family back together. His story was touching, but the events of that morning had given me strong clues as to how the rest of the tale might play out.

Tan Man and I had sat there, on the sand, and talked for quite a while. I told him about my music, about Kendra—I showed him the Galileo letter (still pinned to the inside of my guitar case), which he got a kick out of. "Nobody writes letters anymore," he had said. "Especially not like this." Tan Man examined the construction paper note carefully, turning it over and taking it in.

At one point during our conversation, a guy with an uncanny resemblance to Johnny Depp appeared atop our dune and stood about ten feet from Tan Man and myself, staring out at the ocean through aviator sunglasses and swaying his hips. This mover made wavelike motions with his hands as the breeze blew his hair around beneath a fedora. Tan Man and I tried not to pay much attention to the dancer, but soon he began to inch closer, clearly wanting us to acknowledge him in some way. Eventually, he ended up just a few feet from our conversation, gyrating in the breeze and grooving to some tune in his head. Without breaking his rhythm, he glanced at us and asked, "Hey, either you fellas know the nature in these parts?"

I had no clue what he was getting at, but Tan Man instantly responded with some fish facts and he and Johnny Depp's twin (JDT) instantly started speaking at length about porpoises, crabs, and fluorocarbon lines.

The dancing doppelganger, from Oklahoma, had never been to California before, and had just arrived in San Francisco. He'd driven halfway across the country to see the Pacific Ocean he'd heard so much about. The gyrating dance that Tan Man and I had witnessed was JDT and the mighty Pacific shaking hands for the first time. The three of us talked there on the dune for a bit, and, at about noon, decided to walk up the street and check out a nearby café. Tan Man had mentioned that the place hosted live music, and I figured it would be smart to follow that lead and try to line up a gig while I was in town.

We crossed the great highway, and as I walked on JDT's left, he turned to look at me, uncorking some dormant urge to babble about the moon with a level of fascination I may never understand. JDT's voice fluctuated decibels as he gestured profusely, bursting with lunar enthusiasm.

"Get this, man," he blurted. "This THING is the only moon in our solar system with an almost perfect. Circular. Orbit. AND! It's exactly the right size AND DISTANCE from the earth to PERFECTLY cover our sun during an eclipse."

We walked on as I processed these facts. In that moment, JDT reminded me of a fly, staring at me through those mirrored sunglasses and tilting his head compulsively from side to side, awaiting my response.

I think I just nodded, probably blinked a time or two.

Unsatisfied with my reaction, JDT continued, determined to enlighten me. "Astronauts have *tried* to drill into the surface up there, man—CAN'T DO IT! Too tough. Made outta illeminite THAT'S GOT TITANIUM IN IT! They use that stuff to build damn SUBMARINES!" JDT's enthusiasm was astounding, and I tried not to laugh as he continued. "And what about the towers on the moon? You seen *those*?! No way HUMANS could have built 'em, man. NO WAY!"

I was beginning to think that walking with those guys wasn't as good an idea as I'd initially thought, but I carried on anyways—free entertainment. JDT saw that I wasn't born again via his lu-knowledge and turned toward Tan Man instead. "Hey, you know where I can score some meth 'round here?"

Unphased by this question, Tan Man shook his head. "Haven't touched the stuff in years." he said. "Used to dig it, though. God, I remember this one time..."

I walked along and listened as those two talked about the good ol' days.

Moons and methamphetamine...

"Hey, Jason!"

A familiar voice.

Tan Man, JDT, and I looked across the street to the big, beige monster of a Toyota with the shirtless, sunglassed captain at the helm. Blaze threw his beast into reverse and parked along the curb before hopping out of the cab and strutting across the street to join our band of merry misfits.

"Mornin', gentlemen," Blaze greeted with a smile and swagger, blonde locks in a ponytail. "May I offer you a little of NorCal's finest?" Blaze pinched a bud off of what looked like a little marijuana Christmas tree and pulled a pipe from his jeans. Tan Man studied Blaze.

"Hey," Tan Man said, leaning close to Blaze's face "I lost a pair of sunglasses *just* like those yesterday—tried to surf with 'em on." He shook his head. "Bad call."

Without a word, JDT removed his sunglasses and held them toward Tan Man. For the first time, I caught a glimpse of JDT's eyes—piercing, blue intensity and just as crazy-looking as I'd imagined they'd be.

Tan Man glanced down at the glasses, and then up at JDT. "Yeah?" Tan Man asked.
Without nodding, JDT responded. "Yeah."

Tan Man took the sunglasses and put them on, leaving JDT's blue eyes to burn holes in everything he stared at, starting with me.

"You know what I really think?" JDT asked, abruptly turning toward me and standing much closer than I would have liked. Blaze and Tan Man had started to talk about surfing, leaving JDT and me to continue our fascinating discussion.

"What's that?" I replied apprehensively, taking a step back.

Without hesitation, JDT closed the gap. "I think the moon ain't no moon at all. I think it's a damn SPACECRAFT! I think somethin' PARKED it up there however many thousand years ago, and they're still sittin' up there, sendin' out scouts and MESSIN' UP PEOPLE'S CROPS!" JDT was prepared for an argument, and cut me off at the pass. "Gimme ONE fact of proof that says this ain't possible."

He stared deep into me with those eyes, tilting his head from side to side, waiting.

I didn't feel like having a full-fledged debate, so I decided to try and be funny. "I don't think you can make a spaceship out of cheese, man."

JDT's head stopped moving and he glared at me. For a moment, I wondered if he'd even heard what I'd said. Then I started to think maybe I shouldn't have said it.

This moon business is no joking matter.

Not to this guy...

JDT burst out laughing, a grating cackle that gave my throat sympathy pains. He slapped me on the shoulder. "CHEESE!" he repeated, as he continued to laugh.

The four of us stood there on the sidewalk, smoking and talking, talking and smoking, luckily on to new topics beyond lunar conspiracies. After a little while, Blaze said he needed to go buy a new battery for his "baby" and the two of us made tentative plans to meet up later that night. He said, "See ya," hopped into truckzilla, and rumbled up the street. After Blaze left, I looked toward the water and noticed a girl creeping out from around a nearby corner. She was young, probably in her early twenties, very dirty—raggedy clothes and grimy hair that covered most of her face. The girl looked like she'd slept on the beach for the past year and a half. I was hypnotized by her appearance as she slowly approached—like I was seeing a ghost. And I assumed the girl would just haunt past, but...

"Where the hell you been?" Tan Man asked as he strutted up to the ghoul—I mean, girl.

These two knew each other and began to speak familiarly. She was way out of it, slurring speech and throwing arms around in baggy sleeves as she rambled something shrill. JDT glided toward the ghoul and the two of *them* began to talk. As they did, JDT focused unblinkingly upon her eyes, moving his head in sync with hers like a cobra ready to strike. The two of them rapped back and forth, matching each other's intensity, and sure enough, it wasn't long before JDT began to ramble about the moon again, activating this girl's arm-flailing excitement.

"Oh my goooood," she yelled. "I was juuuuust talking to my friend about that!"

It was time for me to leave.

As I picked up my guitar and walked toward the group to say goodbye, a young woman with a stroller rolled up the sidewalk. Those three amigos parted so the stroller could pass between them. As the mother pushed past, Tan Man pointed to a pack of Starburst candy resting in the top compartment of the baby buggy and asked the already wary woman, "Hey, could I score one of those from you?"

How Tan Man spotted that candy amongst the wide array of sensory stimuli on that street, I'll never know, but the woman accelerated her step and promptly ignored him, pushing her stroller up the sidewalk and pondering the fact that a grown man had just asked her for a piece of her kid's candy.

That solidified it.

I walked back toward the beach, waving to the rambling

threesome as I passed and generating a collective goodbye.

Once back at the sand, I sat down on one of the tall dunes with my guitar, taking in the sun and the surf and the gulls and the good. I looked to my right and noticed two people having sex on a not-so-distant dune—four legs sticking out of the tall grass, one pair spread wide with another in between. The latter pair ended in a partially visible ass that was receiving a strange, pants-half-down tan on that November afternoon. It *was* a beautiful day, and if I had had a willing participant there on the dune with me, I might have been inclined to do the same, celebrate the sunshine.

Good on ya, fuckers.

I then remembered that I *did* have a partner, and she was more than willing. After pulling my baby from the case, I laid her on my lap. The two of us faced the ocean and started making music together, sending sounds across the air to collide with the mighty roar of the Pacific.

We finished our first song, and I took a deep breath of the sea air as th—"Hey, dude!"

A voice shattered my zen.

"Decided to come hang a bit before I grab that battery, such a nice day!"

Blaze had found me sitting on the dune.

"Hey, Blaze."

I was a bit annoyed—as though the disco record had just been screeched to a halt in the middle of a happening dance party (my friends and I have a name for these moments; we call them Errrips, the sound of said screeching record).

"Hey," I began. "Honestly, I think I just wanna sit here for a while and jam on my—"

"Jaaaasoooon."

Enter Dominic, donning shades beneath his Giant's cap. "Got your text," he said. "They let me out of the café early. Good thing. My head is killing me."

Well, shit... That's that.

I placed my guitar back in its case, and the three of us hung under the afternoon sun. I pointed out the couple across the sand, still making babies in the tall grass. The guys got a kick out of this and made some cheering noises. After a while, we walked down to the water. I kicked off my shoes and felt the cold ocean on my toes. Dominic and Blaze got along well. They spoke San Francisco—local music, bars they liked. After about an hour on the beach, Blaze left to buy his battery, and Dominic and I hopped into Ruby to hit a nearby café. Dominic had designed a website for the place, so they gave him a great deal on everything, including the world's most amazing breakfast sandwich—bacon, pepper jack cheese, egg, and avocado, all on a toasted English muffin. It was delicious, and definitely worth the discounted price of three dollars. No matter how tasty the sandwich, though, it still brought my net worth down to fifteen bucks.

Time to go make some money.

After Dominic and I had eaten heaven, he dropped me off at the train platform where my morning journey had begun. Dominic was ready to head home and take a nap. I didn't blame him. After a night like we'd had, followed by an early morning of work, I'm sure he was beat.

"Hey," Dominic said, tapping me on the shoulder as I exited Ruby. "Take this"

I looked down at the key in the middle of his palm. "Seriously?"

"Yeah," he said. "You gotta have a place to stay while you're down here. This way you can get in and out of the apartment if you need to."

"Wow," I said. "Thanks a lot. I got your next forty beers."

Dominic pointed at me. "Careful," he warned. "I just may hold you to that."

I smiled and snatched the key. "Make 'em cheap beers then." I stepped out of the car and grabbed my guitar and stand from the back hatch.

"Good luck, buddy!"

"Thanks," I said, closing Ruby's booty.

With hatch secured, Dominic hit the gas and sounded a single honk as he sailed across Sunset.

Waiting on the platform, I introduced my new key to its chain and looked west to the ocean, feeling an immense wave of goodness wash over me and knowing that right then, I was right where I needed to be.

22

"Siiiiiiiiing me a sooooooong mister guitar man!"

The tuxedo-wearing puppet belted out a custom-tailored tune as I walked by, the puppeteer doing his best Sinatra impression from behind a black curtain that was draped across a small, waist-high stage. The pint-sized performer crooned over a lounge-style backing track that echoed through the Embarcadero subway station at the beginning of rush hour. Here, the worker bees of San Francisco's financial district poured past in a steady stream of suits, skirts, and ties—clocking out for the day.

"Pretty woman... Goin' home from work! Pretty woman... You in the black skirt... Pretty woman..."

The woman smiled at the puppet as she clicked past in high heels, stopping just before she reached the turnstile to fish a dollar bill from her purse. She then turned around and walked toward the performance, dropping the buck into a hat that was overturned on the marble floor. The woman blew the puppet a kiss and continued on her way.

"I think I'm in love!" said puppet Sinatra.

The woman laughed as the escalator carried her down to the train platform.

I walked to the far side of the station and, with guitar in hand and

stand slung over my shoulder, climbed long stairs up to the busy
street. Amidst the rush hour hustle, I asked a passing man,
"Which way to the Embarcadero?" He pointed up the road, and I
walked that direction. The financial district was very much alive in
the late afternoon—heavy traffic, shuffling feet—and sun struck the
concrete between shadows of giant skyscrapers.

I heard what sounded like a jazz band as I neared the ferry
building (which sat at the end of Market Street, on the
Embarcadero) and, as I continued toward the water, passed a man
in a green suit and matching top hat who was playing his bass
guitar in front of a sandwich shop, rocking back and forth between
a pair of speakers. These large speakers were mounted on stands
that stood as tall as he did. The man played solo, but grooved
along to some pre-recorded tracks (drums and an electric guitar)
that were being pumped through the sound system. People eating
their sandwiches at nearby tables didn't seem particularly
interested in what the man was doing, but he didn't seem to care.
He just continued to rock there in his patch of sun.

I walked through a small farmer's market consisting of about
twenty tables in an open concrete park near the ferry building. I
considered stopping and setting up there, but I'd heard much
about the Wharf and wanted to fully explore the area before
committing to any one spot. What I didn't know was that to get
from the ferry building where I was standing to the area of the
wharf where I would end up playing, it was about a mile-and-a-half
walk around the northeast portion of the city. This turned out to
be a nice impromptu workout, and a chance to sweat out some of
the toxins I'd built up recently.

I took in views of Alcatraz, the Bay Bridge, and other sights as I
cruised the concrete with seagulls soaring overhead. At one point I
stopped and sat down on a wooden bench where, facing the water,

Alex Rasmussen

I gave Kendra a call. She and I decided to meet at a spot on Columbus, in the North Beach neighborhood, at around six. That gave me a couple of hours to check things out at the Wharf.

I hiked a little over a mile to Pier 39, a main attraction of waterfront tourists, where a man stood on the brick with a saxophone slung over his shoulder, arranging his CDs on a foldout table that sat in front of a two-story Christmas tree. The sax man explained to me that he was the only one scheduled to play at that spot for the night and no other busking was allowed at Pier 39. He said that I should continue along the water and would find some good spots to play further on. He also told me that I should follow his lead and order a device that could be plugged into my phone so that I could accept credit card payments during my performances (a great idea that I later integrated).

I continued walking along the waterfront, noticing the smell of the sea and, every now and then, a stench of sewage wafting through the air (I imagine all the crap in one of America's most densely populated cities would have to go somewhere—why not the giant body of water surrounding it?).

Speaking of crap, I ran into a guy dressed as a clown (a strange segue, but bear with me). He sat atop a stool with a blank easel beside him and an even blanker expression plastered across his painted face—a caricature artist, looking deflated as a week-old birthday balloon.

"How's it going, man?" I asked.

"Shitty," grumbled the clown. "These fuckin' people are all idiots. If it's not on YouTube, they don't wanna give it the time of day. Half the time they won't even look up from their damn phones, and when they *do*, all I get is this—" The clown looked at me with eyes crossed and mouth hanging wide open. I tried not to laugh as he held this look for much longer than I'd anticipated. After a few moments, he returned to his default grimace and pointed toward my guitar case. "I'd be surprised if you made ten bucks tonight."

I nodded slowly. "Wanna bet ten bucks on it?" I asked, holding out my hand.

"Sure, kid," he said, laughing sarcastically as he shook it. "Good luck."

"You too," I replied before moving along.

I only made it a few steps before I heard the clown's voice again. Wheeling around, I saw him slumped over on his stool, barking at a mother and ponytailed daughter who had stopped in front of his easel. "Well, you gonna stand there and *stare* all day, or are you gonna talk to the artist who's right in front of you?"

The woman tugged on the little girl's hand, and the two of them carried on without being sketched.

Then that stink intruded my nostrils again.

After wandering on for a while, I found myself walking along a street lined with many restaurants and shops. I passed a Ripley's Believe It or Not! museum, an In-and-Out Burger, a T-shirt shop, a candy store, a bakery—bicyclist passing on my left, boats docked in clusters to my right. I scanned the scene, taking in all of th—

"HEYHOWYADOIN'!?"

"Holy shit!" I yelled, nearly dropping my guitar case.

A chorus of laughter accompanied my startled state as I looked across the street to where a group of about twenty people stood clustered together, getting a big kick out of watching me almost go into cardiac arrest. I thought I was on some hidden-camera TV show, partly because of that little crowd and partly because I didn't think that a guy jumping out from behind two giant eucalyptus branches and scaring the living hell out of me was something that would happen on any *normal* Monday evening. But, apparently, in San Francisco this has been happening for years—since 1980, to be precise.

This busker's name, appropriately, is Bushman.

Bushman laughed and crouched back down in front of the garbage can where he had been hiding, letting those big green branches completely cover him and becoming invisible to anyone walking up the sidewalk. I continued on for a few paces and turned around to watch the master at work.

From afar, he really did look just like a bush sitting in front of a trash can. *What an interesting gig*, I thought, as I tried to picture what had driven him to do this. Then I imagined his first day on the job.

Did Bushman hide in other places before deciding to crouch in front of the trash can?

Maybe he just hid inside *the garbage can...*

But then, he wouldn't have been Bushman...

Can-man?

While contemplating Bushman's beginnings, I noticed a happy couple strolling up the sidewalk hand-in-hand. Those of us gathered around that urban stage knew their fate, but the man and woman were oblivious, walking along in their romantic bubble.

"OOOOOGABOOOOOGA!"

The lovers jumped back simultaneously, and the woman shrieked at the top of her lungs before running full speed up the street with beau in tow. Mass laughter erupted once again, and this time I was part of it. Smiling, I walked over to Bushman and tipped him for the entertainment, dropping George Washington into a tin can that sat on the sidewalk atop an eternal piss stain— the product of thirty years of Bushman-induced terror.

"This is great," I said, depositing the dollar.

"Gotcha, didn't I?" Bushman asked with a proud grin, resuming his crouched position. He glanced at my guitar case. "You playin' down here, today?"

"Not yet," I said. "Looking for a good spot."

He nodded across the street. "Try In-and-Out, you'll do good there."

A lead. From a reliable source.

"I will. Thanks."

"Don't mention it," Bushman said, not looking up at me, but instead peering ahead through those branches like a lion stalking its prey in the tall grass.

In-and-Out Burger: I unfolded my stand, opened my case, hung Galileo, strapped on my guitar, and drew a deep breath.

San Francisco busking, take one.

People flowed in and out (appropriately) of the restaurant at a steady place, chowing down burgers and sucking on milkshakes as I played a few choice tunes from my repertoire. Over the course of about twenty minutes, a few satisfied fast food patrons threw some cash into my case, but for the most part the spot was looking like a bust (though I did get one lady dancing to a Red Hot Chili Peppers song as she stepped from a freshly parked car). During what I'd decided would be my last tune at that spot, a man and a woman walked past carrying guitars. I recognized them from earlier. During my initial sweep of the Wharf, these two had been playing to a decent-sized crowd near a seafood restaurant.

I stopped my song.

"You two done playing over there?" I asked.

"Yeah," the woman said. "Have at it."

Hearing this, I quickly tossed my guitar in the case, closed it up, and folded the stand before jogging the few blocks to the seafood spot, hoping that no one would have a chance to set up before I arrived.

Jack's Crab Shack lived on the corner of a busy Wharf intersection. The spot was a bit noisy due to the passing traffic, but housed a cement half-circle of a bench where happy seafood lovers were seated and enjoying their evening meals. I opened up my case and began to play some music for these folks as they indulged—Dire Straits, Tom Petty, a couple of original songs. After about thirty minutes, I was feeling pretty good. Money was coming in steadily, and the energy was high on that lively corner.

"Know any Creedence?" a voice asked.

I looked toward the cement bench. Two guys and a girl, all looking like they were in their mid-twenties, sat and smoked various things as they watched me play.

"Yeah," I said. "I've got one for you."

I found it fitting to play "Bad Moon Rising" for these folks as the sun began to set.

Seagulls sang along as they circled overhead, diving every now and then to peck at scraps of crab on the concrete. The guy who'd requested the Creedence grabbed his girl by the arm, and the two of them began to dance. He'd spin her around, and she would giggle, and the two of them would look toward me and smile as their buddy remained seated on the bench, smoking his cigarette and tapping his feet, sometimes drumming on his legs with his hands. When I hit the last note of the tune, these three walked up and dropped some money into the case.

"You want this, too?" the dancing man asked, as he held a joint toward me.

"Hell yeah, I do. Thanks." I accepted his gift and tucked it into the chest pocket of my blue flannel.

They were from Humboldt County, and the four of us chatted for a few minutes before they took off to see a movie.

I ran through a few more tunes and made a couple more bucks as the sun continued to sink. After about an hour at that spot, I'd earned twenty-two dollars, a joint, and some memories—nothing spectacular, but it was a start. I had officially made my first money in San Francisco, and planned on coming back to the Wharf the next afternoon to give it another go. Right then, though, it was time to catch up with an angel.

I closed my shop for the day and hauled my tools up the hill toward North Beach, as the city began to light up under the cover of a growing darkness.

23

The door opened, and I glanced toward the front of the room, anxious—like a puppy waiting for its owner to come home.

My tail wagged.

A good-looking girl, but not the one I had been anticipating.

I let out a breath and took another sip of my beer before looking around the place—dimly lit, old wooden floors, a long bar, and a good-sized crowd for a Monday night. Seated on the bottom floor, I glanced up at folks chattering between drinks at second-level tables.

I could feel the history there—smell it.

Common knowledge regarded this spot as a regular hangout for Jack Kerouac and other figures of the Beat movement in their heyday; as I sipped my beer, Jack's visage peered at me from a photograph that hung above the bar. I wondered what I would say to him if he were seated on the stool beside me. *What would I ask him?* I'd also heard that parts of *The Godfather* had been written in that room. Taking a deep breath, I lifted my IPA and proceeded to soak in the residual energies of these potent souls.

This was definitely the kind of place I could picture Kendra spending her nights, kicked back in some dim corner with a novel and a cocktail. It had been a little over a month since our night in Seattle, and there I was, moments away from seeing her again.

My stomach did cartwheels.

I pulled a tiny notebook from my pocket and began writing to occupy my mind. I wrote about my morning on the beach and its colorful cast of characters, about the wharf, the bitter clown, Bushman scaring the shit out of me. I wrote about busking and three dancing folks from Humboldt on a crabby corner.

The door opened again.

I looked.

She stepped through the door, wearing a half-smile and the long green coat with the furry hood, scanning the room slowly as she moved forward, appraising faces with a careless ease. I watched from my seat near the back of the bar and let myself fill with warmth, admiring—what a gorgeous thing she was.

Kendra looked my direction, our eyes met, and her half-smile filled out. She quickened her pace and moved across the room as I stood from my stool.

The two of us greeted each other with a hug.

She squeezed tight.

Kendra and I let go for the moment, and she took the stool beside me, hanging her purse on the hook beneath the counter and locking brown eyes onto mine.

"Long time, no see," Kendra said, through perfect lips turned up at the corners.

"Feels like it was just last week," I replied, knowing that it seemed much longer.

The bartender came up to us and I ordered another beer for myself and whatever Kendra was having. "Dark 'n' stormy," she said.

I gave the man some of my wharf cash, and he turned around, popping the drawer of an old register. The thing looked like a beat-up typewriter and made a loud noise when the copper-colored drawer shot open. He set my change on the bar and began to pour our drinks.

With tip, that round was going to eat up a good chunk of my funds. I made a note to myself: *Sip slowly.*

"Thank you," Kendra said, as she glanced toward my guitar case, which leaned against the bar. "How was the wharf?"

Floodgates.

I told Kendra about the subway and the waterfront and puppet Sinatra and downtown and the beach and the Bushman and this and that and blah, blah, blah, blah... Everything that crossed my mind spilled out of my mouth, and Kendra took it all in with an interested ear.

"Sounds like you've had quite the day," she said. "You know, you should go play at one of the trolley turnarounds. I see people performing there all the time, and it looks they make pretty good money—which makes sense, because when you're waiting for the trolleys, you have to stand there a while before they pick you up, so I always get to hear a few songs, whether I like it or not." The bartender set our drinks in front of us. "I think there's one platform down near Powell, on Market Street, and another... Ummmmmm..." Kendra thought for a moment, glancing toward the wall. "Oh yeah! Right at the end of the Wharf."

I opened my notebook and wrote this down—a clue for the treasure hunt.

"I can't believe you're here," Kendra said, grabbing her glass and holding it up. "Cheers. To new adventures."

The clinking of our drinks seemed to activate the sound of the room. Conversations and other noises swelled around us that I hadn't noticed up until that very moment.

"I think it's so cool that you actually came," Kendra went on. "I know you said you were going to, but you never know. You know?"

167

I knew, and nodded. "I love it here," I said. "Such a great city."

"You haven't even been in town two days," Kendra said. "Just wait, there's so much here. So much to do and see..." Kendra proceeded to tell me all about San Francisco: About the Haight-Ashbury neighborhood, with its counterculture history and backpacked travelers who flocked to the area hoping to taste some 60's magic still alive in the grasses of Golden Gate Park. About the Mission District with its vibrant Mexican culture, colorful murals, and rowdy nightlife, bands blaring until two in the morning and drunken twenty-somethings hitting the streets in search of a late-night taco cart. The Panhandle, the Richmond, Chinatown, North Beach. She told me about the Marina, where you could go on a Friday night to count the Lamborghinis and get a fifteen-dollar hamburger (fries not included.) Then there was the Outer Sunset, which led you west to Highway One before shooting straight down the coast to Santa Cruz and beyond. Kendra's eyes lit up as she told me about her city with vibrant enthusiasm, and I soaked up every word, watching the pictures she painted swirl in my mind's eye like some tie-dyed kaleidoscope.

We talked about music, her recent trip to San Diego (where she grew up), the remodeled Bay Bridge; we talked more in depth about where we'd both come from—birthplaces, family history. At one point, Kendra and I got onto the topic of relationships, and she vented about her most recent ex-boyfriend.

"He's a good guy, but he doesn't know how to handle his emotions."

The fact that Kendra spoke about her ex in the present tense perked my ears up and riled a paranoid voice in the back of my head, but I took another sip of my beer and told that noisy bastard to shut up and focus on the angel before us. Kendra went on to tell me about why their three-year relationship hadn't worked out. I filled her in on my situation with Brenna and why the two of us had split up a few months back. I also told Kendra that, since some time had passed, Brenna and I were happily coexisting, and moving toward individual goals (in fact, at the same time I was taking this trip, Brenna was down in New Orleans, exploring a new world of her own). The fact that Brenna and I had maintained a friendship made Kendra feel good, as she hoped that she and her ex could maintain something similar beyond their romance.

Talking about these things made me think about how I would treat Kendra if I were with her.

Could I be with her?
That would be quite the move...

Don't get ahead of yourself. She's talking...

"What was that?" I asked. My inner dialogue had drowned out the last thing Kendra had said.

She smiled and leaned toward me, looking into my eyes. "I said, finish your beer. I want to show you something."

24

"Damn, you're really trying to get me in shape aren't you?" I asked, huffing and puffing up some North Beach hill.

Dozing dwellings and lazy cars—packed tightly together— lined either side of the narrow street.

Kendra looked at me as we climbed higher. "Well, you've got to work off that slice of pizza somehow," she replied. "I'm just helping you maintain your girlish figure."

I grabbed some of the extra flesh around my waistline and jiggled it as we carried on. "About sixty more of these hills, and I bet I could even fit into my prom dress again."

Kendra laughed as I pictured myself wearing a big pink dress and corsage.

The two of us summited the hill and the street ended, replaced by a large, cement platform and two brick staircases, one on either side of the platform, that dove down the steep incline to a street below. This descent was decorated with many large trees and bushes, planted on several cement landings that were placed periodically throughout the downgrade, allowing access to houses that lined the sides of this slope.

"And there it is," Kendra said, pointing out across the open air. "The new Bay Bridge."

Houses in the foreground provided a perfect natural frame for the multicolored lights of the city below, glowing brightly across the western night and rolling all the way to the water where the Bay Bridge shimmered fantastically with twinkling blue lights. These dancing lights ran top to bottom along each of the bridge's vertical suspension cables, spanning from Treasure Island to the city and making the bridge look alive from miles away—like it was trying to communicate with us via some code hidden in the language of the LED.

"Wow," I said, hypnotized by the electric spectacle. "Look at that."

During the day, that bridge was the beast—a marvel of engineering and human accomplishment. It was strong, rigid, and supported all who came and went between the East Bay and Frisco. But here at night it took on a completely different personality: a glittering beauty, looking delicately over her city with pride—a mother cradling her newborn.

Kendra and I stood there, taking in the scene, a stillness between us. I glanced at her, standing to my right. The blondest strands of her hair seemed to glow.

"So, I guess we're even now," I said, the Seattle rooftop adventure in mind.

Kendra looked back at me. "Not quite. But it's a start."

We sat down atop the nearest staircase, and I fished the crab shack joint from my breast pocket. Kendra and I passed the payment back and forth, blowing smoke and words into the air where they floated slowly over that twinkling city. At one point, two older ladies crept up behind us.

"Pardon us, pups."

We scooted to either side of the step so the ladies could pass. They said thank you and laughed a jolly old laugh as they stepped slowly down the stairs onto a cement landing, where they entered a home together.

"Want to help me with something?" Kendra asked, passing the joint to me.

There wasn't much left. I pinched the end of the paper to avoid hot embers.

"Sure," I said, exhaling and rubbing the joint out on the brick next to me. "What's that?"

"I have an old magazine I want to cut up," Kendra said, staring out over the city. "I want to cut a bunch of the words out of the pages—hundreds of words. And I want to lay them all out and scramble them around." Kendra moved her hands in front of her like she was mixing playing cards on some imaginary table. "Then I want to take all of those words and make a huge poem, or maybe even a story."

Kendra looked at me and quickly raised a finger. "But we can only use the words on the table," she continued, leaning close to me. "'Cause that's how life is, you know? You can only use what you're given, make the best story you can with what you've got. You've gotta get creative. See th—"

Kendra stopped. "What?" She asked, recoiling with a shy smile.

I must've been grinning like a dumbass, lost in her. My reply was corny, but that's how these things go sometimes.

"You."

Kendra giggled and shook her head slowly as the two of us leaned close, dissolving the gap between us and picking up where we'd left off, five weeks prior.

Sitting on that staircase above San Francisco, we became locked in some slow and perfect moment.

"Yeah? Yeah, I can be over there in like, twenty, tops..."

The two of us looked to our right, snapped quickly out of mutual sensations.

A business suit stood a few feet from us, one hand resting on a waist-high metal railing at the edge of our cement landing, the other holding a cell phone up to the ear of a man who looked over the city and ruined reunions. Kendra and I looked at each other and laughed, causing the talker to glare at us as if we were interrupting something important before he looked back toward the city and continued his call.

"Not tonight, man! You know that stuff makes me puke every time!"

Kendra and I took this as our cue to move along.

We descended the stairs onto one landing, and then the next one, and the next. Finally, we found ourselves on the road below, safe from lurking, cell-phone-wielding business dicks. Kendra and I thought this as good a spot as any to disappear back into our reunion. We turned to face each other and picked up where we'd left off. Unfortunately, this embrace only lasted a few moments before I caught myself laughing, picturing that same guy popping out of a nearby mailbox or garbage can, blabbing on his phone.

NO WAY! NO FUCKIN' WAY!! I'VE BEEN TRYING TO NAIL THAT CHICK SINCE HIGH SCHOOL!!

Arms still around me, Kendra smiled before looking abruptly over her shoulder and then quickly back at me, eyes wide with pretend fear.

She got it.

This made me laugh even harder.

Earlier that night when Kendra and I had left the bar, I'd left my guitar and stand in the trunk of her car. Good thing, too. That hill we'd hiked was a monster, and I'd had enough of a workout for one day. The two of us decided to head back to her vehicle and continue our evening.

We walked a few blocks through the North Beach night,

not saying much, and not needing to.

Somewhere along Broadway, Kendra and I passed a small pub with an open door where, for a few seconds, we were able to hear "Hollywood Nights" by Bob Seger blasting over the speakers.

"...In those big city nights,
    In those high rolling hills,
        Above all the lights,
            With a passion that kills..."

Hearing these lyrics, I could only shake my head and smile— walking with that angel through a San Francisco dream and taking Seger's words as a cue that the forces behind the curtain had approved of the night so far.

25

"What the hell *is* that thing?" I asked as Kendra pulled the car over.

The two of us stepped out onto the sidewalk to get a closer look.

Darkness hugged the dormant wharf, and salty air crept into my lungs like a familiar friend.

Kendra and I crossed the concrete, walking toward group of about twenty people—visible for only split seconds at a time by the white light of flashing strobes—who had gathered around the thing. As the two of us approached, the sound of banging drums and excited voices echoed through the empty piers.

The blasts of white light came at sporadic intervals from strobes mounted atop four metal mini-towers (about ten feet each) that were placed around the base of an enormous tree, forged from aluminum and steel, two stories tall, thirty feet wide, and looming over a group of entranced bystanders. The top of this tree was split into eighteen branches that arched outward from the trunk and hung down at their ends, giving the sculpture the appearance of a steel mushroom cloud. The end of each metallic branch supported a pseudo-chimpanzee—the size of a full-grown man—in one phase of a simian swinging motion.

Kendra and I watched as the tree-hemoth sat still, flashing in the night, and eight bystanders-turned-percussionists banged on hand drums of various shapes and sizes. The drums had been placed around the base of the monkey umbrella and were connected to it by thick, black cables.

I walked up to an unoccupied drum and picked it up, placing it between my legs and banging out my contribution to the already unorganized assortment of beats that this makeshift drum troop was projecting into the night. A few of the tribal thumpers yelled at the lazy monkeys to "Do something!" hoping that with enough energy put into this collective pulse, there would be some reward.

The woman who had been playing to my left set her drum on the flashing concrete, and Kendra picked it up to take her place. Kendra held the long drum between her legs and smacked it with her palms, looking hopefully toward the tree every now and then, calculating her effect on the scene.

"A SIMULTANEOUS BEAT WILL ACTIVATE THE MONKEYS!"

The group of drummers, pounding out ten different beats, glanced over to see the woman who had abandoned her place in the troop reading aloud from a small sign posted nearby. Individuals of the ensemble looked around and nodded to each other.

Our mission was clear.

Each of us started playing a slow and steady pulse on our respective drums.

At first, the speeds of the beats were similar, but not quite synched up.

A bit slower... No, a bit faster... There we go.

Each of us adjusted the tempo of our hand motions— looking around the circle for cues—and soon, ten drummers had found a rhythm together.

tHUMP... ThUMP!... THuMP!!... THUmP!!!... THUMp!!!!... THUMP!!!!!

The flashing of the strobes intensified—four machine guns firing light—and the whole top of the tree began to move in a slow, clockwise motion.

Excited chatter spread amongst all in attendance, and anticipatory looks shot back and forth. The banging had now become very steady and deliberate, all of us pounding at a uniform pace. Kendra looked at me and scrunched her face with a mock intensity before focusing again on the head of her drum, striking it hard. I laughed as the tree spun faster—faster—and the flashing of the strobes continued to intensify.
 Then we saw it...

Somewhere in the collaboration between the Tommy gun strobes and the tree's spinning top, a sequence came to life—eighteen monkeys swinging branch to branch across the monstrous tree in perfect unison. As the drums pounded on, a green snake (with a human hand for a head) slithered from the tree's trunk. That hand-head clutched an apple as the snake slid up one of the branches, making its scaly way across the steel, and force-fed the fruit into the open mouth of a chosen ape. Cheering and applause filled the air as the king-sized zoetrope came to life. Kendra, banging on her drum, looked to me with mouth gaping in awe before glancing back toward the monkey carousel. As the scene spun, so did our thoughts, weaving interpretations of what this artist had been thinking when they'd created this. *What were they trying to say?*

I noticed a woman standing behind Kendra, gazing at the sculpture in wide-eyed wonder, and asked her if she'd like to take my place on the drum. The woman nodded and smiled as I handed it to her. She then sat cross-legged on the concrete and joined the collective rhythm, picking up where I'd left off.

Kendra stood her long drum up on its wooden base and motioned toward a very small boy who'd been watching with his family nearby. The boy's father placed both hands under his son's armpits and lifted the toddler so he could strike the djembe. That little rock star wailed on the instrument with reckless excitement, grinning ear-to-ear and making chimpanzee noises as he thumped away.

Kendra and I stood back and watched all of this until the spinning scene had sufficiently burnt its way into our synapses. When we'd had our fill, we walked back across the flashing sidewalk, contemplating Eden to the sound of fading drums.

26

We drove through the night.

Along the Embarcadero to Bay Street, shooting up through the hills of North Beach and down into the Marina, where we hit Lombard through the curves of the Presidio. The Golden Gate winked in our rearview as we zipped into the Richmond district. There, we hit Geary—all the way to the Great Highway—and rode along the beach until Taraval Street, where Dominic and I would be playing an open mic at the Swell.

Kendra was a smooth driver, and maneuvered this route with speed and ease while she and I spoke over laboring pistons and low music. City lights and passing headlamps whizzed past our car like multicolored comets.

Kendra parked across the street from the Swell, which was about a block from the beach. As the two of us stepped from the vehicle, I noticed the rumble of the ocean in the distant darkness, beyond a thin fog painted orange by yawning streetlights.

I walked around to the back of the car, where Kendra stood fidgeting with the trunk's handle.

"It's stuck," Kendra complained.

My testicles disagreed with her.

I grabbed the underside of the handle with both paws and gave it a hard vertical yank, putting some leg strength behind my effort and nearly shitting myself trying to prove how manly I was.

Kendra laughed and held out her hands.

"Stop! Stop!" she yelled, pointing her keys toward the car and pressing a button that opened the trunk instantly. "I'm just messing with you." She flashed a satisfied smile.

"Goddammit!" I replied, laughing. I pointed at the car. "You're lucky," I said. "This time."

After I'd grabbed my guitar and closed the trunk, the two of us crossed the street to the Swell.

We opened the front door (blue with an eye-level porthole) and walked into a place that looked like the living room of someone's backwoods cabin. A modest bar occupied the room's right side, and straight ahead, across the old floor, a large brick fireplace adorned the wooden wall. In front of that fireplace lay a large woven rug, decorated with intricate red and white patterns, and above it hung a large painting of an old boat wrestling with the waves. Various other nautical nuances—helm of a ship mounted on an adjacent wall, thick ropes draped across the ceiling—drove the sea theme home. Strangely, amidst what appeared to be a very deliberate maritime motif, a large moose head had been mounted to one of the walls near the back of the room. The taxidermy seemed a bit out of place, so I just assumed the moose was the Swell's security guard, sure to spring to life and gore with mighty horns if someone attempted to duck out on their ten-dollar tab.

"Heeeeeeey," a man slurred as he wobbled from his barstool, heading our direction.

"What's up, Blaze?" I greeted, surprised to see him.

Blaze maneuvered toward us with a bit of difficulty, swaying heavily but trying his best to look composed.

"Kendra, this is Blaze, one of the guys I rode down from Seattle with."

Blaze removed his sunglasses and rested them atop his forehead, revealing eyes that told me he'd been at the bar for more than just a few drinks. He looked at Kendra for a long moment, and then back at me, nodding with squinted eyes and a dumb smile tugging at half of his mouth (I'm not completely sure what Blaze was trying to communicate with this nod, but the excessive amount of time he spent bobbing his head up and down made me wonder if he'd momentarily lost consciousness). I glanced toward Kendra, who looked at Blaze with a sympathetic grin like she was watching a monkey try to solve a Rubik's cube.

Snapping out of his nodding trance, Blaze looked back at Kendra and promptly curtseyed.

"Kendra? It's a pleasure." Blaze resumed his standing position. "Heard a lot about ya from this guy." He hit me hard on the shoulder, and I gave him a reciprocal shove. Blaze wobbled like a floor-weighted heavy-bag.

"The pleasure's all mine, Blaze—if that *is* your real name." Kendra smirked.

Blaze made a face like he'd just smelled dog shit. "Well, it's my *last* name, and, considering my line of work—"

"Jason told me," Kendra interrupted with a smile. "And I'm just messing with you. But he also told me about how you two cuddled on the car ride."

Blaze looked at me. "Dude. You said you could keep a secret." He glanced back at Kendra and laughed to himself.

I felt a tap on my shoulder and turned around. The three of us, standing in front of the door, were blocking the path of a girl with a huge hat who was trying to come inside.

Several raised tables with barstools occupied the left side of the room, so Kendra, Blaze, and I grabbed an empty one close to the fireplace, directly in front of the microphones and speakers that had been set up for the night's performance. Blaze and Kendra sat down as I walked to the bar to order a pitcher. The bartender was bald—perhaps the bald man from my market fortune who was foretold to bring me good luck? The guy was nice, and he poured me some beer. I also didn't have to spend too much money on that beer.

Sounds like good luck to me.

I chalked this up as another prophecy come true.

When I turned around and walked back to the table, I saw that Dominic had joined the group. He and Kendra were catching up as Blaze listened with a grin, swaying back and forth on his barstool.

"Hey, man!" I greeted as I set the pitcher down. "I'll go grab one more glass."

"No need," Dominic said, tapping on a pint of something dark.

"Oh, nice," I said, taking a seat next to him. "How was the nap?"

"Alright," Dominic replied, sounding drained. "Woke up about an hour ago." He raised his beer. "Now, about to do it all over again."

"Well, *you've* got some catching up to do," Blaze interjected, looking like he might fall off his stool at any moment.

Dominic looked disapprovingly at Blaze and shook his head. "I didn't bring enough money to catch up with you."

Kendra laughed without looking up from whatever she was doodling on her napkin.

"I had a night with a boy last week..."

The voice was small, but the room fell silent, like the queen had just addressed the court.

Every eye in the place fixed upon the petite frame standing timidly before the fireplace with hands behind its back. The girl wore black from head to toe, with the exception of a few white flowers sewn into her skirt. Long, ebony hair framed the girl's milky skin, creating a black and white canvas upon which

ruby lips and piercing blue eyes could scream with the
concentrated color of an entire being.

Her fiery mouth burned delicate words into the
microphone.

"I had a night with a boy...

And I've written something about it."

The sound of crumpling paper permeated the silence of the bar
like pint-sized thunder claps as the girl produced a sheet from
behind her back. The poet cleared her throat with frail force and
held the white paper in front of her with both hands, beginning to
read with a shaking voice.

"I can't go chasing opportunities past.

This moment is here and gone,

And it's my fault for not being present,

for letting the darkness creep in

and take me over."

Icy eyes glanced up from the paper, slowly sweeping the
room as the girl took a deep breath and her voice found solid
ground.

"But that's the risk I take...

And I love it."

The poet glanced back at her sheet.

"Walking through the dark curtain to tiptoe along
the edge of the void.

Peeking over... The edge of death...

So close to unconsciousness, complete absence
of awareness...

So close to the abyss."

The girl looked up, throwing her voice across the room
with confidence.

"I've died for a night... Tasted it!

Only to wake reborn, again."

She crumpled the paper into a ball. Dropping it to her

feet and closing her eyes as she clasped the microphone tightly with both hands.

"Here, along this edge, I can see the white thoughts huddled in the nervous corners of my mind...

The invisible ones...

The darkness beckons them."

The girl opened her eyes and held up a finger as she smiled slightly.

"You see... They are afraid of the light.

But in the dark they feel safe to come out and play... To dance."

The poet locked sapphire eyes onto Blaze, who watched from atop his stool.

"And yours, my dear?

Who are your voices, your hidden children?"

The girl smirked, seductive.

"I can show you your secret family."

Blaze had no response. The girl's intensity was contagious, and Blaze was a snake, charmed—along with the rest of the room—by her presence.

The poet looked around the Swell, slowly.

"All we have to do is kill the light."

She closed her eyes and wrapped her arms around her body.

"Kill the light and your thoughts can meet mine in a dark room.

Your mind can kiss mine and mine will strip yours.

And without their cover they can roll around, naked and warm,

Honest."

The girl grasped the microphone again with both hands,

eyes shut, voice hot with a growing intensity.
"Breathing and biting, scratching and clawing,
Digging for something,
For each other.
For ourselves."
The poet released the microphone and opened blue eyes, looking dazed around the room as her voice shrunk back to its initial fragility.

"But when we wake, it fades away,
And in the light, we're lost again."

27

My ears were ringing when I woke up that next morning.

I silenced my alarm and tried to remember why it was going off so damn early.

Six thirty: The sun had just begun to scale the morning sky.

"Oh right. The Civic Center," I mumbled to myself, remembering a conversation I'd had the night before with a native busker.

I laid there for a moment and contemplated the sweet, sweet notion of going back to sleep—waking up around noon to hit the beach—but the voice in my head, which seemed to have much more energy than I did right then, kindly told me to

QUIT BEING SUCH A LAZY PIECE OF SHIT!

The drill sergeant took a mental breath and continued:

Get your ass up off the floor, get out the door, and GO BUSK!

He was a strict one, and I knew better than to disobey.

I forced myself up from Dominic's kitchen floor and folded my blanket before setting it and my pillow in the corner. I took a quick shower and ate a cereal bar from my backpack. After breakfast, I put some clothes on, grabbed my guitar and stand, and headed out the door. It was a bit chilly that morning, walking to the train before the sun had had a chance to warm the air.

Chilly or not, though, considering a blue sky with minimal cloud interference, it was beautiful outside.

The busker I'd spoken with the night before had been wearing a beanie over long hair. I was also wearing a beanie that night and had long hair. Needless to say, the two of us became instant buddies—beanie buddies, if you will. My double-B had said that he now had a "real job" (he made these quotation marks with his fingers while explaining this to me) but had mentioned that he used to play in the Civic Center subway station every weekday when he'd first moved back to San Francisco after busking in Europe for a few years. He said that he'd done very well down at that station and had made enough to pay his rent and buy some food and a beer or two each day. He'd also told me that I should go check out Europe—sounds like they love their street performers across the pond.

Busking Nugget #1: Sometimes busking is like a treasure hunt. One clue leads you to another clue, and that clue to the next. Street performing has taught me to be more aware of my surroundings and to follow the current that brings everything together. It all seems to connect somehow, just gotta know what I'm looking for.

I followed my beanie buddy's clue to the train platform.
As I waited for the L, I set my guitar on the concrete and reached into my back pocket. My wallet felt light, and I peeked reluctantly inside the billfold.
Damn.
Just as I'd suspected: I'd spent all of my money.
There's got to be something left...
I reached into the other back pocket—nothing.
Then into my front left—same story.
Okay, Jason. Last chance...

My stomach jumped as I dug into the final frontier.
After a moment spent denim fishing, I produced four dollars, a receipt, and some change. Those dollars, in that desperate second, looked like a handful of hundreds.
A sigh of relief.

It cost two bucks and a quarter to ride that train downtown. I paid the fare, knowing that if I didn't make any money in the next few hours, I could use my stub to ride the train back to Dominic's, where a peanut butter and honey sandwich would greet me with open arms.

Despite my self-imposed financial strain, it felt good riding to work with the nine-to-fivers that morning. I was officially a commuting contributor to the culture of the city—and the only person on that 7:30 train with a guitar.

The L entered a long tunnel that ran underground, through the heart of the city.
A few stops before the Civic Center, I noticed several folks waiting at a platform in the Castro Street station. No one was playing any music for these poor people, so I took it upon myself to do so. After stepping from the train, I positioned myself on the platform—far enough away from folks so I wasn't blasting them with sound, but close enough that if they were enjoying what I was doing and wanted to show it, they and their money could easily find their way to the case. I began that set with a mellow version of "Won't Back Down" by Tom Petty, strumming the strings softly to accommodate the delicate ears of a morning crowd. The acoustics in that tunnel were great, so it didn't take much to be heard, anyway.

I quickly noticed a difference between the flow of the wharf and the station. By the end of that first song, one guy had dropped a five-dollar bill into the case and a few other folks had tipped singles. Some of the people who didn't tip still passed by smiling, nodding, or even saying thank you.

I began to feel a large weight lift from my shoulders.

Hope has strong biceps.

I played a couple more songs, and the money continued to flow. It'd been about a half hour, and I'd already made fifteen bucks—almost what I'd pulled in during an hour at the wharf.

"You can't be playing down here."

The guy in the reflective vest spoke sternly, and his *Errrripp* (remember the record screeching?) echoed throughout the tunnel. I didn't want to argue with the guy, especially that early, so I asked him where I *could* play in the tunnels. He said anywhere on the upper level, past the turnstile, was fair game.

I scoped the upstairs area of the station, but it didn't look very promising. Many folks were passing through, but there wasn't a decent spot in that wide walkway where I could set up and catch a solid flow of people traveling close to the guitar case.

Nugget #2: The busking game only works if it's easy for people to drop money into your case and grab CDs out of it. If it's too much effort, no matter how much people like you, they won't bother, especially on their way to work.

I decided to go back to my original plan: the Civic Center station.

Once I arrived there, I stepped from the train and rode the escalator up into the main area. Brick tunnels and marble floors promised more great acoustics—*perfect.* Looking to my left as I walked through the turnstile, I remembered a bit of the conversation I'd had with my beanie buddy the night before, hearing his mellow voice in my head:

"*I had this spot right near the escalators where I used to*

189

*make about twenty bucks an hour playin' my whole book of
Beatles covers, A to Z."*

Bingo.

There it was.

I didn't have a book of Beatles covers, but this was a great
spot—an escalator coming down into the station and a brick tunnel
where I could set up, be heard, *and* be close enough to the
passing folks to make my case an easy dollar depository. I also
noticed that I'd be performing close to people as they purchased
train tickets. Considering how long it would take them to do so, I
knew they'd be able to hear a good portion of whatever song I was
playing at the time.

Anticipating the monetary possibilities of my new spot, I unfolded
my stand, opened the case, and tuned my guitar.

Nugget #3: A guitar case always looks more inviting when there
are a few bucks inside. So I took everything I'd made that
morning and spread it around inside the case, surrounding my
CDs like a little green bird's nest.

Over the next few hours, I ran through everything I knew,
Creedence, Bob Marley, Johnny Cash, Neil Young—a few bucks
here, a few bucks there—an original tune, some Marshall Tucker,
Sublime, Tom Petty—five-dollar bill, fifty cents...

"Thanks, have a good morning!"

"You too!"

Minutes ticked by as the San Francisco workforce passed;
and it was my job to get a pleasant song stuck in their head, to put
a little bounce in their step, which would hopefully seep into their
first interaction of the day, maybe with their local barista:

"Hey, how are you?"

"I've got Allman Brothers stuck in my head."

"Oh, I love the Allman Brothers!"

Hopefully this would be a nice exchange and encourage these people to tip their barista well.

And then the barista would have a few extra bucks.

And then that barista could go out and buy themself something nice, like some new shoes.

And then some handsome fellow would see those new shoes and say:

"Hey, nice shoes... Wanna get married?"

And the barista would say, "I do!"

And then there'd be little barista babies and grandbabies, and so on, and on, and on...

That was my job: a third party matchmaker, jamming in the San Francisco subways and making babies from worlds away.

After a couple hours at that spot, I'd made about twenty-five more bucks—nothing crazy, minimum wage—but I was enjoying that space, especially the acoustics. Curious as to what the rest of the station might have to offer, I decided to wander around and scan for other promising places to play. I gathered my things and, as I approached one of the long brick tunnels, heard a violin echoing through the chamber. It sounded very pleasant; as I *entered* the tunnel, I saw the origin of the sound—a tall man with tattered clothes playing beside an open violin case. This case was weathered, decorated with countless stickers, and overflowing with cash.

Further down the tunnel, seated on the marble and leaning against the brick, was a man who wore a long black coat. His eyes scanned the pages of a disintegrating novel while his guitar waited patiently beside him.

I smiled at the violinist as I walked toward the man.

The violinist nodded and continued playing something beautiful.

"Hey there," I greeted.

The guy in the coat looked up from his book.

"Sorry to bug you. My name's Jason. I'm in town from Seattle and just got done playing over on the other side of the station." I nodded toward the violin player. "This looks like a great spot. What's the deal with busking here?"

The man closed his book and stood up. "Jason, I'm Stewart."

We shook hands.

"Seattle?" he said. "I've been meaning to get back up there. My sister is living in Georgetown now, so I've got no excuse not to make the journey." Stewart nodded toward the other end of the tunnel "How'd you fare on the other side?"

"Pretty good," I said. "Twenty-five bucks in a couple hours."

"Hmmmmm," Stewart said, looking around. "It's been that kind of morning down here too, a tad slow."

"You normally do pretty well here?" I asked him.

"Oh, yes," he said. "Once a week I come down here on a day off from teaching and do a full shift in the tunnels. I normally walk away with anywhere between fifty to a hundred dollars."

"That's great," I said, as cash registers rang in my head.

These were quickly replaced by a raspy voice.

"Hey partner, I'm done here for now if you want ta' play this spot."

The violin player had packed his things.

I hadn't even noticed that the music had stopped.

I looked to Stewart, who was next in line, and he pointed toward the tunnel. "Jason, give it a go if you'd like. It'd be nice to get some lunch, and if you're playing here, I'll know the spot's saved."

The violinist tipped his hat and said, "You boys have a fine afternoon," before limping slowly out of sight.

Stewart bent over to grab his guitar and looked up at me. "You'll be playing the entire hour?"

I nodded. "Yeah, this looks like a good spot. Even if I burn out or break all my strings, I'll save it for you 'til you get back."

"Great," he said. "All yours then."

Stewart picked up his case and tucked the book into a pocket of his black coat. Then he walked away, shouting, "Break a leg," as he disappeared around a corner.

The treasure hunt continues.

I set up shop, hung Galileo, and scanned my new surroundings: a brick tunnel, funneling a never-ending stream of changing faces— my customers.

Back to work.

My vocal chords and fingers were beginning to feel a bit raw after the nearly three hours I'd already put in that morning, but the fact that this prime location had fallen into my lap gave me a second wind.

I started by playing a Red Hot Chili Peppers song called "Soul to Squeeze." Anyone walking through that space was able to hear the music for a minute or so before they stepped out of range, and the natural reverb of the marble made my voice and guitar sound very good. During that song, my mind drifted, thinking about what it would be like to record down there (minus the sketchy gremlins and underground dinosaurs that might try to steal the equipment; these creatures lurked in the subway station shadows, as I would soon discover).

Having only an hour, I played the strongest and most recognizable tunes that I knew. At some point during "Billie Jean," a good-looking woman in high heels and a business skirt synched her step to the beat and strutted across the marble to drop a five in the case. I had another girl come by a few minutes later to grab a CD, leaving a crispy ten-dollar bill in its place and mouthing, "Thank you," as she continued on her way to wherever. These women were great, but the highlight of that set came in the form of an older gentleman who walked through the tunnel toward the end of the hour. I had been in the middle of playing "Last Dance with Mary Jane" when the man approached, slowing his stride and listening intently. He stopped walking and leaned against the brick with hands folded in front of him. The man watched me play the remainder of the song and applauded when I finished.

"Sounds good," he said. "Real good."

He walked across the floor and stood in front of my case, squinting to read my sign.

"Ten bucks, eh?" the man asked as he pulled out his wallet.

"Yeah," I said. "Five original songs on there."

The man slid a twenty from his billfold, and I reached into the guitar case, fishing for the Lincoln twins as Andrew Jackson joined the dead-presidential party.

The man waved his hand like he was swatting a pesky fly.

"It's your tip," he said. "But I want to hear one of *your* songs now."

"Thanks very much, sir," I said, smiling. "I really appreciate that. Best tip I've made in this city so far."

"Glad to hear it," the man said as he reclaimed his spot against the wall, hands folded in front of him, holding my CD.

"This is the second song on that disc there," I said, giving myself a "one, two, three, four" before strumming the opening chord of a tune I'd played at the Swell the night before.

28

"Yeah, we've goooooooooot it all!"
Three more chords... Slow it down... Last line.
"Oh, we've goooooo...ooooooooot... it... all..."

Dominic and I let our strings ring out as everyone in the Swell clapped and cheered—loud with so many people packed into that tiny place, making noise together. The energy was electric, alive.

"Thanks, guys." I reached over and grabbed a disc off the stool beside me, presenting it to the rowdy room. "I've got that song on a CD I'm selling here. Trying to get back to Seattle in a few days, and proceeds go straight into the gas tank." I thought for a moment and rubbed my stomach. "Well, the gas tank *and* my belly." I smiled and nodded. "I'll be around if you want one."

I unplugged my guitar and knelt down beside Dominic, who was already returning his instrument to its case.

"That sounded great," I said, sheathing my sword.

"Yeah," Dominic replied with a dull tone, standing up and slinging his case over his shoulder.

"Now, I've gotta learn 'Out of my Head' and hop on that with you!"

Dominic looked at me and forced a smile before adjusting his ball cap and walking toward the back of the room.

I wonder what's up with him...

I picked up my case and walked back to the table where Kendra and Blaze were seated. Blaze had two fresh beers waiting on the table and his right hand cocked, waiting on a high-five.

"Duuuuuuude!" he exploded as we slapped palms.

"Great stuff! Very Seattle."

"Thanks, Blaze, glad you liked it." I leaned my guitar against the wall and grabbed the cold brew, clinking Blaze's glass before taking a sip. "And thanks for the beer."

I looked toward Kendra, seated across the table. She glanced up at me with pen in hand, the tip of which was resting on a napkin doodle.

"I liked that," she said, before a thoughtful pause. "I could feel it—feel you."

I smiled, taking a victory drink and reveling in the fact that Kendra had enjoyed the music I was making. "Whatcha drawing?" I nodded toward her napkin sketch.

Kendra turned the napkin around and slid it across the table.

I peeked down at her ink interpretation of the monkey carousel. "Looks just like it," I said, impressed by the detailed doodle. I glanced back at Kendra, who leaned across the table, looking at me with a thoughtful depth in her eyes.

"I wanna remember it," Kendra said, with some tone I couldn't place. I didn't ask her about it, though. In that moment, it was difficult to think about anything beyond the fact that I felt this girl was much better than I deserved.

Goddamn, she's beautiful.

Kendra's giggle snapped me from my trance. "Spacing out, are we?"

I laughed. "Yeah, yeah. I do that sometimes." I looked around the room before focusing back on her. "Hey, you wanna take a walk down to the beach?"

Kendra looked down at her monkey-tree drawing and then toward her beer. She drank what was left in the glass and folded her napkin before standing up, sliding the doodle into the pocket of her green coat, and pulling its fuzzy hood over her head.

She nodded. "Yes, I do."

29

"How was your set?" Stewart asked as I laid my guitar to rest in its case.

"Great, man," I replied. "You weren't kidding about this spot. Forty-eight bucks."

Stewart smiled and rubbed his palms together. "Nice work. I'm hoping there are some riches left for me."

"Me, too," I said. "'Preciate you letting me play here. Did the wharf yesterday for a few hours and only made about twenty dollars. I definitely needed this."

"Well, I'm pleased to hear that it worked out for you." Stewart pulled a business card from his pocket and handed it to me. "Here's my card. If you'd like, there's a website on the back where you can check out some of my music."

"Thanks, man," I said. "Here..." I knelt down and reached into my guitar case, taking a CD from the middle compartment and handing it to Stewart. "You can have one of these."

Stewart took the CD and studied the sleeve. "Jason Mayes. Thank you, sir."

"No problem, Stewart." I threw my stand over my shoulder and picked up my guitar. "Well, I'll let you get to it. Thanks again."

Walking slowly up the tunnel, I caught the first few lines of Stewart's rendition of "Peaceful Easy Feelin'," his pleasant voice fading with each step.

"I like the way your sparklin' earrings lay...against your

skin so brown...
And I wanna sleep with you in the desert
tonight...with a billion stars all around..."

Once back in the main area of the station—my office—I took one
last look around the floor, teeming with folks en route to various
destinations. Amidst the hustle, a very dirty man slept on that
floor, curled up in a tight ball against the brick and somehow
managing to snooze through the automated announcements that
blared over the station's speakers.

"Outbound train... L... Taraval...
Arriving... in... three... minutes..."

Thanks, robot lady.

That was my ship.
I pulled a few bucks from my fattened wallet and bought
myself a ticket for the train. Then I stepped through the turnstile
and rode the escalator down to the lower platform; the train
arrived shortly thereafter. I stepped onboard, set my things down,
and rode that baby back to the beach with some money in my
pocket and Eagles in my head.

The train stopped a few blocks from the water. I stepped onto the
sidewalk and popped into a little restaurant that had a giant plastic
blue bull's head mounted on top of the sign. The menu at this
place was one of the strangest compilations of entrees I'd ever
seen. A bacon cheeseburger occupied the same lunch list as
spaghetti and meatballs, chicken teriyaki, barbeque ribs, and
pepperoni pizza. It was risky, but I opted for the bacon
cheeseburger and a chocolate milkshake to celebrate my first
successful day of busking in San Francisco. The milkshake tasted

great, but the bacon cheeseburger was slimy and soggy—floppy bacon, bun saturated in grease. It was bad, but my momma taught me never to waste food, so I took that whole thing down (along with its little French-fried buddies) and chased everything with that delicious chocolate shake.

Speaking of mom, I gave her a call to let her know how things were going in San Francisco.

"Eighty-eight dollars?" she had asked.
  "Yeah, not a bad morning."
  "Okay, that's good... But how *often* do you make that much?"
  "Well, today was definitely a *good* day. But I'm hoping that I can keep those good days coming by playing in the subway. That seems to be the place to profit."
  There was a slight pause.
  "You're playing in the subways?"
  "Yeah."
  "Jason..."
  "Mom, I assure you, it's safe down there—no more dangerous than playing at the Market."
  She took a deep breath. "Isn't there somewhere else you can play? A nice coffee shop or wine bar or something?"

I told her I'd look into these places, knowing that it'd be very tough to book anything on such short notice. Hearing this made her feel better.

"So, how much money do you *have?*" she asked.
  "Let's see, I've got about..." I hesitated. "Eighty-eight dollars."
  "Jason!"
  "Mom, I'm goo—"

"Jason, let me send you some money."

"No, I have to do this. Trust me. I'll be fine."

There was a long pause.

"Jason, I want you to promise me something..."

I laughed.

"I'm not joking," she said sternly. "If you get into a situation where you need money, where you have like, four dollars left—" I smiled. "—I want you to promise that you'll call me and let me help you."

I exhaled heavily.

"Jason..."

I didn't say anything.

"Jason!"

I chuckled again and crossed my fingers.

"Okay, Mom. I promise."

I could almost hear her relief.

"Good. I love you."

"Love you too."

I paid for my meal and stepped outside. The afternoon sun—coupled with a light breeze blowing from the ocean—felt good on my face. I carried my guitar across the Great Highway and onto the sand, where I stopped for a moment to watch the waves crashing in countless rows ahead of me.

Seagulls glided back and forth through the air above, riding the breeze.

"Nice work today!" they squawked in seagull-ese.

"Thanks, guys!" I yelled back.

How nice of them to notice.

I hiked up onto what was quickly becoming my favorite dune—the spot where I'd hung out twice the previous morning and the spot where, later that night, Kendra and I had spent some time together. Waves slammed the misty shore as I traced the coastline north, thinking about what Kendra and I had said...

30

"Naked?" I had asked.

The corners of Kendra's mouth turned upward. "Super naked," she replied.

I smiled. "Okay, I'm officially intrigued. What *was* this naked ritual of yours?"

"Well," Kendra said, "last year, I had a lot of beliefs, a lot of behaviors that I wanted to get rid of—things that weren't serving me any longer, things I needed to change."

The ocean churned before us, dark and vast in a slow and steady rhythm; a natural backbeat for Kendra's tale as she and I sat atop that late-night dune.

"I went to the store and bought six red balloons," Kendra continued, looking out at the water. "They were all filled with helium, and a tiny string was tied to each one. I waited until midnight, and then I put them all in my car and drove down past Pacifica to one of my favorite little beaches." Kendra looked over at me, reminding me of an Eskimo with that hood covering half her face. "You'd love this place," she said. "You have to park on the highway and hike down a hill to the sand."

Kendra focused again on the darkness ahead of us. "I brought my flashlight and went down to the beach with the balloons to sit by the sea. It was *such* a nice night. And there were *so* many bright stars shining. I sat there in the sand and thought about what I wanted to change in my life, listening to the water." A slight breeze blew as Kendra spoke. The air was warm. "When I pinpointed something I wanted to change, I meditated on it, and then I wrote it on one of the balloons with a black marker."

"So when did this whole *naked* thing happen?" I prodded.

Kendra smirked. "Typical boy," she said, shaking her head. "After I got all six balloons marked up, I—"

I interrupted. "Why six?"

Kendra processed my query with a thoughtful, "Hmmmmm," before deciding, "It was the right number," and following the answer with a nod, as if she were agreeing with herself. "Now," she said with a playful grin, "if you'll let me finish... I had all *six* balloons marked up. So I took all of my clothes off and walked over to the edge of the water. Then I took the balloons, one at a time, and meditated on each one. I thought about what the idea on the balloon looked like in my life, and then I pictured what my life would look like without that behavior. Then, as soon as I had that image in my head, I let go of the balloon and watched it sail into the sky." Kendra stuck a closed fist out in front of her and opened it slowly.

"I did that with all six balloons"

She looked up at the sky, and I looked with her. A few stars twinkled above.

"I love your crazy," I said. "I can't believe you did that."

"It felt amazing," she said. "I think there's a lot of power in ritual—a physical representation of your intention."

"Did it work?" I asked. "Are those things gone from your life now?"

Kendra looked at me, sincerely. "It's been tough," she said. "A lot of work, and some days are harder than others." Kendra turned fully toward me, legs crossed in the sand. "Sometimes I find myself slipping back into the old, but I try to catch myself. I try to move from a different space—a space of '*I am*' instead of '*I want*' or '*I need.*' I'm trying hard to realize that everything I could ever want, I already have." Kendra looked toward the water. "I *have* the power to move," she said. "I *have* the power to be, to create—it's all in me. I *am*. And when I feel that, and *know* that..." Kendra glanced back at me with a grin. "That's when I'm invincible."

31

"Naked with balloons, huh?" Dominic shook his head before taking a sip of his beer. "That's a new one."

He spoke slowly and sounded a bit off—*rough day maybe?*

"Yeah," I said. "She's a trip."

Dominic had just finished his shift at the café, and the two of us had met at a spot called Shaeffer's, which was a few blocks from the beach. I'd vowed to buy him a few brews with the spoils of that morning's Civic Center success and was making good on my offer.

He and I were half of the crowd that afternoon, including the woman running the show. The pub was dark but the front door, propped open, allowed some curious light to peek inside.

"You know you kind of moved in on her that night in Seattle, right?"

I was mid-sip when Dominic said this, and swallowed before looking at him.

"What?" I asked, wondering if I'd heard him clearly.

Dominic's expression was cold as he spoke with unfamiliar intensity. "I met Kendra at the bar that night," he said. "I bought her a drink, and then *I* brought her back to the table—and who goes and runs off with her?"

The bartender and lone customer paused their conversation to look our way.

Conscious of our audience, I leaned closer to Dominic and spoke quietly. "How come you haven't said anything about this until now?"

Dominic took a quick sip, setting his glass down with a thud that startled me back to my original position. "I let it slide, buddy. I let it slide that night. We were all getting crazy and having fun. I get it. But now you're down *here* seeing her, bringing her to the Swell. Rubbing it in my face."

A knot tightened in my stomach. "Shit, man," I said. "Look, it's not li—"

"It is what it is," Dominic interrupted (which was probably best because I was having trouble finding words). "Like I said," Dominic went on, "I get it—and now it sounds like you two have some sort of connection. But, I just don't understand. I mean, I..." Dominic was visibly frustrated and stopped speaking to take a long drink. After he'd swallowed and set his glass on the bar, there was a silence as he stared straight ahead. I would have broken this silence, but my tongue wouldn't work.

"Okay, look." He turned to face me, speaking in a calmer tone. "That night in Seattle, before the two of you ran off, Kendra gave me her number." The bartender and patron resumed their chatter. "So for the past month I've been trying to get in touch with her, and she kept telling me, '*Oh, I can't meet up this weekend,*' or '*Sorry, maybe next week.*'" Dominic rubbed the back of his neck. "So I'd given up, even though I thought it was a crazy coincidence that on my birthday trip up to Seattle I'd met a beautiful girl from San Francisco." Dominic stared at his half-empty glass before slapping a palm on the bar and snapping himself out of his trance. "So, yeah, I'd given up, but then, lo and behold, I sign us up for an open mic at the Swell and who walks in the door with you? Ms. Next Weekend: Kendra."

As I processed this, the bartender scooped a cupful of ice from the bin. Then she stood on her tippy toes to grab a bottle from the highest shelf.

"Look, man," I said. "I'm sorry. I didn't know you felt that way." I shook my head. "I got swept up that night in Seattle—I mean, we both talked to her, but I didn't realize you had a thing for her too." I thought back to the rooftop. "But you saw the two of us run off that night. Why would you try to get a hold of her after that?"

Dominic glanced at his hands, folded on the bar, rubbing fingers together. "I didn't know you'd stay in touch with her," he said. "Figured it'd just be a little fling."

I nodded. "Makes sense."

There was silence again as Dominic drained his beer and set the empty glass on the bar. "It's just a pride thing," Dominic said, shaking his head. "I'll get over it." He adjusted his ball cap. "I had to get that off my chest, though, Jason. Sorry for bumming the mood."

I clinked my glass on his empty pint and killed what was left. "No worries. Glad you said something about it."

"You boys need two more?" the bartendress asked, appearing in front of us as if out of nowhere—perfect timing, very magical.

"Yeah, I got 'em," I said, pulling the wallet from my coat and sliding the paper equivalent of my CD across the bar.

Dominic knocked on the bar. "*Gracias.*"

"No problem, man," I said. "Thanks for the hospitality."

Dominic patted me on the back and smiled. "Don't mention it. It's good to have you—even if you are a prick sometimes."

I smiled back. "Shut up."

As our beers were being poured, I scanned the walls. The owner of the bar must've been from Pittsburgh; there was Steeler's crap all over the place.

Wait a second...

I looked toward Dominic. "If I see her again is it gonna bug you?"

Dominic shook his head. "No... Sounds like you two actually have a pretty nice thing going. I'm happy for you. Like I said, I just needed to get that out."

"Cheers, boys." The bartender set two fresh beers in front of us.

I raised my glass and said, "*Salud.*" Dominic saluded back.

With tensions settled, the two of us went on to talk about songwriting. Dominic mentioned something about a fluid inside every artist that needs movement, like each creator is a cup full of blue liquid. He talked about how that cup can sit, untouched, atop a white sheet of paper for a year straight and nothing will happen; but if you shake that cup, start to push it one way or another, eventually some of that liquid is going to spill over the rim; and then you'll have yourself a little blue painting.

After entertaining the image of that creative cup full of blue liquid, Dominic and I finished drinking our amber liquid and stood up to leave. As we did, Dominic peeked at his phone. "Hey, buddy," he said. "It's only two o'clock..." He looked at me with eyebrows raised. "You wanna see that beach she was talking about?"

32

We blasted fast around the bend as the water rolled out before us.
The Pacific Ocean—a slightly darker shade of blue than
the cerulean sky above—stretched as far as our eyes could see.
Dominic hit the gas, and Ruby rode the curve, as the two of us
watched the California coast unravel for miles ahead, revealing the
city of Pacifica with sea cliffs beyond—beautiful country, the edge
of the west.

"Damn. Look at that!" I said, taking in that picturesque
panorama for the first time.

Dominic glanced at me and smiled as though this was
exactly the reaction he'd anticipated. He cranked the stereo (Pearl
Jam's new album) and accelerated to the tempo of the song,
allowing Eddie Vedder and the boys to become our cruise
control.

Ruby swooped down a long hill before gunning beneath an
overpass, shooting through Pacifica, and passing a peaceful beach
on the right. Then up into the hills, winding and climbing a
narrow road shaded by trees that gave off a potent aroma. Once
this eucalyptus forest opened up, sunlight kissed the crimson car
as we hugged the hillside and shot across a small canyon. Ruby
rode that bridge into a tunnel that took us straight through the
middle of a large hill. As we erupted from the other side, the coast
opened up again, stretching forever toward a great blue nothing.

Dominic pulled a panting Ruby to the right, letting her

cool down on a patch of gravel. "I've gotta show you something."

The two of us unbuckled our seat belts and stepped from the car, greeted by the sound of cars whizzing past on Highway One. I gave the thumbs-up to a NO TRESPASSING sign as we tramped along a small dirt path that stretched about a hundred yards to the edge of a cliff.

"What's that building?" I asked while hiking the slight incline, seeing nothing but blue sky and ocean beyond the subject of my inquiry.

A small concrete structure—only about ten feet tall, but raised another ten feet off the ground by the rock it had been built on—waited for us at the edge of the cliff, appearing to have once served some purpose before becoming this lonely shell perched over the Pacific.

Dominic answered my question as we moved closer. "This was an old lookout post back in World War II. Soldiers used to sit in there with binoculars to keep an eye on ships passing by."

Dry dirt and popcorn rocks crunched beneath our shoes as we approached the old lookout. To my left there was nothing but coastline; to my right were tall, jagged cliffs—green grass sloping down into orange rock that dove headfirst into the churning sea below, massive natural monuments, sentinels standing tall, appraising those sailing east across the Pacific.

Dominic and I walked to the edge of a bluff along the right side of the structure and peered down at the sea as it cried out for attention. Pacific tantrums were funneled into small arenas between the rocks where water splashed enthusiastically upward in an attempt to climb the cliffs.

I looked from bursting waters toward the structure, noticing graffiti of many different styles decorating the building's form. Spray-painted on the upper portion of the north wall, a cartoon man glared at me with hands on his hips, sporting spiky hair and yellow skin like a Simpsons character. A speech bubble floated from his open mouth, encouraging all who looked upon him to "Die Trying."

"Here, check this out," Dominic said as he led me around the west side of the lookout. This wall bulged outward like a beer belly (as opposed to the other sides of the building, which were all flat) and loomed above the small sliver of ground that lived between the lookout and land's edge.

I made sure to keep a close eye on my footing. Though a swim on that sunny day would have been nice, a fall from that height would have put a real damper on the day. Dominic and I successfully navigated around to the south side of the structure and looked upward. A long slit, about two feet from its top to bottom edge, ran the length of the lookout's sea-facing side. I pictured men in camouflage holding binoculars and hanging out of this gap, making sure Pacific waters stayed friendly.

Turning toward the ocean, I took a deep breath and a moment to appreciate the magnitude of the beauty before me.

"Up here," yelled Dominic.

I spun back around. Dominic had climbed the rock onto the structure and was hanging from the lookout's seaward side, hands grasping the inside edge of the long slit. The opening was slightly larger at its ends (about three feet from top to bottom before it narrowed). With hands planted inside, Dominic kicked his leg up into this wider part of the opening and squeezed himself horizontally through the slit.

"Nice!" I ran toward the rock, looked around, and, finding some sturdy holds, climbed the ten or so feet onto the structure. Once on the building's south side, I stepped onto a small, concrete rim (about a foot wide) that ran along the perimeter of the entire building. Once my feet were planted firmly on this small ledge, I was able to shimmy around to the western face of the lookout. I grabbed the inside edge of the chest-high slit and continued shuffling my shoes along the ledge, making sure not to lose my footing as I turned and looked down at four-hundred-something feet between me and the Pacific.

My stomach screamed at me: *Pay attention!*

I obeyed.

Sliding my right arm deep into the slit and freeing my left, I turned and looked across the ocean. The sun kissed my face, and a warm wind blew my hair. This tandem embrace launched me into a state of simultaneous powerlessness and invincibility, which I enjoyed for a moment before turning back around and grabbing the inside edge of the opening with both hands. Taking a deep breath, I kicked my right foot into the chest-high slit, and squeezed through the small aperture.

My feet found solid ground and, as I dusted off my shirt, I noticed Dominic on the other side of the small concrete room, using light from his phone to illuminate spray-painted walls. He glanced over his shoulder with a grin. "Welcome to the Highway One graffiti gallery."

"Wow." My voice echoed through the dark space. "How cool is this?"

Empty cans of beer and spray paint littered the concrete floor like spent shells. Kicking one of these every few steps, I walked the room, using my phone's flashlight to breathe life into the work that had been left by phantom artists.

Among these creations I found a robot flashing a peace sign, a row of orange aliens with various cartoon facial expressions, and a man and his dog slumped forward beneath the phrase "Looking for love." Taking up most of the wall furthest from our makeshift entrance was a spray-painted tree with a rope swing hanging from its largest branch. Upon that branch sat a mischievous cartoon fellow with a water balloon in hand, cocked and ready to soak any would-be swinger. Names, dates, bands, gangs, sports teams—some in Spanish, some in English— in countless colors and styles of street art were peppered amongst various larger and more intricate works. Upon completing my circular tour of the room, I came across a final message, left above the entry slit for the chosen to ponder:

Stay Forever.

White paint fading into the past.

"This stuff always changes," Dominic said. "There's new art every time I come here."

"This is great," I said, as I made eye contact with a spray-surfer, throwing the shaka as he rode a massive blue paint wave. The cartoon breaker-chaser reminded me of Blaze.

I gazed out at the world through the concrete gap—a world whose blues and greens were made even more vibrant in contrast to the darkness surrounding the two feet through which it was viewed.

I felt a hand on my shoulder. "Ready to roll?" Dominic asked.

I nodded, and the two of us pulled ourselves carefully back into the sunlight through the concrete opening, making sure to avoid a misstep that would send us sailing onto hungry rocks below. We climbed down onto the crunchy ground and took one last look around the majesty of our surroundings before beginning our trek back to the car.

We walked toward the edge of a cliff on the graffiti palace's south side. "There's the beach," Dominic said, pointing to a sandy shore below.

Glancing down at a small strip of land tucked into a little Pacific cove, I was able to pick out the forms of a few people lounging on the sand and a little dog running along the water's edge. That shore was definitely secluded, just like Kendra had said it would be.

I scanned the dirt around me for the remains of red

balloons.

"Wanna go check it out?" Dominic asked.

"Definitely."

As we walked toward the road where Ruby waited patiently, I looked at the hills towering over the highway and imagined climbing them.

Once inside the car, Dominic started her up and peeled out, giving wings to gravel as we shot down a steep slope and made an abrupt left into a small dirt parking lot. Dominic parked the car and the two of us walked across the dusty lot to the highway. We waited a moment to cross, watching cars whiz past at sixty-five miles an hour, and bolted to the other side of the road as soon as we saw an opening.

As we walked along the highway, a heavy guardrail protected us from yet another long fall from Pacific cliffs. Soon this downward drop turned to solid ground and the barrier came to an end, revealing a dirt path that wound down a slight incline. This trail led us through tall grasses to an old wooden staircase flanked on both sides by blackberry bushes and descending all the way down to the beach below. With every step I took down those rotting planks, I pictured Kendra with her flashlight and balloons, navigating that same course on her midnight mission.

Upon setting foot on the soft, white sand, I instantly removed my shoes and socks. Carrying them, I trekked toward the water, beach between my toes and sun on my face. The shore was private and quiet; and only a few other folks shared the secluded space, lounging on the sand or walking around carefree. I looked up at the graffiti palace, perched atop the bluff which towered over the beach on my right. This sat adjacent to its counterpart, looming epic to the left.

Together, these twin cliffs created a tight cove.

As Dominic and I stood there taking in the scene, a little dog zipped across the sand, blasting between Dominic's legs and huffing hard, tongue out. Dominic laughed as the dog ran a few excited circles in the sand and stood in front of him, staring upward with tail wagging vigorously.

The dog barked.

"Hey, buddy," Dominic said, kneeling to greet the pup.

"Gizmo! Come here!"

Without hesitation, the little dog jetted across the sand to its owner, a man lounging on a towel several yards away.

"This is awesome," I said, surveying the scene. "I can't believe this is so close to the city."

"Yeah," said Dominic. "Welcome to my escape."

Blue sky...

White sand...

The smell of the sea, the sound of the waves...

"I call it my zen zone," Dominic said. "If I need to clear my head, I just come and spend an hour or two down here—works every time."

"Looks like you're not the only one," I said, pointing to a man standing at the water's edge, wearing nothing but a long gray ponytail. The man tilted his head back and photosynthesized, arms outstretched.

I closed my eyes and did the same—with clothes on, though—letting the sun's rays warm my face. A few seconds of this bliss beckoned a satisfied sigh—a soulgasm—deflating some pent-up pressure I didn't know I was carrying until it had been released.

I thought of Kendra's balloons.

The dog barked again, and I opened my eyes to see him standing at the water's edge, blasting back and forth in short bursts of puppy power.

"Whoa!" Dominic said, pointing toward the water.

Before I could ask "Whoa, what?" he took off running

across the sand. I followed and caught up with him near the water, where Gizmo stood rigidly beside us, barking at broken intervals and wagging his tail in savage spurts.

"What's up, man?" I asked, catching my breath.

Gizmo barked once more before zipping back toward his owner.

Dominic's eyes were fixed on the water ahead. "Wait for it..." he said.

I didn't have to wait long.

The thing rolled around in the waves about fifty yards out, and it wasn't alone.

At first, all I could see was a small fin, but then a little black body, glistening in the sun, surfaced and slowly resubmerged. A few yards away a large spurt of water shot upward with an audible release, and a huge, black hump broke the surface, gliding with grace and revealing a tail that rose regally before disappearing slowly into the sea.

"No way!" I blurted.

Dominic flashed a goatee-framed smile and pulled a phone from his jacket. Then he snapped a few pictures of momma and baby whale as they swam around, bobbing up for air when they felt like it and not appearing to be in any kind of hurry—no 5 o'clock appointment with their whale estate agent.

"Those humpbacks?" a voice asked.

Turning around, I was surprised to see the naked guy, in all his shriveled glory. He held one hand over his forehead, shielding his eyes from the sun; the other rested on his hip.

"I'm not sure," I said, maintaining steady eye contact.

"Yeah," Dominic answered. "They're the only species that swim around here this time of year."

"Groovy," said the naked guy.

Gizmo zipped back to the water's edge; his owner trudged through the sand wearing board shorts and black dress shoes.

"I bet he'd love to sink his teeth into one of those," the owner said as the whales breached simultaneously.

Gizmo barked in puppy agreement.

The five of us (including the pooch) stood there on the shore. We didn't say much—just little comments every now and then on the whales at play.

After a while, when shiny humps stopped breaking the water's surface and the sun had officially clocked out for the day, we said our goodbyes and went our separate ways. Dominic and I hiked back up to the car and shot north on Highway One, Gizmo and his owner shook the sand from their towel, and the naked guy continued to be the naked guy.

None of us traded names or backgrounds or stories; we didn't need to.

We were just there, in that moment, sharing something good.

33

"No!"

I knew I had to be stern; otherwise I wouldn't penetrate his fog.

The man looked from the guitar case back to me with glazed, bloodshot eyes.

I locked my stare onto his and didn't break the gaze. I also didn't stop playing "Dock of the Bay" (though I had stopped singing momentarily, keeping my mouth free to handle this situation).

The man had a string of yellow snot running from his nose into a scraggly beard; the mucus had worked its way deep into those coarse hairs. He was very thin, very dirty, and standing about a foot from my guitar case, eyeing the dollar bills inside like they were a medium-rare rib eye.

"NO!" I commanded again, louder this time.

I stopped playing.

The man took a step back, facing me with hands dangling limply in front of him—a subway tunnel T-Rex. There was no emotion on his face that I could recognize, but I saw him thinking, evaluating risks and benefits of the situation, eyes darting back and forth between me and the money.

I made his decision easy.

Reaching out with my left hand, I flipped the lid of the

case shut and continued to look him in the eye. The T-Rex broke away from my stare, glancing curiously at the now-closed case, cocking his head to one side—processing.

He looked back at me with dark eyes.

"Inbound train... N... Judah..."

The robot announcement startled the creature into movement, and he looked suddenly toward the ceiling, then back to me.

"Arriving in... five... minutes..."

The man made a sound that landed somewhere between a grunt and a growl as he turned quickly and scampered across the marble floor to the other side of the subway station, where he found a spot near the stairs to pace back and forth, shooting nervous looks in my direction at sporadic intervals.

I opened the case back up.

Noon at the Powell Street subway station, and I wasn't making much money.

I'd been playing there for about two hours and only had about fifteen dollars to show for it.

Defeated, I decided to take a train toward the Civic Center station where I'd had great luck the day before, leaving my current spot to the T-Rex.

I packed up my things and made my way down to the platform to catch the N train.

Once I arrived at the Civic Center, I rode the escalator up to the main area and walked back to the tunnel where I'd made most of my money the day before. No one was playing there, but a man who looked like he'd just taken a mud bath sat cross-legged at one end of the tunnel. He was holding a cardboard sign and had placed a small plastic cup on the marble in front of him.

"Shit," I said to myself, stopping in my tracks.

Nugget #4: It's bad for business to have someone begging close to you. It's tough enough that the general population already lumps street performers in with panhandlers, but the opportunity for visual association almost guarantees that passing folks will shut their ears—and their wallets.

I walked over to the escalator where I'd played my first set the day before. It smelled a bit like piss, but there was no one playing or panhandling there. I looked around—not many people passing through the station. The place was quiet.

It felt lonely.

Folks who *were* coming into the station were wet—folding dripping umbrellas and pulling back saturated hoods as they took a much needed break from the rain. The marble was slick from soggy shoes slogging across it.

I unfolded my stand near the brick wall and placed the open guitar case on top, taking a large breath before slinging my guitar over my shoulder, tuning it, and beginning to play.

My first tip was all coins—a few silver shiners, but more pennies than anything. I heard the change jingle when the trench-coated man tossed it into my case and muttered, "Get a job." He refused to look at me while he said this, and afterward continued to walk quickly across the station.

Already fed up with the day, I stopped playing and reached into the case to grab a few of those pennies. Remembering my short stint as a little-league pitcher, I threw them as hard as I could in the man's direction, yelling, "Get a life!" as he rounded a distant corner.

A young boy wearing a backpack clutched his father's leg and looked at me with frightened eyes.

Once the father had paid for a train ticket, he shot a glance of disapproval over his shoulder and took his son's hand before pushing through the turnstile.

I shook my head and sat down on the marble floor.

"Outbound train... L... Taraval...
        Arriving... in... seven... minutes..."

Empty station.
        Just me and the robot lady.
        I slowly scratched a fingernail across the spruce top of my guitar.

"Don't get... down... Jason...
        I see... what... you're... doing..."

I glanced toward the ceiling.
        "Huh...?"

"I know... *why*... you... do it...
        You... want it all to... *mean*... something..."

Two business suits with briefcases strolled past and she changed her tone.

"Inbound train... N... Judah..."

I rubbed my face, contemplating the effects of exhaustion on a human brain.

After a moment, not quite ready to let my robo-fan down, I decided to stand up and resume playing.
        I ran through some popular songs, hoping a familiar

melody would be the catalyst for some incredible tip, but the majority of folks just walked right past. Any money that *was* coming in was trickling slowly: a buck here, some coins there.

It's not about the money, I kept reminding myself. *If you were looking to make money, you'd be a doctor.*

Food was nice, though. And, unfortunately, I needed dollars to trade for food.

Maybe I could bring my guitar through the grocery check-out line?

Play a song or two in exchange for my cereal...

Picturing some angry checker paging her manager was enough to burst that fantastic bubble and snap me back to the reality of that stinky subway. There was a friction between where I was and where I wanted to be—I could feel it. Singing beneath the streets of San Francisco wasn't the pumped up crowd of 40,000 screaming fans that I saw when I slept at night, but I played on anyway, knowing that I'd much rather be there than working some dead-end job.

Maybe Neil Young is on his way downtown?

There's a nice thought...

He'd walk by—head down, wearing some cool hat—and hear my angelic voice moments after the opening act on his upcoming tour had called him to say they needed to cancel.

Then I'd be his hero, a penniless knight in flannel armor.

He'd offer me the gig, we'd hop on a tour bus, and that would be it: the dream come true.

Fantasies like these kept me company as I strummed along, that big break just around the corner.

Another thing that made me feel worthwhile was the fact that every CD I sold was out there in the world, keeping some set of eager ears company. After those discs left my case they continued to do their job, whether I was there to supervise or not. Those songs were my soldiers, hardworking little guys, clocking in every time their new owner hit play.

The CDs and I were in the middle of playing "Turn the Page" when a man in a wheelchair rolled up and parked a few feet in front of me. He was a large man, proud owner of a mighty gray beard that was yellowing in sections. Wearing a green sweatshirt and camouflage pants, he sat against the brick smiling toothlessly, nodding, and giving me a thumbs-up about every twenty seconds or so. As folks passed between the two of us, this man began mouthing Seger's lyrics, looking like he had some sort of engine revving inside of him.

Then, when the second chorus hit, he couldn't hold back any longer.

"HERE I AM!"

Goddammit....

"ON THE ROAD AGAIN!"

The man started singing along with me, belting Bob at the top of his lungs in slurred bursts of gravelly belligerence. Once he got going, he didn't stop. The wheelchair wonder and I proceeded to perform the finest version of "Turn the Page" I've ever heard, bringing tears of joy to the eyes of every passerby. In fact, the afternoon crowd was *so* moved that every single one of them forgot to tip—minds fully blown, neural connections between brains and wallets fried.

The song ended, and, despite the obvious chemistry between the subway idol and me, it seemed necessary for me to carry on alone.

The world wasn't ready for that level of awesome.

I grabbed a dollar from my case and walked over to the camouflaged crooner. He flashed a big smile. I had been wrong when I thought he was toothless—there were still about six left.

"SOUNDID GOOD, BRUTHER!"

"Thanks," I said.

A cup containing a few coins rested between those camouflaged legs. I dropped the dollar bill in there.

"AWWW, MANN!"

My performance partner gazed up at me, smiling through gray-yellow hairs as he gave me another thumbs-up and then retracted the thumb, turning his closed fist sideways.

Apprehensively, I pounded his fist with mine.

"THANKS, BRUTHER!"

"No problem, man." I almost added "Pleasure singing with you," but I didn't want to encourage him to stay for another song, so I just said, "Have a good one."

The man gave me one final thumbs-up, grabbed the wheels on his chair, and rolled across the marble to the other side of the station, singing the whole way.

"Here I am,
        On the road again..."

Wow, I thought, watching him disappear into a tunnel. *What a morning.*

I walked back to my spot and resumed playing. Every few songs, someone would drop a dollar in my case, but after another hour, I'd made only a meager six bucks (one of which I'd given to the rolling wonder for his vocal services).

This was definitely not the day I'd hoped for. I'd had grand visions of repeating the previous day's profits, maybe even improving on them. *A hundred bucks?*

Maybe more...

Nope. Several hours and I wasn't even close.

Final Nugget: Busking is full of ups and downs. You can make fifty bucks in an hour or fifteen bucks in a day. Nothing is certain. The feeling of accomplishment when things *do* go right is a high beyond words—a sense of truly *making* your money, earning it with every fiber of your being. But when the money isn't flowing, the people aren't listening, and you watch some dirty gremlin steal a train ticket from a guy who's mid-purchase at the machine in front of you—

That's when it's time to find a new spot.

34

"Why don't you try Haight Street?" Dominic suggested over a sizzling bacon symphony.

I spread some barbeque sauce onto a slice of white bread. The burger patties—pepper jack cheese melted on top—had already been cooked and sat, succulent, atop a plate, awaiting the piggy-ribbons that would be the finishing touch for the early evening treats.

"Yeah, man," I said from the kitchen table. "I still haven't been to that part of town."

"You need to go," Dominic said, facing the stove. "You'll love it. There's all sorts of crazy people running around down there—lots of street kids, travelers..."

"Sounds interesting," I said, as Dominic poured grease from the skillet into the sink.

Few things make me happier than the smell of freshly cooked bacon. I glanced out the window as a gray San Francisco day turned to night.

"Have you talked to Kendra, at all?" Dominic asked, setting the plate of bacon on the table and taking a seat.

"Not since the other night," I said. "Tried to call her yesterday after you and I took that drive, but didn't hear anything back."

"Weird." He grabbed the barbeque sauce and squirted a healthy dose onto his burger.

"Yeah." I placed a patty on my bread, laid some bacon on

top, and grabbed the stack with both hands, admiring the impending deliciousness before me. I gave the burger a good sniff before taking my first bite.

It smelled great, and tasted even better.

I tried not to think about the fact that I hadn't heard back from Kendra.

After all, it's only been two nights.

As often as I told myself that, though, I couldn't get her off my mind. There were moments I didn't think about her, but every time I got a call or text, I immediately reached for my phone hoping to see her name.

"Why didn't you guys keep hanging out on Monday night?" Dominic asked.

"She had to work early," I said. "But she did mention something about wanting to see each other again, so I'm trying not to sweat it."

Dominic took a large bite of his burger. "Yeah," he said, chewing, "I wouldn't worry about it."

The two of us ate our burgers in the silence of mutual meat nirvana.

After we'd finished, I washed the dishes and Dominic went to the bathroom to take a dump. Once the dishes were clean, I pulled my guitar out of its case and started playing, sitting at the kitchen table and staring out the window at nothing in particular. After a little while, Dominic came down the hallway with his guitar to join. He sat down at the table, and the two of us began to work on one of Dominic's tunes called "Out of my Head." We played around with the song, trying new things, repeating verses and choruses.

"What's that chord?"

"No, that doesn't fit."

"How 'bout this?"

"Yeah, that sounds great!"

Eventually, I'd added a guitar part and some vocal harmonies that Dominic and I were both happy with, and after an hour or so of working on the song, the two of us decided to play its latest incarnation at an open mic across town.

We hopped into Ruby and shot over to the Richmond district.

This "open mic" actually took place at a café with no sound system, and therefore no microphone. Those playing would sit on a stool at the front of the brightly lit room where spectators would become respectfully silent as soon as a tune began. This courtesy was a rarity for most live music venues, and seeing it in practice was a breath of fresh air.

A number of talented musicians played that night, many of whom I was beginning to know after running into them at various spots across town. The San Francisco acoustic music scene was rapidly revealing itself as a tight-knit, but very warm and welcoming, family. Players sat in on each other's songs, sang along to each other's lyrics, and dove into what everyone else was creating, offering feedback and insight. I instantly felt welcome there, almost more welcome than I'd felt in the Seattle scene. There was camaraderie in that community I hadn't experienced before, and the cherry on top? People really seemed to be enjoying my music.

Toward the end of that night—somewhere between Dominic and I playing "Out of my Head" together for the first time and a male/female duo giving me chills for three songs straight—thoughts started spinning, and I entertained the possibility of coming back down to San Francisco and spending more than just a week.

Hell, maybe I'd spend more than a month.

It was strange, but I was beginning to think that maybe the other cities on my list could wait.

35

"How about 7 o'clock?" I asked.

"Perfect," she said, voice sweet as ever, bouncing from some satellite into the phone at my right ear.

"Cool... See you then."

"Great!"

I hung up the phone with a smile and slid it back into the pocket of my jeans, noticing that someone had dropped a dollar into my case while I was talking to Kendra—another sign that the first round of Haight Street busking was going just fine so far.

I took a drink of water in the sunshine, a block from the intersection of Haight and Ashbury. I had set up the case in front of a smoke shop painted psychedelic orange, purple, and red. The visage of Jimi Hendrix, watching from above the shop's entrance, greeted those passing on that warm afternoon. After playing this spot for a little over an hour, I had already made forty bucks (my first tip of the day being a twenty-dollar bill from a father and son who strolled past with bags of groceries from the nearby market). The father had given the bill to his son of about three, who proceeded to slam-dunk Andrew Jackson into my guitar case like a tiny NBA star.

Yeah, that was more like it—no lingering piss smell, no T-Rex drooling into my case. Nope, just sunshine, happy people, and hippie history.

I was pleased to find that folks on Haight Street, not

hurrying to any office or meeting, were actually willing to stop and listen for a song or two. Some passersby would even sit on the concrete for long chunks of the performance, closing their eyes and rocking back and forth to the music. At one point during that first set, a young couple sat together on the sidewalk—the man reclining against the base of a light post, the woman sitting between the man's legs, leaning into his chest—relaxing and listening for a half hour before tipping five dollars, thanking me, and moving on.

I took a moment to reflect on the flow that had brought me to that sidewalk. Sometimes I think of it as a little piece of dental floss wrapped around my heart that gently tugs me in the right direction.

After entertaining this image, I bent down to grab a treat from the box of donut holes someone had given me as a tip.

"You like green?"

The voice was deep and smooth, a friendly tone.

I thought to myself: *Green?*

Green money?

Green weed?

Green beans?

So many options...

Before I addressed this query, I decided to gather all of the facts.

I stood up with my donut hole and smiled at what I saw.

The man was large, black, and built, wearing sunglasses and a very tight red shirt that made his muscles pop like some action star.

"Green?" I asked.

The man grinned before clarifying in a delicate tone, "Your hat." He nodded toward me with left hand behind his back.

I took a bite of my donut hole. *Oh,* I remembered with a mouthful of good. *I'm wearing my green beanie* (I was so close when I thought green *beans*). "Yeah," I said, answering the initial question. "This is my favorite hat."

The man smiled widely, showing off bright white teeth, and said, "I like green, too," as he brought his left hand around from behind his back, revealing the long, scaly iguana lounging in his palm.

To say that I was surprised to see the lizard would be a colossal understatement.

The man held the creature a few inches from my face, and I leaned closer, staring fascinatedly into its orange eyeball. The iguana stared back at me. A row of spines running down its back made it look like a tiny dinosaur.

I peered past the lizard, to its owner, who was still grinning. "That's great," I said in awe.

My inner child, still infatuated with all things scaly, ran excited circles around the reptile zoo in my mind.

"Go ahead," Iguana Man urged, holding the lizard closer to me. "You can pet Charlotte."

I stroked her rough scales. The pretty little lady didn't seem to mind my touch.

"Wanna go get some ice cream?"

I shifted my gaze from the tiny dinosaur to its owner, who waited patiently for my reply.

It was a tempting proposition, but I decided to continue with my set. "No thanks, man." I said. "'Preciate the offer though, and you letting me pet your little lady."

The man pulled the iguana close to his bulging chest, looking down as he began to stroke it. He lowered an ear to Charlotte's scaly head, waited a moment, and then glanced up at me.

"She likes you," Iguana Man said. "We both do." He reached out with a beefy arm, gently touching my shoulder with his huge hand. "Have a spectacular day."

"Thanks," I replied. "You too."

"Oh," he said, taking his non-lizard hand and lifting

sunglasses so I could see his bright, blue eyes, "we will." He pulled the glasses back over his eyes, smiled, and sauntered down the sidewalk with little dragon in tow.

"What an interesting fellow," I said to myself, shaking my head.

A breath, a reflection, a look around; a double-decker San Francisco tour bus packed full of people.

Back to work.

I gave myself a four-count and began to play "Time of the Season" with a brand new memory burned into my brain—more valuable than any amount of money that could populate my hungry case.

36

I opened my eyes and was immediately startled by how close he was standing to me—inches away.

About twenty years old, sipping something through a straw plunged into the plastic lid of a large, paper cup.

I took a step away from the sneaky fellow, but my back found the smoke shop behind me.

The corners of his mouth turned upward around the straw lodged firmly between his lips.

"Hey, man—" I began.

"What?!" The guy interrupted angrily, glaring at my open guitar case and then back up at me. "I can only watch if I contribute?"

I wished Iguana Man were there instead; he had been much kinder.

"No," I said, keeping my voice calm, still playing the chords to my song "You can watch; I've just gotta ask you to give me a little bit of space here."

The guy took another sip. A tell-tale scent revealed there was more than just soda in that cup. "You know what I think?" he slurred. "I think *you're* a piece of shit." He shot fire from his eyes, too close for comfort.

I kept playing the chords to my song and glared back with a contagious anger.

"Well," I said, "how 'bout you go fuck yourself?"

The guy didn't say anything else. He just took a big sip of whatever was in the cup, aimed the straw toward me, and shot a stream of some fizzy drink directly at my face, I moved to the right and turned my head away, but not in time to avoid the entire attack.

I was hit.

The liquid was warm.

People made loud noises, and I turned to see the sneaky bastard scrambling toward Ashbury. A man, walking with his family, attempted to grab the shooter's shoulder, but the assailant was too quick and ducked beneath his arm.

"Fucking dick," I muttered.

I entertained the notion of chasing the spitter down and beating him with my box of donut holes, but I figured it wasn't worth the trouble. The sun was starting to go down, I was making great money, and in a few hours I had a date with an angel. Best to keep the vibes high.

"That was messed up."

I glanced in the direction of the voice.

What a gorgeous girl...

"Yeah," I said, wiping my cheek with my sleeve. "A real asshole."

I'd seen this girl stroll past my spot with her guitar a few times that afternoon. She had long brown hair and wore khaki shorts, a black tank top, and what I can only describe as a tie-dyed purple cape that flowed behind her as she cruised along. Large purple earrings in the shape of crescent moons dangled from her ears, and a purple band brightened her hair. She owned an interesting look and an extremely confident and powerful energy—some estrogen gravity.

"Wanna take a break?" The girl asked, green eyes locked into mine. Her lips parted slightly, and she watched my mouth, awaiting my answer.

I'd been at it for a while and had quite the haul at that point—somewhere around eighty bucks for the day. I felt I deserved a bit of a break, especially after my unexpected shower.

"Yeah, sure," I answered as I extended my hand. "I'm Jason"

"Summer," the girl said as she shook it. "I'm meeting my friend Cameron in the park, if you wanna come cool with us."

"Sounds great," I said, undoing my guitar strap and laying my hardworking lady back into her case. I knelt and grabbed the box of donut holes, holding it toward Summer. "Need one?" I asked.

She smiled and said, "Duh," before taking a powdery pastry and popping it into her mouth.

Oh, to be a donut hole...

The two of us, carrying our guitars, wandered up to Ashbury and turned the corner. The whole neighborhood was alive with people enjoying the early evening warmth. A four-piece band—female wash-tub bass player, a fiddler wearing an American flag vest, young blonde boy on guitar, and man with sunglasses playing the banjo and singing—played in front of the ice cream shop across the street. There was a line down the block for that ice cream. *Perhaps that's the spot Iguana Man had in mind?*

Something about that band reminded me of playing in front of Starbucks at Pike Place. I thought about home, about the gospel boys doing their thing at that very moment. I also imagined that the band at the ice cream shop was making very good money with a long line of captive listeners like that.

Summer and I walked down Ashbury, toward the panhandle park. We passed unwashed teenagers with sleeping bags and backpacks, smoking on the sidewalk; we passed a little girl, skipping in pink and blowing bubbles with her family walking behind her. At one point a guy with blonde dreads flew past with a grinding roar, cruising down the middle of the street on his skateboard.

The air was fresh, and bright colors exploded everywhere: green trees, blue sky, bright paint gleaming from Victorian houses. On the front steps of those houses, people laughed and passed bottles back and forth, reading palms or playing cards while music blasted from somewhere inside.

With every breath I took, San Francisco seemed to be reeling me in further.

Summer and I crossed a busy street and walked into a long, grassy park. Basketball games raged on twin courts while a football flew between the hands of sweaty thirty-somethings. A petite girl, dancing in a patch of sun, twirled a hula hoop around her body in ways I didn't even know possible. Gracefully, she bent elastic, moving fluidly while the bright blue hoop orbited her body with vicious obedience. A young man lounged on a nearby blanket beside a boom box, smoking a cigarette while watching the girl's every move.

"There he is," Summer said, pointing to the base of a large tree across the grass.

The two of us walked toward a man seated cross-legged beneath the tree. His eyes were closed beneath wire-rimmed glasses, and he wore a long, black trench coat over a purple tie-dyed T-shirt. A mass of long red hair and a crimson beehive beard made Cameron's head look like it was on fire.

As Summer and I approached, Cameron's eyes opened slowly beneath his glasses, green and calm.

"A new friend," Cameron said, glancing up at me and smiling.

"Hey, man," I said. "I'm Jason."

"Hello, Jason. I'm Cameron." He fixed his gaze on Summer. "And an old friend."

Summer leaned her guitar against the tree and knelt

beside Cameron, throwing a hug across his left shoulder and kissing him on the cheek. I set my things on the grass and plopped down across from them. That place was a green oasis wedged between two very busy roads. Cars zipped all around us, but their noise didn't penetrate the peace of the panhandle park.

"How was the wizard breathing?" Summer asked as she made herself comfortable on the grass.

I looked at Cameron, intrigued. "Wizard breathing?" I also noticed a large green crystal hanging from around his neck.

"Try this," he said, straightening his shoulders.

I crossed my legs. Cameron spoke slowly and deliberately, closing his eyes. "Breathe in for five seconds—deep, with your stomach... Feel it expand... If your shoulders move, you're doing it wrong."

Cameron inhaled slowly for five seconds; so did I.

Summer closed her eyes and followed suit.

I watched as silent cars and invisible people moved all around us.

"Then, hold for five seconds..."

The three of us held our breath for five long seconds.

"Now, release for five," Cameron instructed. "Slowly..."

As Summer began to release, she opened her eyes and caught me staring at her.

She smiled and continued to exhale.

"Now," Cameron said, "hold the nothing for five..."

We held it, and I felt the world slow down.

"Then..." Cameron calmly opened his eyes. "You repeat."

He stretched his arms outward—palms up, reminding me of Jesus in that painting of the last supper.

"And that, my friend, is wizard breathing."

"Why do you call it wizard breathing?" I asked.

Cameron smiled. "Because it sounds neat."

Summer giggled.

"I'm just joking," Cameron said. "My friend Amon taught me that technique when the two of us were working on a farm in Peru. He calls it wizard breathing, so I call it wizard breathing. But he also has another name for it: temple breathing."

"Why temple breathing?" Summer asked, looking at me with a smirk as if she knew she was anticipating my next question.

Cameron straightened his shoulders again, taking a deep breath and closing his eyes. "Because your body is a temple, and air is a guest in that temple..." Cameron exhaled slowly. "And it's much easier to hear your thoughts without noisy guests around."

37

The sun had almost fully set as I made my way up the Ashbury incline.

Cameron, Summer, and I had had a great time trading stories on the grass. Our time together was a fitting celebration for a very successful day of playing in the Haight. As we'd said our goodbyes, Summer had given me a pouch containing some small crystals that she said would bring me good luck. I had dropped one of these into the sound hole of my guitar to let that magical afternoon soak into the rosewood.

Hiking back toward Haight Street, I passed two little girls selling lemonade on a small table in front of their garage—a dollar a cup. My mouth was dry and the deal was too good to pass up. I set my guitar on the concrete and bought two Dixies full of sugary goodness, tipping each workin' girl a buck.

"Thank you, ladies!" I threw back both shots before tossing the empty cups into a small garbage can beside the table.

"Yer welcome, mister!" The oldest one said, beaming with a missing tooth and blonde pigtails. The younger one jolted with tiny excitement, jumping once in place and laughing.

I smiled at the little entrepreneurs and tipped the brim of an invisible hat before picking up my guitar and continuing up the street.

What a great day it had been—and it was about to get even better.

I would be meeting Kendra in an hour at a place called

Divine's on Haight, and I was feeling pretty divine indeed, like everything was really lining up. I'd found a decent spot to make some money in the city, discovered an amazing music community, and found a solid friend in Dominic. All signs had led me to San Francisco; now, I was beginning to feel like those signs were telling me to stay.

The thought of potentially relocating made me happy, getting to know a new town, a new life. I felt there was much more to be explored than a week would allow. It also made me smile to think that if I *did* take an extended trip to San Francisco, Kendra and I could possibly pursue something deeper. I stopped for a moment to picture us together—our days and nights spent exploring beaches, bars, highways, mountains, lakes, trails, Monterey, Big Sur...
  Yes.
  I wanted to see it all with her.
  And I decided to tell her that night how I felt.

I sat facing the door with my notebook and beer on the table, looking onto Haight Street though big windows. A couple of travelers—complete with hundred-pound backpacks—strummed their guitars and sang in front of a closed storefront across the street. Every now and then someone would stop to talk to the duo and they would take a little break and smoke something.
  I took a drink of my beer—a nice reward after a full day of busking. The icy glass felt good on sore fingertips, and the cold brew soothed my weathered throat. I enjoyed the opportunity to sit in silence and stare at nothing, writing down random thoughts as they popped into my head and taking sporadic sips.
  I had been writing something about wizard breathing when a purse hit the tabletop.

I looked up.

She was smiling, framed by lights shining through the open door.

"What are you writing?" Kendra asked.

I stood up. "I'll grab you a drink and tell you all about it."

"This place is famous for their rum punch," Kendra said. "You should try it."

"How 'bout I get you one and you let me have a sip of it?"

"Deal."

No green coat that night. She wore a slim, gray sweater, hugging curves and showing her form in a new light.

I walked up to the bar and ordered one of the famous rum punches for Kendra and another pint for myself, paying the bartender in ones. When I returned to the table, Kendra was seated with her back to the door. I set the mini-fishbowl punch glass in front of her and took my spot against the wall.

"Thank you," Kendra said as she fished a cherry from the punch and popped it into her mouth.

"You're welcome."

Kendra chased the cherry with a sip of her drink. "Mmmmmmmm." She held the little fishbowl glass toward me. "Here," she said. "Try it."

I took the glass and did as I was told. The pink drink was good—very fruity, but good. I chased the punch with my IPA and handed the little fishbowl back to her.

Kendra laughed. "You don't like it?"

"It's good," I said. "Very fruity, but good."

Kendra smelled the punch and said, "That's what *makes* it good," before taking another sip. Then she set the glass on the table—followed by her elbows—and leaned forward, resting her chin on one palm. "So. How have you been the past few days?"

You probably know the drill by now: floodgates. I won't

bore you with the exact details of my ramblings, but in short, I told her about the Civic Center and Haight Street and Iguana Man and wizard breathing and the T-Rex in the subway and the highway and the beach and the whales...

"I knew you'd love that beach," Kendra said.

"I kept my eye out for the remains of little red balloons," I said, "Didn't see any, though."

She smiled. "They're still floating around out there somewhere."

I took a sip. "What have *you* been up to?"

Kendra removed the orange slice from the rim of her glass and answered the question between citrus nibbles. "My friend Mandy and I drove up to Mount Tamalpais yesterday—a one-day, no-phone challenge. It was absolutely amazing. You'll have to go up there at some point. San Francisco looks like a little speck from the summit."

"Where is that mountain?" I asked.

"Just north of the city, across the Golden Gate. It's such a great way to escape for the day. We watched the fog roll in from the east side of the peak and then drove over to the west to watch the sun set over Stinson beach—gorgeous purple. It was so peaceful, and it was *so* nice to see her. The two of us haven't had a chance to catch up for a few weeks. We're always so busy, so it was a real blessing that we had a day off together."

"That sounds like a great way to reconnect," I said.

"It was," she said, nodding slowly.

A painting above my head caught Kendra's attention, and I watched as she admired it for a moment before scanning the entire wall, taking in every little detail. She then leaned forward and gestured toward something on her left. "Date night, 2013," she whispered.

I looked to a table near the window where a couple—man and woman—sat together, staring at the screens of their phones and not saying a word to each other.

"That creeps me out," I whispered back, leaning toward her. "I can't stand it; it reminds me of some sci-fi movie."

Kendra nodded slowly, eyes wide. "Totally," she said. "Sometimes I ride the BART at rush hour, and it'll be *full* of people but absolutely silent. Everyone is staring at some sort of screen—iPad, iPhone, iBook. But nobody *talks* to anyone." Kendra thought for a second, staring down at the table before looking back up at me and saying, "It's sad." She took a sip of her pink punch. "I think people are scared to be human these days."

Kendra pulled a phone from her purse and held the screen toward me. "This is safe," she said. "In this world, you have all the time you could ever need to craft the perfect, witty response to whatever comes your way." She set the phone on the table. "But here..." She looked around the room before quickly lurching forward and punching my shoulder.

I laughed and held my fists up like a boxer as she continued. "Here you have to react in real time. There are consequences, *emotion*—tone of voice, passion, fear. It's all real. And this..." Kendra tapped on her phone. "This hides you from it." She gestured toward the couple. "Those two over there have everything they could ever need to be happy. They have each other, and each of them has a universe of knowledge and experience to share, an unlimited number of questions to ask. But where are they? They're online, on Facebook, somewhere else, somewhere more entertaining than their lives. Maybe they're playing some meaningless game, tending a fake farm or killing zombies, racking up points that don't amount to anything when it's all said and done. Can you imagine that on someone's tombstone? Here lies so-and-so, the best darn video gamer we ever knew, making his whole family proud by holding the high score for three consecutive years." Kendra shook her head. "I just don't believe it, Jason. Sometimes I want to walk right over and snatch those things out of people's hands, put them all in a big bag and throw them from the top of some giant building." Kendra made a motion as though she were swinging some heavy sack in front of her. "I'd be doing everyone a favor." She let go of the sack and watched it sail into some imaginary night. After the load hit the concrete and burst into a million cellular pieces, Kendra looked back at me. "I know the technology is convenient, but what's the price? I mean, people can't even find a date in person anymore. We're trusting our most primal urges to some stupid hard drive." She sighed heavily. "Meeting other humans has become like shopping, like choosing a pair of shoes. Here are the stats—date of birth, favorite movies—and here's a witty, one paragraph summary of their entire existence." Kendra fluttered her fingers as though she were typing on a keyboard. "Do your research, prepare your essay. No need to discover any of these facts through a *conversation*. Who's got time for that, anyway? Not in this busy world. Plus, what if I say the *wrong* thing. Well, Jason, you know what *I* say?" Kendra leaned forward. "I say, let it fly—ramble, stutter, pause. Say the wrong word and correct yourself, for Pete's sake. Who cares? Own it. It's part of being a human, part of being alive." She leaned back into her seat. "But we're forgetting that. We're *voluntarily* forgetting that."

I nodded thoughtfully. "I like the fear," I said, leaning forward. "I like knowing that something is on the line. Feeling it." I gestured toward the bar. "Seeing someone across the room who stirs that in me and knowing that I have to do something about it— take action or be eaten by regret. No dating profile, no bullshit... Just you, me, and that primal fire..."

Kendra grinned. "Did I do that to you? Fan the primal flame?"

I looked her in the eye and nodded slowly. "You're doing it now."

Kendra continued to look at me for a moment before taking a deep breath and glancing down at her glass. She lifted the little fishbowl and moved it clockwise, punch and ice cubes swirling around inside, then set the glass on the table and watched as the mini-whirlpool began to slow.

"I want to show you something." I laid my guitar case on the floor and opened it. Kendra leaned over the table to take a peek.

"No way!" she said, seeing Galileo pinned to the inside of the case. "That's so cool!"

I closed the case and leaned it back against the bench.

"I can't believe you're using the letter like that!" Kendra said with twinkling eyes.

"I love it," I said. "It's such a cool image, and a great message. I figured it would be a nice break from the usual '*I'm a musician, give me money*' busking sign."

"I'd give you a dollar," she said. "Maybe two on a Friday."

I smiled and stared at Kendra, taking a sip of my beer. She smiled, staring comfortably right back.

What a beautiful girl, blonde and beautiful—no makeup, hair slightly messy. Kendra's allure was all *in* her, all in who she was.

"Hey!" Something popped into her head.

She looked down at my beer, then up at me. "Finish that," she ordered.

Though I should have been used to Kendra's spontaneous bursts of enthusiasm by then, I was still intrigued. "Yeah?"

She nodded. "You know the other night? When I showed you the bridge and you asked if we were even for what you showed me in Seattle?"

"Yeah," I said, raising an eyebrow.

"Well," she said with a sly smile, "it's time for me to get even."

38

"Almost there." Kendra spoke from up ahead, leading the way as we climbed the darkened trail. I turned to glance at her car, sitting on a peaceful street below and appearing tiny from our position near the top of the steep slope. Houses around the vehicle slept soundly, unaware of sparks flying in the nearby night.

"Up here." I wheeled around to see Kendra standing at the summit, hands on hips, her back to me. I hiked quickly to catch up with her. *Just a few more steps...*

"Goddamn..."

(This is the extent of the poetry I was able to muster in that moment.)

With the last step I took onto the hilltop, an explosion of light filled my vision. The entire city of San Francisco glowed before us in the darkness. A few eucalyptus trees reached toward the night sky from the grassy plateau atop which we stood, but with the exception of these, the view of the city's nocturnal majesty was unobstructed. Lights of the Bay Bridge glowed bright blue to the right, the Golden Gate stretched out lazily to the left, and, in the center of everything, a massive cluster of monstrous skyscrapers radiated from the city's metropolitan heart, shooting veins of light across the darkness in every direction.

"Now we're even," Kendra said.

San Francisco winked at me.

"This is amazing," I said. "What a view."

"Yep," Kendra said, looking out across the night. "I knew you'd love it."

A single wooden bench watched over the city from a patch of nearby grass. Kendra and I took a seat as I inhaled a large helping of high-altitude air.

"I think I'm falling in love with this place," I said, watching an airplane blink across the night sky.

"I had a feeling that might happen," Kendra said.

Glancing toward her, I noticed there was no breeze that night—Kendra's blonde hair sat still.

It was time.

I leaned forward, resting my elbows on my knees, and looked at Kendra on my left.

She looked back.

"I'm thinking about moving down this way."

As soon as this statement left my lips, a swarm of stomach butterflies stirred into action.

Kendra nodded slowly and looked toward San Francisco, appearing deep in thought.

There was a long pause before she said, "Really..."

I scooted closer to her.

"Yeah," I said, stretching my arm toward the skyscrapers. "I love everything about this city. I love the people, I love the coast, love the music scene..."

I glanced at Kendra. "...and I'm starting to become pretty fond of you, too."

I smiled, but Kendra just stared ahead at the city lights in silence.

I began to hear a familiar ringing, and my stomach started

to tighten.

"Look..." Kendra began, her tone unfamiliar. She looked back at me, and I could tell from her eyes that something was wrong. "I have to be honest with you..."

I swallowed the stone in my throat.

"These last few days, I didn't call you back, and I'm sorry for that, but I've been sorting some things out." She glanced back toward the city, and I started to feel weak, like some fire inside was running out of fuel.
She spoke slowly. "I talked to my ex-boyfriend the other day..."

No, no, no...

"...and the two of us are going to give things another try."

I went numb.
Like I'd heard the words, but didn't know what they meant.
I did, though.
I *felt* what they meant—something sharp in my chest, something cold.

My brain didn't work, my mouth wouldn't move. I just stared silently at San Francisco, glowing there below; the city that, moments ago, was the most beautiful thing I'd ever seen.
Now, I wanted to watch it burn.

"I'm really sorry," Kendra continued. "I almost didn't even want to meet you tonight, but I figured I had to tell you in person."

I breathed deeply—wizard breathing, temple breathing, something—trying to wrangle at least one of the thoughts ping-ponging around in my head so I could send it out my mouth. I felt Kendra looking at me, but didn't feel like looking back. I just sat there with my elbows on my knees, hands folded, looking at that fucking city, hoping she'd change her mind, wondering why...

There's a thought.

"Why?" I asked.

Kendra looked hurt.

I sat up straight. "I thought you'd had it with him."

The static cleared for a moment and Kendra bowed her head. "Don and I have been off and on for a while now, and, after three years together, neither of us is ready to give up on our relationship yet."

I looked out at San Francisco as if the answers to all of my questions were spelled out somewhere in the lights below. "What about this?" I asked, looking toward her. "Us?"

Kendra glanced back at me, breathing deep before answering. "You're great," she said, "and I have so much fun with you..." She looked down at her hands, folded in her lap. "I feel like you understand me on a level not many people do, even when *I* don't know what I'm trying to say, I feel like you get it." She met my eyes again. "And that makes this hard, because I love spending time with you." I nodded slowly and bit my lip. "But I don't know where you're at," she said. "Where you're going to be. I know you've got this grand adventure planned for yourself, traveling and playing your music..."

God. Dammit.

Hypnotized by the city, I saw every light down there at once— pulling me out of myself.

I floated for a moment, thinking about telling Kendra how I could move to San Francisco and the two of us could be together; how we could share everything and see it all—live and love and laugh—and life would be fine and great and beautiful.

But Kendra was right.

I wanted something else.

Part of me begged for a home—that city, with her—but somewhere deep down I knew that at some point I'd long for something new and leave everything behind to find it, searching for something I'd never understand but felt compelled to seek, only to reset and play the game all over again once I arrived—trapped in solitude by the same ambition that made me feel so alive.

Sitting there, atop that hill, the two of us locked eyes.

Kendra looked so beautiful.

My chest felt heavy

And Kendra said, sadly:

"I don't want to hold you back from that."

39

On the walk from Kendra's house to the bus stop, my case felt like it was full of bricks. The late night street was silent except for the sound of my footsteps and the thoughts screaming between my ears. I was sure the sleeping neighborhood could hear the voices, and I tried to keep them quiet so as not to wake anybody from peaceful dreams.

Words that Kendra and I had shared echoed in my head.
Scenes replayed themselves over and over again. *What could I have said differently?*
What could I have done?
I couldn't help but feel led on.
By everything—the letter, the offers to stay at her place, the late nights, the vistas, the kisses, the phone calls, the fun, all of it—happening only to lead to her decision to go back to her ex.
I felt angry. Angry and sad.
But in a way, I understood.
Kendra did what I might have done in her situation—what I *had* done before in fact—and now I was feeling it from the other end. Many times, I'd been swept up in people—in their energy, in being with them—riding everything to a breaking point and then realizing that feelings were building and attractions were growing.
Kendra did what she felt was right for her, and I got that.
I wished the outcome were different, but I got it.
She and I had made a few memories together and shared

a valuable thing: our time. And that, in itself, was beautiful. Maybe the two of us would see each other again at some point, but for now, it was goodbye.

I started to softly sing a song I'd heard the night before, the lyrics enjoying a new potency as I slogged along that late-night street.

"So I'll be here and you'll be near, and we'll marvel at the day,
and if the tide decides to take us apart,
we're just a memory away...

"Just a memory away."

As I repeated this last line, I thought of the final hug that Kendra and I had shared before she'd climbed the stairs to her apartment, the kiss she'd planted on my cheek, and the depth in her eyes when she'd said goodnight with an unsettled something in her voice.
The two of us would always wonder.

"Just a memory away..."

I thought about everything I'd seen and all the people I'd met in the past few months. What a ride it had been. I thought about Iguana Man, about Dominic and Ruby and Highway One, about the whales and Gizmo and the naked guy on the beach. I thought about Boulder and the hand drummer and the rappers in a circle of midnight dancers; Dante howling at the moon, soulgasms. I thought about Jaclyn, Blaze, and a carful of adventurers rocketing through the sunrise toward some unknown horizon; about the T-Rex, the Bushman, wizard breathing, the subway dwellers, the beach creepers, and all my fellow crazies of every shape, size, and color.
It had been a hell of a trip—and it was far from over.

Alex Rasmussen

After all, San Francisco was just one city on a
long, long list.

I set my things down on the sidewalk in front of a silent bus stop
on a silent street and looked around. No cars, no people,
nothing—just the shells of sleeping houses. Taking a deep breath, I
glanced upward, toward the light shining from a nearby window,
and saw the silhouette of someone peering down at me.

Then, just as the two of us realized we were looking at each other,
the shade was drawn.
And they disappeared.

40

"Wait, keep playing that," Jaclyn urged, swaying back and forth, barefoot and cross-legged in the sand. Dominic and I, seated on either side of Jaclyn, obeyed, continuing to strum our guitars as she closed her eyes in an attempt to tap into some creative vein. The three of us sat atop a very familiar dune and played a private show for the Pacific Ocean, which applauded enthusiastically with each set of crashing waves.

Beyond those waves to the west, the sun had lost its grip on a slippery sky and began its slow slide toward the horizon, painting purple streaks across the clouds.

Jaclyn—done with work and ready to enjoy herself—had met us on the beach about an hour previously. She plucked a bottle of beer from the sand and took a satisfying sip before grinding the glass back into coastal grains.

She took a deep breath, closed her eyes, and refocused.

"Set me down in a new place..."

She crooned, slow and sensual, over flowing chords. Dominic and I shared a glance of approval as we continued to play our instruments.

"Let's take a ride through this new space..."

Jaclyn's sunglassed eyes remained shut as she swayed slowly from left to right with hands on her knees, receiving musical transmissions from somewhere unknown and letting them

pour from her lips.
"Lay me down in this new place…"

Left, right, left, right…

"And feel the sun on my new face."

Dominic picked a simple lead over cruising chords as the medium received her next jolt of inspiration.
"Oh, it goes on—and on and on—and on and on…
It goes on—and on and on—and on and on…"
Jaclyn's melody fit beautifully over the guitars, inspiring Dominic and me to harmonize.
The three of us locked in, singing together on the sand.
"Oh, it goes on—and on and on—and on and on…
"It goes on—and on and on—and on and on…"

Water, waves, chords.

"It goes on and on and on—and on and on…
Oh, it goes on—and on and on—and on and on…"

Voices rested for the moment, but the guitars persisted—on and on—a downstroke accented every now and then by the splashing of the sea.

The three of us played on that beach until the solar wick had burnt its last breath, leaving twilight embers glowing in a darkening sky. Opening my guitar case with a satisfied sigh, I glanced toward Jaclyn, whose eyes were wide, love-glazed and gazing across the Pacific as night fell on our last day in San Francisco.

"Seven, four!"

A lit cigarette bounced up and down in the man's mouth as he called out his bid. He looked to the player on his right, seated on a barstool and staring back at the smoker with an air of playful competition.

"Eight fours," the second man said as he turned to *his* right, facing Dominic with a hand still grasping the porcelain cup that was overturned on the bar in front of him. Dominic carefully studied his opponent—a middle-aged Chinese man, drinking in a business suit, tie loosened and many of the buttons on his blue shirt relieved of their daily duty.

"Bullshit," Dominic declared with a slight grin.

Eight porcelain cups decorated with red dragons were lifted simultaneously by eight hands, revealing dice belonging to the eight individuals playing this game at some after-hours bar in Chinatown. The bartender, a tiny Chinese woman of about fifty, stood rigidly behind the bar with one hand resting on an empty shot glass and the other wrapped around a bottle of baijiu, cocked and ready. The woman slowly scanned the bar left to right, awaiting the result of Dominic's claim as eight players scrutinized the dice in front of them.

I examined mine. Of the five dice that had been hiding beneath my cup, only one showed a four. I picked up the chosen one and set it apart from its six-sided brethren as the other late-night contenders surveyed their dice and did the same. The bartender silently counted the results and then smiled as she looked toward Dominic.

She poured the clear liquid into the glass. "Eight." She spoke sternly, sliding the shot across the wooden bar. "Drink!"

A mixture of laughter and chatter filled the dark room as Dominic lifted the glass with an apprehensive hand. The man sitting to Dominic's left, who had been on the receiving end of the round-ending accusation, beamed a smile as he slapped Dominic across the back.

"*Ganbei,*" he said with glee.

Dominic glanced toward the man, shook his head, and raised the shot. "*Ganbei.*"

Once Dominic's empty glass met the bar, the eight of us scooped our dice back into our cups, shook them up, and slammed them back down onto the wood. This created a staggering, eight part thud that sounded like a pack of firecrackers exploding beneath a plastic bucket.

After a few more rounds of liar's dice—and a few more shots of the white devil—Dominic, Jaclyn, and I decided it was about time to wrap things up. We said goodbye to our fellow players, paid our tabs, and stood up to head out the door. It was nearing three AM, and—as per usual—Dominic had to work in a few hours. The bartender shuffled around from her post behind the bar and unlocked the front door. As the three of us were ushered outside, we said "*Xie xie*" to the bartender and she smiled, nodding and waving as she released us back into the Frisco night.

"The café's just a few minutes from here," Dominic slurred, stumbling out the door. "I'm just gonna sleep in the car."

"Probably a good idea for all of us," Jaclyn said, glancing upward as we walked beneath a series of red paper lanterns that had been strung above the Chinatown Street. Not a sound, only our footsteps tramping past closed storefronts adorned with foreign text. Every now and then lone wanderers would cross our path, hands in their pockets and a shadow glued to their face.

"You guys going home tomorrow?" Dominic asked as we navigated the late-night maze.

"Yeah," Jaclyn said. "Unfortunately. I totally want to come back though. There's so much I didn't get to see."

Dominic, not breaking his stride, jumped to smack the low-hanging sign of a Chinese market.

"So Jaime's really staying down here?" I asked Jaclyn, referring to her coworker who was supposed to be riding back home with us the next morning.

"Yup," she said. "He wants a change, and has a ton of money saved up. He'll at least be staying for a couple weeks. We went out last night and he said he was falling in love with this city."

I took a deep breath of the warm night air.

"This place seems to have that effect on people..."

The three of us rounded a corner and were greeted by Ruby, parked beneath a lone street light.

"There she is!" Dominic shouted, running toward the red station wagon and hugging it, face pressed against the driver's side window. Jaclyn giggled as we continued toward the happy couple. Dominic opened Ruby's back door, threw his Giants cap and jean jacket across the seat, and turned to face us with arms spread wide.

"Come here!" Dominic demanded with a baijiu glow.

Jaclyn, Dominic, and I squeezed together, making noises like we were taking a simultaneous shit.

After we'd flushed, I said, "Thank you for everything," and pulled the keychain from my pocket, removing Dominic's key and holding it toward him.

Dominic grinned through his goatee.

"You coming back to San Fran?" he asked.

I nodded. "Yeah. Hopefully soon."

Dominic nodded toward the key. "Keep it, then. When you come back to town, you'll have a kitchen floor to sleep on."

"The life of luxury," I said, smiling. "Thank you, man. I really appreciate everything you've done for me."

Dominic and I shook hands. "Don't mention it, buddy. Forty beers, right? That means we've still got about thirty to go."

"How 'bout thirty shots of baijiu?" I proposed.

Jaclyn laughed. "If Mr. Bullshit here keeps playing liar's

dice, that'll happen anyway."

Dominic faked a gag, shook his head, and said, "The white devil," before turning around and climbing headfirst into the backseat of the station wagon.

Lying across the seat with his head resting on a balled-up jean jacket, Dominic gave me a thumbs-up as I closed the door to his suite at the Ruby Inn. Jaclyn and I then left him to enjoy a glorified nap before he woke in a few short hours to feed caffeine to equally groggy zombies.

"Jason..."

A muffled voice echoed through the fog as I rode the scaly, green dragon across the Atlantic. Metallica blared from speakers mounted on the back of the creature's head as we zipped over the crystal water—land up ahead, mountains and trees...

"JASON!"

I woke up.

Darkness... Couch...

Something smells like gasoline...

"Jason," Jaclyn repeated, peering at me over the top of the Marquis' front seat.

"Hello," I grumbled from my makeshift bed in the back.

"Jason, I've been thinking..."

I rubbed my eyes. It was still dark outside.

"...I don't want to go home."

Intrigued, I lazily propped myself up on my elbows.

"I've been looking online," Jaclyn continued, "and there's

a ton of jobs in Austin. We could get there in a few days...." She paused for a moment to gaze out into the night. "I'm just not ready to go back to Seattle," she said. "We're already out here, exploring..." She glanced back at me. "Why not keep going?"

I sat up and looked at Jaclyn, resting her chin on arms folded across the top of the seat. No headband or sunglasses right then, just green eyes radiating something I recognized all too well.

"I hear it's a great music town," she added with a smirk.

I *did* have a decent wad of cash, and no Seattle obligations.

Just a quick phone call to the artist I sold for at Pike Place, and I'd be clear for take-off.

If anyone would understand a spontaneous flight in the name of creativity, it was Zoe.

There's also that friend in Austin I haven't seen in a while...

Feeling flint strike steel in my stomach, I nodded once and smiled.

"Let's do it."

We woke with a purpose the next morning, parked on some slanted street in North Beach.

I took the first shift at the wheel, smiling as the key brought Thelma roaring to life—no coffee necessary for the workhorse of the group. I stepped on the reins, and she galloped across busy streets where commuters began their daily grinds with sleepy eyes.

Our phantom threesome snuck between routines, coloring outside the lines.

We felt like we were breaking the rules, like we'd won the game.

The prize was freedom, fluidity—evolution per circumstance, per whim.

Jaclyn cranked the eight AM stereo up loud as Thelma greeted the Bay Bridge like a familiar friend. The morning traffic's molasses tempo amplified the anticipation burning inside us, and the car crept along at a snail's pace, giving me a long moment to utter psychic goodbyes to San Francisco, waving farewell from across the water.

Goodbye, Dominic.
  Goodbye, Ocean.
      Goodbye, Iguana Man,
Haight Street,
    North Beach,
       Golden Gate....
              Beautiful and crazy people all over...

Goodbye Kendra...

We roared through the Yerba Buena tunnel and the traffic began to thin.

Thelma growled, gaining speed—eating pavement for breakfast, one mile at a time.

Past Oakland, past Berkeley, east across golden hills, further east—onto the interstate...

And there we were again.

Eighty-five.

White lines ticking past the Marquis to the beat of some grooving tune.

Cars and trucks—our travel companions, flying just a few feet away—hurrying into the horizon, a school of fish swimming swiftly across land.

The road. Progress. Forward momentum.

Jaclyn rolled her window down and stuck a ringed hand into rushing air as I weaved past the left-lane straggler who was doing sixty.

Yes.

Eighty-five.

Our church.

Onward to something new—testifying on the edge.

The edge of it all:

The next move.

The next mile.

The next sound.

The next smile.

Amen.

God lives blurred between white lines on the pavement, in the massive snowcapped mountains silhouetted against the scarlet sunset, and in the vast black of the New Mexico desert at night.

Shout it from the top of the mesa (tie-dyed orange and red) that the messiah rises again through the chorus of the song, sending chills up my spine as Jaclyn, Thelma, and I round the next bend into the unknown.

Alex Rasmussen

Coloring Outside the Lines

Thank you, Anna Eklund. You did an amazing job editing this. I really appreciate your ability to streamline the text while staying true to my intended vision. I wish you luck in all of your future undertakings; not that you'll need it.

Special thanks to Michael Bliss and Kayla Jayne for opening your house so I could lock myself in a room and write a book. Also, to my family and friends for the encouragement and unwavering support.

To those who read the story, or parts of the story, before it was finished—Alina Shanin, Lauren Rasmussen, Irma Zuckerberg, Mom, Matt, Brendan Shea, Ben Rouse, Theresa Idone, Carrie Cole, Bridget Bennett, Kory Khile, Steph Chinn, Johnny Sawyer, Liz Watson, Iris Liu, Iris Chamberlain, Tim Dunn, Jacob Lopez, Brie, Erik and Andrew, Barbara Parissi, Natalie Hammers, Christopher Stearns, Geli Wuerzner, Aaron Brouliette—thank you. Your feedback was invaluable and helped to shape this book.

Also, a huge thank you to those who contributed to the publishing of this novel via Kickstarter:
Gerard Boulanger, Mary Hulva, Buddy Jolly, Nancy Gardner, Erik and Andrew, Ashley Mead, Melody Price, Barbara Parissi, Wendy Reid, Sarah Reid, Rebecca Strothers, Rachelle Kauffman, Jennifer Wilmoth, Ben Rouse, Chase Baldwin, Mia Allen-Stockman, Judie Skagen, Erin Dodge, Ian and Elise Travitzky, Debbie Beekman, Myles Koser, Pete Yore, Vanessa Latrimurti, Jeffrey Krieble, Joshua Swanson, Alina Shanin, Patty deCamp, Linda Thompson, Debbie Meadows, Brooke Lip'dem, Brendan Shea, Carol Brock, Miranda Marks, Jamie Rose, Mom and Matt, Iris Chamberlain, Denise Zuckerberg, Jacob Lopez, and Chris Krona.
Without you, you would not be holding this. Pat yourselves on the back.

Cover art by Johnny Sawyer.
johnnsaw@gmail.com
SAW and SawNw on Instagram.

Edited by Anna Eklund.
aeeklund7@gmail.com
@dazed_starling on Twitter

Design sugar by Iris Chamberlain.
www.startheredesigns.com

Alex Rasmussen sings and plays guitar in a band called
Alex Rasmussen and The Road. Their music can be found here.
www.alexandtheroad.com
"Alex Rasmussen and The Road" on Facebook.

You can also email Alex here.
alexsroad@gmail.com

Made in the USA
Middletown, DE
15 August 2023

36510543R00158